Legend
of the
Blue Eyes

B. KRISTIN MCMICHAEL

The Legend of the Blue Eyes
Book One
The Blue Eyes Trilogy

LEXIA
·PRESS·

Lexia Press, LLC
P.O. Box 982
Worthington, OH 43085

ISBN-10: 098912181X
ISBN-13: 978-0-9891218-1-1

Cover design: Ravven, http://www.ravven.com
Editor: Kathie Middlemiss of Kats Eye Editing

Sixteen is an age of freedom, when you finally get to drive a car.

Sixteen was the age my life changed and chained me to a fate I did not know existed.

—Ari

ONE

"Auntie, I'm leaving now," Arianna called into the busy diner kitchen from the stairwell. Her dark blonde ponytail bobbed up and down as she jumped back onto the next step to avoid a passing worker. The short, black-haired woman in the middle of the mob of people, dirty pans, and food only nodded. To avoid the early dinner crowd, Arianna hurried out the back door of the diner into the alley. It was Friday, the one day of the week Arianna Grace did not help with the diner run by her guardians, Aunt Lilly and Uncle Dean.

"Don't forget to come straight home. We need to leave tonight at midnight to catch our plane," a large man yelled from behind her. Arianna briefly nodded and waved to her uncle as she turned the corner.

Arianna ran to the nearby bus stop and ducked into the shelter to escape the light rain. Raindrops accumulated on the plastic enclosure and trickled to the ground as she waited. Across the street, an old man shuffling along with his small, black dog waved to her as he continued to be led by a much younger dog. Every Friday, Arianna took the same bus to meet with her friends at the movie theater. As the rain picked up, Arianna rushed from the bus shelter, and darted through the open door of the waiting bus.

"Hi, Fred," Arianna said to Robert, the portly bus driver, as she swiped her pass.

"Five o'clock movie, Ethel?" he replied with a wink.

"Is there any better time?" she responded as she passed the normal riders: the dark-haired, tall girl always dressed in ripped, purple fishnet stockings that matched the streak in her hair; the clean-shaven, young, bald businessman wearing a suit and tie; the older, gray-haired couple who shopped each Friday near the theater; the two twenty-something boys she always assumed were brothers that went to the gym to play basketball; and the cute blond-haired, blue-eyed boy from her math class that always sat in the back corner. Just like Arianna, they all rode the five o'clock bus to the parking lot next to the theater.

"What's playing today?" the young black man asked.

"It's Mary Ellen's choice," Arianna answered, sitting behind him. "So, I'm guessing it will be that new teen romance. I dunno the name."

"Something Roses, I think," he replied, putting his business papers away at her arrival.

"It's my choice next week," Arianna replied. "I'll make sure to pick something bloody, with a lot of action to make up for this week." The man smiled and chuckled. To the outside world, Arianna was just a shy fifteen-year-old, but around her friends, she was her normal, bubbly self.

As they neared the parking lot, Arianna walked to the front of the bus. "Fred, can you let me off by the theater before you turn?" The driver nodded as the rain poured down faster. He checked each of her hands. "No umbrella. I didn't know it was supposed to rain," she explained.

"Have fun, kiddo," he replied as he stopped the bus as near to the door as he could get. "Keep dry." Arianna smiled and waved as she ran from the bus to the theater door. The driver smiled back as he pulled from the curb. Everyone on the bus knew life hadn't been easy for Arianna, but despite everything she was always cheerful and friendly.

Arianna hurried through the door and out of the rain.

She scanned the lobby, but her friends hadn't arrived yet. As she had each time since she started Friday night movies with her two best friends, Arianna went to the concession stand and ordered her usual large popcorn and small drink. As he had each week for the past six months, the teenager behind the counter filled the empty popcorn bowl that was sitting alone near the drinks instead of one from the stack near the popcorn. Arianna nodded her head in thanks as she took the bucket and carefully swiped her hand beneath the cardboard edge. She cautiously pulled the note from the bowl and slipped it into her sleeve.

Arianna sat down in the lobby and waited for her friends. She was eager to read the note, but she had to be careful. The writer had warned her if anyone found out about the notes they had been exchanging, she would get into trouble. It had been over six months now since she received the first one. In the beginning, she thought it was a prank done by her friends, but both Mary Ellen and Tish had no idea what she was talking about therefore she didn't respond to the notes. It was obvious the person knew who she was, but not knowing who the writer was, Arianna had only glanced at the early messages. It wasn't until the person told her that they knew her mother and father that Arianna began to seriously read each one. She had only a very faint memory of her father, who died when she was four, and none of her mother, who died the day she was born. No one, including her aunt and uncle, would talk about either of her parents. Arianna didn't even know if her guardians were siblings of her mother or father. They were the only family she had ever met, and neither talked about their families or her parents. The complete silence about her past, and lack of any family, often disappointed Arianna as a child. Though she never felt sorry for herself, she couldn't help but be interested in notes from someone who claimed to know her parents.

Her return notes began with little questions Arianna had always hoped someone would answer. What color were my father's eyes? What color was my mother's hair? Was she pretty? Each week, she got answers to her questions: blue like yours; dark brown; extremely. And again she would think of more questions. Last week she finally got the courage to ask the writer to meet her in person. Arianna knew the dangers of meeting a complete stranger, but she had so many questions that remained unanswered and the note-writer had all of the information she could want. There was nothing she had thought yet that he or she could not answer.

Arianna tapped on the full popcorn bowl as she waited for her friends. She scanned the room as always, studying each person. Could the middle-aged man in the corner with the blue button-down shirt be the writer? Or was it the flamboyant woman with bright red lipstick bending over the concession counter, trying to get free food? Arianna examined each of them while she waited, but she had yet to see the same person twice at the theater. Not even the teenager behind the counter was the same.

"Hey, earth to Ari," Mary Ellen said as she tapped Arianna's head. "You were supposed to wait for us outside the theater," she reminded her friend. "We were going to pay for you this week for your birthday."

Arianna shrugged as she stopped searching the room. "But it isn't my birthday yet."

"Today is close enough," Tish replied.

"Only forty-eight hours and you'll be sixteen. Do you feel any older?" Mary Ellen teased.

"Terribly," Arianna replied. "Soon I'll be an old maid, just like you." Mary Ellen pretended to frown.

"You leave tonight then?" Tish asked, sitting next to her friend.

"Yeah. They still haven't told me where we're going. They said it's a surprise," Arianna complained. It wasn't that she disliked being surprised, but from the way her aunt and uncle were acting, they were purposely hiding something from her. Arianna hated secrets, and this was a secret, not a surprise.

"Well, you're still just a child," Mary Ellen replied, patting her shorter friend's head. "Children don't need the details." Mary Ellen grinned, trying to make light of the situation. Everyone always assumed Arianna was years younger than her friends due to her height.

"You should talk. You're only two weeks older than me. I may be shorter, but at least I look older than you," Arianna responded, tugging her friend's dark brown braid. "The worst of this whole trip is the dress Aunt Lilly bought. It's pink and shiny and has lots of lace. She said I needed to have a formal dress. I thought she meant something you would wear to prom or homecoming, but instead she brought home this very ugly dress. I've no idea where she plans to make me wear it, but when I finally get my hands on it, I'll have fix it as much as I can. It really seems quite hopeless right now."

"The lace should be easy to get rid of, but you can't change the color or fabric so easily," Tish replied, knowing her friend hated light pink. Arianna had spent years being referred to as a little kid by everyone, including strangers, due to her petite frame; pink didn't help the situation any. Even though Arianna looked young, she wanted to be treated just the same as everyone else her age.

"We should go find seats," Mary Ellen suggested.

Arianna stood to follow her friends, but quickly changed her mind.

"Here," she said, handing her drink and popcorn to Tish. "I'll be right back." Normally Arianna waited until after the movie to read the note, but she was too anxious today.

Heading to the bathroom, Arianna ran into the nearest empty stall. She pulled the delicate paper from her sleeve. She carefully opened the note and memorized it.

Meet me at nine o'clock, behind the diner. Offer to take out the trash, and make sure to wait out of view of the back door. Don't wear anything electronic, or any jewelry, or they will track you.

PS: When you pack your bags for your trip, take anything of value with you.

Arianna threw the note into the toilet and flushed it away. Early on, the writer had informed her that her movements were monitored by an unnamed person. She had always wondered why her aunt would buy her such an expensive cell phone when they didn't have a lot of money until she found it had GPS tracking in it. The person writing the notes was correct. Aunt Lilly could be overprotective, but Arianna had never given her a reason to be. The only thing that made sense was that it had to do with the past that both her aunt and uncle refused to talk about. Hopefully her mysterious correspondent would answer the questions Aunt Lilly would not.

Arianna hurried back to her waiting friends. She hated to lie to them about the notes, but she kept reassuring herself that she wasn't lying, just withholding information. From the initial note experience, her friends thought she should tell her aunt about it, and if she told her aunt, she would never get the answers to her questions.

Arianna sat patiently though the movie, daydreaming in

her own world. Who was this person that knows so much about her mother and father? Was he or she a friend or someone trying to set her up? How could they know so much, and yet, her own aunt and uncle always replied that they didn't know the answers? As a child Arianna could tell from early on that the subject of her mother and father was painful for her aunt to even listen to, so she turned to her uncle. He, on the other hand, just outright refused to answer any questions. When Arianna searched the home for photos or memorabilia of her parents, she found nothing. She always thought it strange that the photo albums started when she was five. Later, through her correspondence with her mystery friend, she found the photos were all a year after her father died. Arianna couldn't understand how there could be nothing of her parents or her life before those albums.

"So, you leave tonight?" Mary Ellen asked as they walked outside into the wet air and fading sunlight.

"Yep. It's a bit strange, but we leave at midnight," Arianna replied as she halted near the bus stop.

"We can give you a ride home," Tish offered, as her mother pulled a car to the curb and waved to the girls.

"Don't worry about it," Arianna replied. "I live in the opposite direction. Fred should be back soon, anyway." Arianna had found, after her first few trips, that the bus she rode to the theater could make its loop in three hours and return to bring her home. Her friends climbed into the waiting green car.

"We'll see you in a week," Mary Ellen called. Arianna nodded as she waved to her friends.

She had told her friends she would be home in a week, but her aunt had only said it was possible they would return in a week. The whole trip was very strange. They refused to explain why they were leaving so late, where they were going, where they were staying, how long they would be gone, or even why they were going in the first place. Arianna was beginning to feel that even her secret correspondent knew more about her trip than she did. For weeks they refused to even give her a time they would return. It wasn't until Arianna bugged her aunt every ten minutes for an entire day that she was finally given a tentative return date.

"So, was it good?" the bus driver asked, opening the door.

"If you like that lovey-dovey stuff," she replied.

"Your choice next week?" he asked, as she sat down near the front door.

"I'll be gone next week, but the week after I'll choose something much more interesting." Arianna sat and stared out the front window. She had ridden the bus so many times she could picture each stop without looking out the window. The rain began again, lightly. Arianna sat in silence for the remainder of the ride home. Who was this writer? Was it safe to just go meet someone who obviously didn't have her guardian's approval?

The rattling of the empty bus didn't help calm her nerves. Arianna always knew she was an orphan. Every time she was asked what her parents did for jobs, she would have to explain that they were dead. Her lack of parents affected her attitude, and made her want to please her aunt and uncle. Without them, Arianna felt she would be homeless. This was the first time she had ever thought of deceiving them.

"I'll see you in two weeks, Fred," Arianna said as she cheerfully bounced off the bus. The driver nodded.

"Then have fun in those two weeks, Ethel," he replied. "By the way, happy birthday, kiddo. Soon enough you won't need me to drive you around." Arianna smiled and waved to the older man as the door shut.

Arianna ran around the diner to the back door. It was

past eight o'clock, so the front door would be locked by now. Briefly, Arianna peered into the kitchen before heading upstairs. As expected, it was almost empty. Aunt Lilly was done for the night, and was in the living room folding laundry as Arianna opened the door to their apartment.

"How was the movie?" she asked.

"Okay, if you like love stories," Arianna replied.

"You just wait," Aunt Lilly responded. "Someday you'll fall in love, and your opinion on love stories will change." Arianna rolled her eyes. Aunt Lilly always preached about the benefits of falling in love and how love can change a person. "Have you finished packing yet? All the laundry is done, so if you need something here, just take it."

"I'm almost done," Arianna replied, walking through the small living room to her bedroom. "I can help downstairs after I pack the rest of my stuff." Aunt Lilly nodded. Lilly and Dean had never asked Arianna to help with the diner, but she always offered. Small tears trickled down Aunt Lilly's cheeks as her eyes glazed over. Arianna moved across the room quietly and put her arms around her aunt. It didn't happen often, but when she began to cry, it was a sign that Aunt Lilly needed a hug. "I love you, Aunt Lilly," Arianna said quietly, as her aunt tried to quickly wipe the tears away.

"I can't believe it's been ten years already," Lilly said as she hugged Arianna back. "Time goes by so fast. I wish I could sprinkle some magic dust on you and keep you a child forever."

"Now do you really want that?" Arianna teased. "I thought the last time we had this talk you told me how proud you were that I was growing up."

"I wish I could have both," Aunt Lilly grumbled.

"I better finish my packing and get the diner cleaned with Uncle Dean," Arianna said, letting go of her aunt. Aunt Lilly smiled at Arianna. Arianna might not be her biological child, but Lilly had never doubted for a moment that Arianna loved her like a mother.

Arianna walked into her room and plopped down on the bed. She had already packed everything days before. Because of her aunt and uncle's refusal to tell her how long they would be gone, Arianna secretly packed up everything she couldn't live without. She fell back into the pillows and began to wonder how long it would be before she would be back in her bedroom in their small apartment above the diner. She studied each familiar crack in the ceiling, these same, comforting flaws that she had spent years staring at. She felt as though her life was about to change, but she couldn't understand to what extent her life would be turned upside down. Arianna glanced at the clock: 8:52. It was time to meet her mystery friend.

Following the instructions, Arianna offered to empty all the trash bins. As she brought out the last bag, she quietly slipped behind the large, green, alley dumpster and waited. The rain had stopped again, and a fog was beginning to rise. Arianna stared at her watch. One minute to go. Patiently she waited, keeping out of view of the back door. In the light mist, she didn't see the person nearing her. In just a flash, Arianna felt her knees weaken and her body fell only to be caught by two large hands.

"Who?" she tried to ask, but the hands gently scooped her up and her world dimmed without seeing the mysterious person's face.

TWO

Arianna rubbed her eyes and carefully opened them as she regained consciousness. The old, plaid couch she was lying on was worn around the edges, and the knit blanket placed over her had a distinct blue and green pattern. She didn't recognize the dim room that came into view. Realizing she was in an unknown location, Arianna bolted up to look around the room more. Across from the couch was a TV and an open doorway. Arianna stood to walk to the door, but she immediately changed her mind as the room began to swirl.

"Sorry about that," a deep, male voice said from the shadows. "I was just going to bring you with us, but they already arrived to escort you to the airport. They could easily track you if you were awake."

"They? Those people Uncle Dean was talking to?" Arianna asked, as the man moved to sit next to her on the couch. Before she had left the diner to find this man, Arianna had caught a glimpse of several other people inside the diner. Arianna studied the man's face while he moved and talked. He was older than she expected. His dark brown hair speckled with gray. Arianna's gaze stopped on his large, weathered hands.

"They were sent to pick you up," he replied, unable to tell if Arianna feared him or not.

"Sent?" Arianna asked. "By whom?"

"Your grandfather," he answered, waiting for a reaction.

"I don't have any living relatives," Arianna replied automatically. "Where am I?" she finally asked, realizing she had been essentially kidnapped. While she had met him willingly, she was now somewhere unknown.

"Who told you that you didn't have any living relatives?" he responded, not answering her question, yet staring at her in disbelief.

"My aunt told me all my relatives were dead." Arianna tried to assess her situation. From what she knew, she was alone in a house with a strange man obviously more than three times her size. The view through the open doorway into the hall showed that they were on the second floor. Arianna could only see treetops out the window in front of her.

"I wonder what her explanation will be when you arrive at the Randolph manor tonight?" he replied, noticing Arianna glancing around the room. He expected her to be more afraid when she realized the situation, but she was calmly assessing her possibilities.

"Such would be expected of your father's child," he added to himself, as he stood and walked to the desk near the TV. Arianna caught his comment, and stopped searching the room. He was the answer to all her questions. He opened a drawer and removed a book. "You asked where we are." Arianna nodded. "You really don't remember anything?" Arianna shook her head no. The man handed her the book before returning to his seat on the opposite side of the couch.

Arianna carefully opened the old book. In the front cover there was an old paper that had yellowed over the years. Arianna skimmed the document, and realized it was a deed to a property that she had never heard of. At the bottom was a signature, signing the house over to Arianna Grace by a

Travis Grace.

"Is this here?" she asked in disbelief.

"Yes," the man replied. "Your father gave this home to you after your mother died. This is your home."

"Why didn't anyone ever tell me about this?" Arianna continued to stare at the document.

"Probably the same reason they never answered your questions," he replied honestly. "They didn't want you to know they have all been lying to you. Lilly and Dean are not related to you. In fact, they are not even husband and wife, but brother and sister. Lilly was your mother's best childhood friend. When your mother and father died, your grandfather tried to raise you, but it was best to have Lilly and Dean take you instead. Lilly had a daughter a few months younger than you. She died around the same time as your father, which made it easy for Lilly and Dean to take you in without anyone knowing." Arianna felt her heart begin to race. This man had answered every question she had asked, and somehow she knew he was telling the truth. How could Aunt Lilly and Uncle Dean lie to her? Were they really not family? How could this man tell her these things? Was he lying to her also? Who was telling her the truth?

The man waited for Arianna to understand what he had said. "Would you like something to drink or eat?" he asked kindly. Arianna stared at the older man. Could she trust someone who kidnapped her? "Patrick, go get some sodas," he said, and a man behind them moved. Arianna jumped as she realized they were not alone. The younger man had sat so quietly in the window that she didn't notice him the first time she looked around the room. "Patrick is my son," the man explained. "He's your father's cousin."

Arianna turned back to the older man. "But, that would make you my great uncle," she responded in disbelief. "But I don't have any living family," she repeated.

"I'm sure they meant it figuratively about this side of the family," the man replied with a chuckle. Arianna couldn't understand his amusement with their lie. "Let me introduce myself. I'm Gabriel, your paternal grandfather's younger brother. Go ahead and open the book. I think the answers you have been looking for are there."

It was hard to shift her gaze from the man sitting next to her. Arianna carefully opened to the first page. She had no memories of her father, and tried to look for some sort of resemblance to herself in the photos. As she gazed down at the pictures, she gasped. Staring back at her were two faces she had seen so many times in her dreams. Arianna felt tears begin to trickle down her face, but she didn't move to wipe them away. She was both sad and happy at the same time. Her father and mother stood arm in arm, smiling happily for the picture.

"It's really them," she said in shock, as she gently touched the pictures. She had spent so many years trying to see their faces clearly in her dreams.

"They were around your age when that photo was taken," Gabriel explained. "They met as teenagers, and, against the wishes of my brother and your maternal grandfather, they married as soon as your mother finished high school. Your maternal grandfather, Lord Randolph, disowned your mother the day she married your father." Arianna turned the page and continued to look at the pictures of her parents. "He has never been too fond of our side of your family. You have no family on your mother's side besides him. As a matter of fact, he is your only living relative on your mother's side of the family, but there are plenty of us alive on this side."

"Here," Patrick said quietly, handing Arianna a soda can. "We don't use this house too much, so there weren't many choices." Arianna took the drink without looking up from the pictures on the next page. Her parents had only been a dream before. She had no real memories of either her mother or father, only faint pictures in her head of what they would have looked like. The pictures in front of her were so much more real than anything she had ever imagined.

"We will leave you alone for a little bit," Gabriel suggested, as he stood and followed his son out of the room.

"Is it safe to leave her alone?" Patrick asked quietly just outside the doorway. "She looked like she was going to run away only moments ago. She would be fine in this neighborhood, but out of it …"

"We are not holding her here as a hostage," Gabriel responded, knowing she was listening. "She is free to leave any time she likes."

Arianna relaxed, knowing she hadn't really been kidnapped. She turned the page and continued to watch her parent's life unfold in pictures before her eyes. Her father and mother as teenagers, then their wedding, next her mother pregnant, and finally a picture of their family: her mother, her father, and Arianna, all grouped tightly together, smiling. Engrossed in the photo book, Arianna hadn't noticed the time that had passed, or her uncle, who had returned to sitting beside her.

"I took that picture the day you were born," he said quietly, trying not to startle her.

"But my aunt said my mother died during childbirth," Arianna replied, as she realized the truth of the photo in front of her.

Gabriel chuckled again. "I knew your father said he was going to lie to your grandfather, but I thought he must have told him the truth about your mom, Tiffany, for Randolph to so openly accept you." Arianna stared at Gabriel. She didn't understand what he was talking about. "We lied to everyone about your birthday," he explained. "Both sides of your family have been feuding for hundreds of years. We knew something could happen to either your father or mother at any time because they were crossing the divide. That's why only I was called to help when you were born. Your father and mother trusted no one. I was reassured when nothing happened the day you were born, but the next day your mother was murdered. It was an attempt to end both her life and yours. We still have not been able to find who did it. Nor have we found who killed your father." Arianna stared at the older man. His melancholy sigh indicated to her that he was telling the truth.

"Why would they go against their families if it meant they could get killed?" she asked.

"Because they loved each other," he replied. "A true life Romeo and Juliet romance. In reality, you can't help who you fall in love with."

"If my grandfather is alive, and so are you, why was I raised by Aunt Lilly and Uncle Dean? Because no one wanted me?" Arianna asked, questioningly.

"No, dear, don't ever think that," Gabriel replied, taking her hands in his. "You have been loved and wanted since the day your parents married. It's true your grandfather would have probably never accepted your father into his family, but he couldn't deny you."

"Then why was I given away? Did you not want me?" Arianna could not help but ask.

"I would've taken you in a heartbeat," Gabriel replied. "It was you father's choice to send you to your grandfather's. After several attacks on his life, he didn't feel it was safe for you to remain here with me. I tried to convince him that I'd protect you with every hair on my body, but I knew I couldn't change his mind. I now see that he didn't trust your grandfather completely either, since he lied about your birthday."

"Then does that mean Sunday isn't my birthday, or that my mother didn't die on that day?" Arianna asked, confused.

"Your birthday is tomorrow, or, rather, in less than an hour," Gabriel replied. Arianna glanced around the room for a clock.

"What time is it?" she asked.

"Almost time for you to leave," Gabriel replied.

"Randolph's dog is here," Patrick said from the window. "He's just down the street."

"The order to not touch him was sent out?" Gabriel asked, as he and Arianna joined Patrick in looking out into the dark street. Arianna could see a person in the distance, leisurely walking down the street. "Take the letter in the back of the book, Arianna. Your father wrote it the day you were born. It's for your eyes only," he instructed, as the mysterious person neared the house. Arianna quickly grabbed the letter and placed it in her coat pocket. Hesitantly, she followed Gabriel and Patrick down the staircase. Arianna stopped in the doorway and stared at the person standing just outside the gate of the picket fence. The rain began to fall again, and he opened the umbrella he was carrying.

"Here," Gabriel said handing Arianna a sealed envelope. "Give this to your grandfather for me, would you?"

Arianna took the letter, but remained on the covered porch. She stared at the young man, who waiting for her to join him. He stood silently outside the white fence encircling the yard. In the dim light of the nearest streetlamp, she could barely make out any of his features. From the distance, she didn't recognize him. Arianna gazed back to her uncle and cousin standing just inside the doorway.

"Go on," Gabriel urged. "He will take you back to Lilly and Dean."

Arianna still hesitated, standing out of the rain and watching the young man, who was, in turn, watching her. Arianna didn't fear meeting the mysterious letter writer, and even after waking in an unknown house, she still wasn't afraid, but now she couldn't help but worry about the situation she had gotten herself into. Arianna's stomach began to churn as she worried over what she should do.

"But," she started to complain. The young man offered his open hand to her.

"Go now; he is safe," Gabriel promised.

"Will I ever see you again?" she asked, turning to her newfound family.

"Any time you wish," Gabriel replied.

The tumbling of her stomach didn't stop as she slowly stepped into the light rain, towards the unknown man waiting for her. The young man opened the picket fence as she neared. Arianna stopped suddenly as she recognized the young man's face. He was the same blond-haired, blue-eyed boy from her math class, who rode the bus north every Friday night, the same as her.

"You're from my math class," she said in shock, as he took her arm and pulled her under the umbrella with him. He didn't respond but directed her down the street. "You also ride the same Friday bus as me." Arianna waited for a reply, but he still didn't speak. His clear, blue eyes darted around, searching the shadows as they walked. She was feeling worse now as her stomach churned. "I think I'm sick," she said, as she slowed her walk. Arianna quickly stepped away from the unnamed boy and puked into the grass. "Just my luck," she said, trying to break the heavy silence. "I turn sixteen and get sick at the same time." The boy escorting her stopped.

"Your birthday is tomorrow," he responded, still carefully watching around them. Arianna should have been surprised he knew, but she was too sick to care.

"Nope, I just found out from my uncle back there that it's today," she replied, as the sick feeling continued. The boy took her arm and began to walk more brisk. In their haste, Arianna failed to notice the small group of men that had begun to follow them. She saw the first man as she stumbled trying to keep up with her escort. "My feet are going numb," she complained, before realizing they were completely surrounded. The young man helped her to her feet and handed her the umbrella.

"Hang on to this for a moment," he instructed, as he moved in front of her. Arianna closed her eyes as her head began to throb. She reopened her eyes in awe. The men surrounding them were extremely muscular, and all had long white hair. Arianna turned from face to face and realized they looked quite similar. *Brothers,* she wondered. "It's best if you just keep your eyes closed for a moment," the young man with her said, as he gently placed his hand on her eyes to shut them. "This should only take a moment." Arianna nodded. Between the sicknesses she was feeling, and the fear that was beginning to form in the pit of her stomach, she was hoping that if she closed her eyes, she would wake up in her own bed, and it would all be a dream. Arianna held her eyes tightly closed as she heard movement around her.

"I'm assuming you are all acting on your own?" the young man said loudly to the men around them. "I'm pretty sure Gabriel wouldn't approve of this."

"Gabriel is an old fool. That girl is one of us, she belongs here," one of the men replied. Arianna heard movement again as the young man momentarily left her side and instantly returned.

"I'd advise you to let us pass," the young man said. "None of you here have enough power to stand up to me. If your friend in the shadows were to join you, it would be a different story, but the six men here now are not enough." The young man prepared to fight six men at once. "Since he isn't protecting you, I'll assume I'm correct in that Gabriel has given us safe passage out of here."

Arianna fell to her knees as the pain in her stomach

increased. The young man quickly knelt to catch her from falling further.

"I wouldn't call this a nice birthday greeting," the young man said to the men surrounding them as he scooped Arianna into his arms. "Her sixteenth birthday," he clarified.

Arianna opened her eyes as she heard the movement around them stop. She saw only a glimpse of the men disappearing into the shadows. As the last man vanished, a new person stepped out, and bowed to Arianna before he followed the rest of the men. Arianna gripped her escort's shoulder tightly as the pain increased. It was beginning to feel as if her internal organs were ripping apart.

"Miss Arianna," the young man said, quietly staring at her as she shook from the pain. "We need to get you to a safe house immediately." The man reached into his pocket and removed a small, glass bottle. He drank the red drink. "Keep your eyes closed," he directed, and she felt him begin to run down the street carrying her. As the pain momentarily subsided, Arianna realized the wind was whipping against her face quite severely. Suddenly, the pain began again, worse than before. Arianna gripped the young man's shoulder as it continued. Arianna was numb to the world around her, while the pain continued to grow worse. The man stopped running, and darted into an alley between two stores. He carefully set Arianna down against a building with an overhang to protect her from the rain. Arianna glanced up as he moved a few feet away and turned his back to her. The pain grew worse, and she shut her eyes as he spoke on his phone.

"We won't make it there in time," he said into the phone. "She's already turning." Arianna waited, trying to distract herself from the pain by listening to the rain. "My tracker is on, get here as soon as you can." The young man knelt beside Arianna.

"Can you make the pain stop?" she begged. He nodded.

"I was trying to make it to a safe house, but we're still at least a mile away from the nearest one." Arianna nodded, though she didn't understand what he was talking about. "You need to feed, or the pain will get worse."

"Feed?" she asked, confused. Arianna felt a jolt of pain rip through her body and she closed her eyes. With one fluid movement, the young man pulled a knife from his pocket and cut his own wrist. "What...?" Arianna began to ask, as she opened her eyes to find his bleeding wrist near her face. Arianna felt an urge come over her. Her eyes glazed over as she stared at the blood. Without thinking, she reached for his arm and licked the blood away. Arianna felt the pain inside her subside. The world around her dimmed, and she passed out.

THREE

Arianna laid still, listening to the sounds around her. Outside, it sounded like there were birds chirping, along with the sounds of unknown people talking. Closer, possibly in a nearby room, she could hear her uncle and aunt quietly talking. At the sound of their voices, Arianna quickly sat up and opened her eyes, expecting to see her room at home, but instead, found herself in an enormous, dark room. Arianna first focused on the bed she was lying in. The grand, four-post, king-size bed was not her normal, small twin bed at home. The room was dark due to the curtains covering the windows across the room, but she could clearly see everything. Arianna gazed first to her right. There was a door directly next to the bed, and one on the wall to her right. Her aunt's and uncle's voices were coming from the door next to her bed. Arianna tried to move, but fell back into bed. Her body was sore. What had happened the day before to make her so physically tired?

Arianna then realized that the day before hadn't been a dream. Arianna pondered the images she had all jumbled in her head. There was a meeting with a man who told her about her parents, the photo album that contained proof that he knew them, the deed to the house, and then the young man from her math class waiting outside the gate for her. She had seen him so many times before in school, and on the bus, but he never spoke before. In fact, she had never seen him speak to anyone before.

After he picked her up, Arianna's memory grew even fuzzier. There were large men with long white hair and ripped clothing. She could also remember the rain hitting her face as the young man carried her. *What happened after that,* she pondered. Arianna tried to remember as she lay there, but no concrete images came to mind. All she could remember was how it felt. First she was sick, and then she was thirsty, very thirsty. And after that, she was sleepy. What happened to make her so tired?

"You should stay in bed for now," a voice next to one of the large curtained windows called out to her. Arianna turned to find the young man from the night before sitting in a chair, watching her.

"Where am I?" she asked, trying to will her body to move.

"The Randolph Estate," he replied.

"What happened to me yesterday?" she asked. "I feel like I got run over by a truck." Arianna tried to stretch, and found she was quite sore.

"You're so little, there would be nothing left of you if you were actually ran over by a truck," he replied. Arianna scrunched her face in disgust that someone she just met would so comment on her size. "You don't remember last night at all?" he asked, ignoring her reaction.

"I met with Gabriel, and you picked me up to take me home, but nothing much beyond that. My mind feels all fuzzy-like," she paused. "Did you drug me?" she asked, accusing the young man who sat calmly smiling at her.

"It would have been easier if I had," he responded without changing his smile. "You are picky. Did you know that?"

"Me, picky?" Arianna replied, still not understanding. "What are you talking about?"

The young man removed a pin from his shirt and pricked his finger. The blood beaded up on its tip. Arianna felt a wave of thirst come over her. Her eyes glassed over as she stared intently at the blood. It smelled delicious.

"Stop teasing her, Devin," a female voice ordered from the left side of the room. Devin licked the blood off his finger and smiled.

"As much as we went through last night, I should get to

23

tease her a little."

"Who are you?" Arianna asked the familiar young woman now standing next to her. The purple streak in her hair made it obvious that she was also one of the Friday bus riders Arianna had seen so many times.

"I'm Molina, the head of your personal security," she explained. "This is Devin; he is my second in command." Arianna stared from one to the other.

"Personal security?" Arianna pondered, still not understanding the situation. "Whose personal security?"

"Yours," Molina replied. "We're part of the seven-member team trained to make sure nothing happens to you," she explained. "The team has been watching over you for over a year now. Your grandfather was worried about you, so we were assembled earlier than normal. You've met everyone at some point except Mori, our computer specialist. We've been taking turns following you, and making sure nothing happens to you."

"Following me? Why would anything happen to me?" Arianna questioned.

"Your grandfather is a very important person. You, being his only grandchild, are a perfect target. Along with a few other details, you have been watched for many years not only by us, but also by other groups intending to kidnap you," Molina explained. Arianna stared at Molina. Her direct talk and thoroughness were in stark contrast to her laid-back-rocker image. "You don't seem surprised when I mention your grandfather," Molina added.

"Gabriel told me about him last night. If my grandfather disowned my mother, why does he want anything to do with me? I'm still my father's daughter," Arianna asked.

"Your grandfather is a proud man," Devin explained. "He can't take back what he did to your mother, but he wants to make it up to you." Arianna turned to Devin. It was clear that he knew her grandfather quite well.

"Devin will feed you, and then you need to get more rest," Molina instructed. "Lord Randolph is anxious to meet you. He wasn't supposed to return until late this afternoon, but with everything that happened last night, he is returning early today." Molina left the room, and Arianna only had the strength to sit and stare at Devin as he approached her.

"What is she talking about, feeding me? I'm not a little kid," Arianna said. Devin sat on the foot of the bed without responding. "You look so familiar," Arianna commented, as she stared longer at Devin. His blue eyes seemed to want to give a response, but he remained silent. "It's as if I'd met you before, and I don't mean at school."

"You have," Devin replied, but didn't elaborate. Arianna wanted to know more but the pounding in her head was distracting her. Arianna listened to her aunt and uncle talk to Molina. Even in their hushed tones, Arianna could hear them. Outside that room, Arianna could hear more people talking and the clicking of the heels of women walking down a long hallway.

"It's so noisy here," Arianna complained. "There must be over a hundred people in this house talking and walking around, and the walls must be thin." Devin stared at Arianna. Arianna's suite in the Randolph estate was directly above her grandfather's, so Devin knew the walls to each room had been built to be soundproof. Devin moved closer to Arianna as she covered her ears. He reached down and touched her face gently. Arianna did not move as she concentrated on all the sounds and numerous conversations she could hear.

"Is it true, his granddaughter has returned?" a young voice asked.

"I hear she was targeted for assassination before she was even born," an older woman responded. "They say she could be the one."

"What one?" the younger voice asked.

"The one with the blue eyes," the older woman replied in hushed tones.

The clanking of dishes brought Arianna's attention to another conversation.

"How are the preparations coming?" a shrill voiced asked.

"Perfect ma'am," a young boy responded.

"It better be, or it will be your job," the shrill lady replied. "Everything must be perfect for Miss Arianna's coming-out party tonight."

Arianna listened to the various conversations as she finally stopped by listening to her aunt and uncle outside the door.

"Is she really alright?" Aunt Lilly asked Molina. "Is it possible to change without needing a sacrifice?"

"Devin checked her over last night," Molina explained. "She didn't take much blood, but she took enough to start the process. She needed more, but once we got her to the safe house, she refused everything given to her. We would have to put an IV in her, but we didn't have time."

"But why would she refuse?" Uncle Dean asked. "I thought, when someone turns, the blood doesn't matter as long as it's blood... and our Ari has never been picky about anything in her life before."

"We don't exactly know why she refused. But you have to remember, she's special," Molina replied.

"Is the prediction is true?" Aunt Lilly asked. "She really is the one everyone has been waiting for?"

"Yes, Devin confirmed our guess last night. She is the one in the legend," Molina responded.

"What legend?" Arianna asked as she finally opened her eyes and found Devin holding onto her. Devin pricked his finger and Arianna felt a warm sensation begin in the pit of her stomach. Her cheeks flushed as she smelled the scent of his blood.

"You need to feed now," he said, gently stroking her head as he waited.

"I don't know what you're talking about," Arianna replied, trying to keep her eyes open. She was beginning to feel light-headed and didn't want to pass out again.

"Just follow your instincts," he replied calmly. "You were born knowing how to feed. Everyone of your kind is." Confused, Arianna stared into his eyes. The tenderness in his voice made her want to follow his directions, but she didn't understand what he was talking about. "Close your eyes," he said quietly, placing his hand over both her eyes. Arianna closed her eyes. The scent of his blood seemed to become more powerful as she did so. Suddenly, without opening her eyes, she could see a faint outline of Devin sitting next to her. A light pounding began to thump in her ears. *Ba dump, ba dump, ba dump.* With each thump, she could see his body better. He slowly extended his arm to her. "Here." He offered the finger he had pricked.

Arianna wanted to refuse, but quickly found herself licking the tip of his finger. The sound of his heartbeat grew louder as she continued to hold onto his hand. The blood flowed through his veins to his wrist. Arianna tried to stop herself, but she was gently licking the throbbing vein in his wrist. Without understanding why or how, she lightly bit down, releasing blood into her mouth. Against her wishes, Arianna felt her world dimming.

When she finally opened her eyes again, Arianna was lying alone in the strange new room. Slowly sitting up, she realized that her strength had returned. She walked to the nearest large-curtained window and pushed aside the plush, white velvet. Arianna stared into the expansive garden that spread just outside her bedroom window. The large fountains were dry, and the trees were still bare because it was the end of winter, but she could not help but be in awe of the enormous garden. Behind the garden, Arianna's attention focused on the mountain range. There were no mountains in the Midwest where she was from. Arianna turned back to the room and continued to look around. The room was ornately decorated, and everything was in pale blue and pink. It had been decorated for a child, and she could vaguely remember part of the room from her childhood.

Arianna noticed on the chair next to the window was a pile of clothing and a note.

Please dress in these when you get ready. Your grandfather is a bit old-fashioned, and believes young women should wear skirts.

Arianna smiled at Aunt Lilly's handwriting. At least something in the room was familiar. Arianna picked up the clothes and wrinkled her nose at them. From the plain, boring style and choice of pink, Arianna knew immediately that Aunt Lilly had chosen the child-like outfit. The jingle of a chain and the click of boots as Molina approached the bedroom door caught Arianna's attention. Molina stopped before the door and prepared to knock.

"Come in," Arianna replied, still staring in horror at her aunt's choice of clothing.

"How do you feel?" Molina asked as she opened the door.

"Much better," Arianna replied. "But I blacked out again. Maybe something is still wrong with me."

"That should go away in a bit of time," Molina replied. "Your grandfather returned home an hour ago. He's waiting to meet you." Molina stared at the clothing Arianna was holding in disgust. "Your aunt has an interesting taste in clothes. Pink, huh? I don't recall ever seeing you wear that color."

"Tell me about it," Arianna replied. "I've tried for years to train her, but I don't think she will ever want me to wear anything but pink and lace. What sixteen-year-old wants to wear baby pink and lace all the time? Are my bags here somewhere?"

"All of your things have been put away in the closet," Molina said, moving across the room to the left side of the bed. What Arianna had assumed was a wall covered by a tapestry, was actually a door. Molina pressed the button next to the nightstand, and the tapestry folded to reveal a large walk-in closet.

"As long as it's a skirt, it's all right?" Arianna asked, and Molina nodded. "But you aren't wearing a skirt."

Molina smiled. "I don't think your grandfather views me as a girl. He hasn't since I was little. Besides, I'm in your employment. So your word trumps his. Will you order me to wear a skirt since you must also be tortured?" Arianna smiled as she pretended to contemplate the idea. "Take your time getting ready. I know you said you feel better, but it's best not to push it. Even if he arrives early, your grandfather can wait." Arianna nodded.

Arianna sifted through the clothes in the closet. Everything she had packed was neatly hung in order. She easily found a skirt and shirt she wouldn't be embarrassed wearing and threw them on. Quietly, she opened the door to her room to where her aunt and uncle were talking before, but found only Molina sitting in the room alone.

"Where is everyone?" Arianna asked. "I heard my aunt and uncle out here before." Arianna could smell the lingering scent of her aunt's perfume.

"We wanted to make sure you got some rest, so they went to meet with your grandfather already. I told everyone you were awake now, and they are waiting in the formal living room," Molina explained. "I'll lead the way."

Molina stood and opened the door on the farthest wall from Arianna's bedroom. Turning to the left, Molina led Arianna down a long hallway. Her shoes clicked on the light brown marble floors. Arianna tried to count the doors as they passed room after room. Large oil paintings were interspersed between the gold and white trimmed doors. At the end of the hallway, Molina paused at a large door before pressing at a space on the wall. A panel swung open to show an elevator pad.

"How big is this place?" Arianna wondered out loud.

"Right now I think it stands at sixty-four guest suites, along with four family apartments," Molina replied.

"No wonder I heard so many voices before," Arianna added.

"Before?" Molina wondered.

"Yes, right after I woke up. There were voices all over the place," Arianna replied, not understanding Molina's shock. "The walls must be thin," Arianna added as the ding of the elevator told them it was opening. Arianna stepped inside the door behind Molina, and watched through the glass as it lowered to the ground level. To the left was a large portrait hanging over a grand split staircase. Arianna paused in the elevator as she stared at the painting.

"Mom," she said quietly, knowing immediately who the person in the painting was. Arianna turned to follow Molina out the elevator, but she stopped suddenly as she remembered the letter from Gabriel. "I need to go back upstairs," Arianna said. "I forgot; I have a letter to give to grandfather. It should be in my coat pocket from last night." Molina turned to rejoin Arianna in the elevator. "You don't need to come with me. I'll be back in a minute, and don't worry, I can find my way back this far. Besides, I can hear someone talking in my room. Auntie and Uncle must have come back looking for me."

Molina stepped into the elevator. "I'll wait in the elevator for you," she explained, as the door opened to the floor Arianna's room was on. Arianna gave a quick wave and ran down the hallway. It was easy to find her room as it was the last door on the right.

"Auntie?" Arianna asked, opening the door to the sitting room. The room was empty. Arianna looked around, as she was sure she had heard two people, including a woman, talking in the room as the elevator reached the floor. Arianna hurried into her bedroom and quickly opened the closet. Hanging on the right side was her winter coat. Arianna found the letter from Gabriel, but accidentally dropped it as music began to play. Arianna turned and stepped into the doorway of her closet to find that on her desk, a music box was propped open. Arianna stared at the little ballerina girl who twirled in circles to the familiar tune. Quietly behind her, a man approached. With one swift movement, he bent down and covered her face. In an instant, Arianna was unconscious.

FOUR

Arianna kept her eyes closed as she regained consciousness. From the feel of cold stone beneath her face, she had been moved to a new location out of her carpeted bedroom. She could hear two men gruffly talking only feet away from her, and she heard a dripping near her head that kept a beat to their conversation. The cold, damp floor she was placed on felt nothing like the ornate rooms she had seen in her grandfather's house. She was somewhere else. The damp smell of mildew around her made her immediately think of a basement, but she didn't dare open her eyes and look around.

"That went easier than planned. Since this girl has not met Lord Randolph yet, he will definitely not be able to tell the difference," a deep, rusty voice said. "It has been years since the old man has seen his granddaughter."

"Still, we need to watch out. You know her guards were all chosen to be the very best, but they only met her last night for the first time," the younger raspy voice replied. The clanking of a large latch being opened made Arianna want to open her eyes, but she remained still, feigning sleep.

"How did it go?" the younger voice asked.

"Serine got in fine. No one seemed to even notice," a third man's voice said as he walked into the room. Arianna heard him near her. "She's still out?" he asked his two comrades as Arianna felt something drop on her back.

"Yes if she were a dearg-dul, she'd be awake, but she's

human right now after all," the older voice replied. "Then what is the plan to do with her?"

"For now, everything is set. At tonight's party Serine will turn. After receiving Lord Randolph's blessing, we won't need this girl any more. Just leave her here and make sure all the exits are properly locked," the leader said.

"But," the younger man said with a trembling voice. "This one will also turn tonight, and if she doesn't get blood," he trailed off, imagining the outcome.

"It's a horrible way to die," the older voice said, finishing his younger comrade's sentence.

"Does it matter?" the leader responded. "Actually, we need her dead. If they find out Serine isn't Lord Randolph's granddaughter, everything will be ruined, but it will be especially worse if this brat is alive. Without an heir, Lord Randolph will have to go on with the act of Serine as his granddaughter." Arianna could feel the reluctance in the two follower's voices as they grunted their agreement. "Besides, she's an orphan. She has no one besides her grandfather. Who's really going to miss her?"

"Can Serine really pull this off?" the younger voice asked.

"We've been grooming her since the day Randolph sent this one away. With all the surgeries, no one will be able to tell the difference physically. She is a perfect replica of the girl we have here. The only way this plan will fail is if they find the real Arianna," the leader explained. "This girl must stay hidden and die, no matter what."

Arianna waited until she heard the man in charge leave before finally opening her eyes. In the darkness of a single candle she could see that two men were huddled over a table in the middle of the room. She could faintly make out cards in one of the men's hands. Without making a sound, she peered around the dim room and cell. There were metal bars separating her and the men with an ancient and oversized large lock on the door. The other three walls surrounding her were made of stone. She was in some sort of old-fashioned cell. Arianna was certain that the only way out was through the locked door. Arianna lifted her face from the cold, damp floor and watched the two men. Neither noticed that she moved.

"Where am I?" she bravely asked.

Startled, both men immediately turned to her. "Doesn't matter," the younger one with the raspy voice replied. She could see he wasn't much older than her, and the scar across his throat accounted for his voice.

"Why did you kidnap me?" she asked.

"None of your business," the older one now replied. Arianna stared at the long scar that ran from his left eye to his right cheek. "Keep quiet."

Arianna moved to sit against the stone wall. She was trapped. They intended to kill her, but there was no way out of her jail cell. Arianna looked around the outside room. Only one door led into the small, cramped space. Arianna went back to lying on the ground. With her palms down on the surface, she listened to the vibrations of people walking. She was definitely underground, in an area filled with tunnels. No one spoke as they moved, silently turning down individual tunnels to their destinations. Arianna listened to find any friendly voice. Without a person talking, Arianna continued to listen to the footsteps. Arianna sat up as she recognized the faint click of Molina's boots. *Three people coming for me*, Arianna thought.

"What time is it?" she asked her guards to judge the distance of Molina from her prison cell.

"Doesn't matter," the older scared man replied.

Arianna leaned against the wall and listened to the footsteps of Molina while the two guards ignored her. She was still far away. Arianna began to quietly tap on the wall as she anxiously waited for Molina to near. When the footsteps were close to the outside door, Arianna heard Molina pause. Arianna stood and walked to the bars.

"Hey, are there any bathrooms around here?" she asked the two men who both turned towards her. "I really have to pee," she lied, as Molina quietly opened the door behind the two men. The younger of the two men stood and walked toward Arianna.

"Stop that," the older one ordered. "She's not to leave the cell." The younger one stopped halfway between Arianna and his fellow guard. As he began to turn, Arianna noticed Devin also entering the room. *I need to buy time*, she knew.

"Wait," she said to the younger guard. Across the room, Devin and Molina quietly moved into position to subdue the two guards. Arianna watched helplessly as a fight broke out between the four people. In the darkness of the room, she thought there was a slight change in Molina's features as she dove near Arianna.

"Forget these two. I'll take them. Kill the girl," the older man said to the younger one. The younger man nodded as he moved his fight with Devin closer to Arianna's cell.

"Where's the third person?" Arianna asked. "There were three of you coming this direction."

"Three?" Devin asked as he neared.

In his slight hesitation, Devin was only able to place his hand in the direction of the knife that was flung by the younger man at Arianna. The knife plunged through Devin's hand and slightly sliced into Arianna's shoulder. The blood dripping from Devin's hand didn't hinder him as he moved, in one swift motion, to remove the blade from his hand and use it to pin the young man to the ground. At the faint scent of Devin's blood, Arianna could feel a warmness in the pit of her stomach, and the thirst began to compel her closer to Devin. The pain of the cut on her shoulder dimmed as she felt herself warming up. Molina moved and caught the man she was fighting between herself and the bars. With his face pressed into the bars, Arianna heard the crack of his arm being twisted behind him. He didn't seem to even notice or care as he stared at Arianna.

"Blue... blue... it can't be... blue eyes," he stuttered as he stared at her. In one movement, a hand fell across his head, and the man fell limp to the floor as Devin quickly opened the door to Arianna.

Devin paused as he stared at the cut on her arm. "Does it hurt?" he asked quietly as he gently touched her. Arianna cringed as she finally noticed the pain, but stopped as Devin placed his hand near her face. The dripping blood distracted her. "Take some," he offered. Arianna shook her head, *no*. Her blackouts were connected to following Devin's orders. Devin shrugged and reached for her, scooping Arianna into his arms, he followed Molina out the door. Arianna looked down at her ripped shirt to see she was no longer bleeding. *Wasn't I just stabbed?* she wondered.

As they exited the prison cell, Arianna struggled with Devin to put her down.

"We need to leave now," he explained quietly. "You are in no condition to be walking. If there's a third person following us, they didn't come with us and can't be too far behind. Our goal is to get you out of here safely."

"Lock the door," she ordered, grabbing the keys from him. Molina took the keys, and locked the door as Arianna had ordered. "The man that was in earlier told them to leave me there and lock the door. This way if he comes back now, he won't know I'm not there." Devin nodded. Arianna threw her arms around him as he began to quietly move through the tunnel behind Molina. Arianna closed her eyes and listened to the footsteps. The third person was still following them. As they came to a fork in the tunnel, Molina began to lead them to the left.

"Stop," Arianna said quietly. "There's a group of five men that way." Molina nodded and began going to the right. "Five more that way," Arianna explained as the group turned to go back the way they came. "The one person following us is that way."

"Our chances are better against one than five," Molina said as Devin nodded and followed her. As they began to backtrack, Arianna heard their follower stop. Arianna opened her eyes and stopped listening to the people walking around the tunnels as they neared the unknown person.

"Gabriel?" she asked quietly, as she made out the older man's figure in the dimly-lit tunnel. Molina moved to attack Gabriel, but he instantly vanished.

"I'm not here to fight," he said to Molina as she continued to swing at him. Devin held Arianna closer. "You're being tracked from each direction. Their intention is to kill Arianna. We need to move now to get her out of here."

"Why would you help us?" Molina asked. "She's another of those purebreds you hate so dearly."

"Because she is his niece," Devin replied. "He wants her alive as much as we do." Gabriel nodded and smiled.

"I was wondering why you were the only one who knew where to find her last night," Gabriel added. "So the old man told you about Arianna's parents?" Devin nodded. Gabriel placed his hands on the stone floor, as Arianna had done earlier, and listened. After deciding the best route, he stood.

"I smelled your blood earlier. Are you okay?" he asked Arianna. She nodded as she stared down at the now-healed place the knife had pierced her. Gabriel followed her gaze and nodded. "Follow me." Devin moved to be between Gabriel and Molina. Gabriel led the way through the maze of tunnels. At each turn, he cautiously listened before turning the corner. As he twisted through each, he brought them closer to the surface. Arianna could begin to hear voices outside. Gabriel finally stopped at a large, solid wood door.

"This leads into the east-side garden," he explained. "From there, use the servant entrance to keep her hidden. This is a list of those involved." Gabriel handed the list to Molina, who was still glaring at him.

"What's the real reason you are helping us?" Molina asked. She knew the list wasn't needed to get Arianna to safety, but he was offering them something to save their time.

"I want access to Arianna whenever she wishes to see me," he replied. Devin smiled. Gabriel was not one to offer information without a catch. Gabriel took off his coat and wrapped it around Arianna.

"As long as Lord Randolph says that it's fine," Molina replied.

"He already did," Devin answered. "I found your letter to Lord Randolph when we met the fake Arianna in the house. He has agreed to all of your demands for access to Arianna." Gabriel nodded as he opened the door.

Molina looked out the door and into the darkness. Placing an earphone into her ear, she began talking to someone on the other end. Arianna turned back to her uncle standing in the doorway.

"I hear she's picky," Gabriel said to Devin. "There's a pack in the coat pocket. If she's anything like her mother, she probably has a taste for a bit of something else."

FIVE

Molina and Devin quietly escorted Arianna back to her grandfather's house. Their caution indicated that they didn't wish to meet anyone along the way. As they twisted and turned through new passages in the ornate building, Arianna was, once again, being led to an unfamiliar place. She stared at the walls they passed as they became less and less ornate. The surroundings had changed to normal, simple decorations. Molina pushed Arianna into a room in front of her, and turned to secure the room. Arianna stopped in her place and stared at the five extra people sitting in the room.

"Meet your Personal Protection Unit: Jackson, Nelson, Mica, Nixon, and Mori," Molina introduced the five men. "Including Devin and me, we make up your PPU."

"Why are all of you here?" Arianna asked, not understanding Molina. Sitting in the dingy, dark room, several familiar faces stared back at her. Jackson was the businessman that rode the Friday bus with her, along with Mica and Nelson as they went to the gym to play basketball. Mr. Nixon was Arianna's teacher for several classes at school. Mori was the only unfamiliar face in the group.

"Your grandfather hired us about five years ago to watch over you. We started twenty-four-hour protection a year ago," Molina explained. "Mori should be the only unfamiliar face because he mainly stays by his computer."

"Hired you? But why would he do that?" Arianna asked. "Is there something I don't know about?"

"A lot," Devin said, offering her a seat next to him. Molina flashed Devin a quick glare, and he smiled in return.

"I don't know if you noticed yet, but you come from a very prestigious, ancient family," Molina continued. "For people like you, it's fairly common, around their sixteenth birthday, to be assigned personal guards."

"Personal guards?" Arianna started to protest. "This doesn't make any sense."

Molina shrugged. This was going to be harder than anyone thought.

"She doesn't know anything?" Jackson asked, rubbing his bald head in surprise. In jeans and a black shirt he didn't look anything like the businessman she was familiar with. "Hasn't anyone told her yet?"

"No," Devin replied. "Lord Randolph was going to talk with her this afternoon and explain everything."

"Then who gets the honor of having 'the talk' with her?" Nelson, the blond, basketball-playing brother of the duo, asked.

"Not me," Jackson quickly said. "Particularly since I'm not one of you." Jackson stood and moved to Molina. "Did you find out which group took her?" he changed the subject.

"Yes," Molina replied. "Mori, can you find these people?" Molina handed the list Gabriel had given her to Mori, and he hurried to the closed door on the left of the room. "You four go take care of this," Molina ordered, and the rest moved to the same room. "Devin and I will watch over Miss Arianna." Arianna could see the relief in each face as they followed Mori into the additional room.

"We get to have 'the talk' with her?" Devin asked with a sly smile.

"'The talk?'" Arianna asked. "Don't worry. Aunt Lilly already had 'the talk' with me," she added, remembering the embarrassing way she had to actually help her aunt make it through their talk.

"Not the same talk," Devin replied. Molina looked from Devin to Arianna. Arianna could see her confusion. Devin just smiled to see her squirm. "Sorry, I'd love to be the one to explain sex to you, but this talk is about who you really are."

Arianna felt her face turning several shades of red before she comprehended what he had said.

"Arianna Grace?" Arianna questioned. "Who else could I be? Did you guys all lie to me about my name also?"

"No, that's your real name. It's not so much who, but rather what," Molina corrected.

"A girl? Homo sapien?" Arianna responded. Molina sighed. It was going to be hard to have a serious talk with Arianna if she kept answering every statement.

"Three have already arrived at the dinner," Jackson said, returning from the side room. "The other six are not attending, but they are on the complex."

"We will take Miss Arianna to the dance, but we will wait for your signal that the threat has been eliminated. Lord Randolph will be anxious to see she's alright," Molina replied. Jackson nodded and left the main room followed by Nixon, Mica, and Nelson.

"Why does everyone do what Molina says?" Arianna asked as Devin relocked the doors.

"Because she's the boss," Devin replied, before laughing at Arianna's shocked face.

"But she looks younger than everyone except you," Arianna responded.

"I am," Molina replied.

"But by ability, she far outweighs them combined," Devin replied. "We're running short on time," Devin said to Molina. "We should get her ready, and then tell her about everything, if we have time. We really shouldn't keep Lord Randolph waiting to meet her." Molina nodded.

Molina escorted Arianna into the room on the opposite side of Mori's room. Arianna stared into the dimly lit room to find it was a bedroom. Two sets of bunk beds lined the left wall, and a full-sized bed was near the right wall. At the top of the wall in front of her were small windows that were six inches from the ceiling. Shades covered the windows, and they didn't allow Arianna to see where she was. Molina walked over to the trunk by the full-size bed. Inside, she removed several pieces of clothing, throwing them lazily on the bed before she found what she was looking for.

"This was my sister's," Molina explained. "She was about your size, so it should fit. I know it isn't that wonderful pink number your aunt picked for you, but it should do."

Arianna took the deep green, strapless dress. It was so much better than the pink frilly dress Aunt Lilly told her she would be wearing. "What is this for?" Arianna questioned.

"There's a masquerade dinner and dance being held in your honor tonight. Once everything is settled with those who planned to kidnap and kill you, you can finally meet your grandfather," Molina explained. "You can change in here, and the bathroom is that door," she said indicating to the right. "Once you are dressed, I can do your hair and makeup." Arianna looked shocked. "Contrary to what your grandfather wants to think, I'm a girl," Molina joked.

Molina left the room, and Arianna was alone. Quietly, she sat on the bed. In the farther room, she could hear Mori clicking away on a computer, periodically stopping to talk to an unknown person. Molina and Devin sat silently waiting in the main room. Arianna stared at the dress lying beside her. *I'll finally meet him*, she thought, and she began to get nervous. Until two days ago, she didn't even know she had any family. Now she had an uncle, whom she had met twice, and a cousin, along with a grandfather who had disowned her mother. Arianna contemplated not meeting her grandfather, but he held the answers to too many questions, just as Gabriel did.

Once dressed, Arianna soundlessly opened the door to the main room. Molina ushered her to a seat and began to comb her hair. Arianna waited patiently, pondering what they needed to talk about. Devin did not look up from his papers once as she got ready. After Molina finished her hair, she began to put makeup on Arianna. Arianna wanted to ask about their talk, but knew she needed to stay still while the makeup was being applied. When she was finally finished, and Molina approved, Arianna turned to Devin. Devin smiled as he placed his papers down, but just as quickly became serious again.

"We don't have much time to explain this to you, so please don't interrupt," he began. Arianna nodded. "You come from a

41

very elite family that can trace their ancestors back hundreds of years before they came to this country. Both you and your grandfather are direct lines to the Randolph family, and therefore very important to this community." Devin paused, thinking of how best to explain everything to her.

"Did Gabriel tell you anything about the baku?" he asked, and Arianna replied by shaking her head no. Devin paused again, staring at Arianna's questioning, bright blue eyes. She wasn't making it easy for him.

"Do you see many horror movies?" Molina asked, interrupting Devin, who obviously didn't know where to take the conversation.

"Sometimes, but not much because Tish gets too scared," Arianna answered.

"Did you know many things in horror movies are based on partial fact?" Molina asked. Dumbfounded, Arianna stared at her. She couldn't understand to what Molina was referring.

"Really? Like what?" Arianna wanted to know exactly what Molina wanted her to ask.

"Like vampires," Molina replied, and Arianna laughed.

"Sure, and the tooth fairy too," Arianna said flippantly, after she stopped laughing. Devin and Molina both stared at Arianna, neither of them laughing.

"Remember, I said we needed to talk to you about what you are," Molina added. "Rather, what your family is? Well, that would be the answer." Arianna turned from Devin to Molina, and then looked around the room.

"Is there a hidden camera somewhere?" she asked, lifting up the pillows on the couch near her. "Where is the person that's going to jump out and say surprise?" Arianna continued looking around the room. "Did Mary Ellen and Tish put you guys up to this?"

"We're not joking," Devin answered. "Molina is telling you the truth."

Arianna's laughter began to turn to fear. She was sitting, locked in a room, with these two people she knew very little about somewhere in her grandfather's home. How many turns did they take to come down to this room? Could she find her way back through the halls to the outside? Could she make it out of the room before Molina and Devin caught her? She had seen them fight. They were both strong. Devin cautiously moved from the couch across from her to sit beside her.

"You are looking for a way to escape," he said quietly. "You may leave at any time you like; we won't stop you. Just know this, we may sound a little crazy to you right now, but we are the safest people for you to be with at the moment. We don't want you dead like those men that took you." Arianna stared at Devin. His kind voice and actions made her feel safe, yet she still was hesitating. "I promise you, we're not crazy," he tried to assure her. "Your grandfather was going to explain everything to you this afternoon when you met him. Your grandfather, like both you and your mother, is a dearg-dul. To be exact, you are a purebred dearg-dul." Arianna was still confused. "Or what you'd call a vampire," Devin added. Arianna continued to stare at him in disbelief. How could he talk so calmly about such a crazy idea?

"She still doesn't believe us," Molina replied. "Which part is hard to understand?" she asked Arianna. "The part about vampires existing, or that you are one?"

"Both," Arianna replied.

"Well, then we'll start with the existence of dearg-duls. I can prove that to you," Molina replied. "Because I'm one also." Arianna unconsciously moved towards Devin as Molina's face slightly changed. Her features grew more refined and elegant, her dark hair lengthened, and her incisor teeth grew longer. It was the face she saw in the dark cell moments before. Devin placed his arm around Arianna as she began to slightly shake in fear. Molina instantly reverted back to normal as she could also tell she shocked Arianna.

"You asked this morning, when you woke up, about last night. I was told not to answer those questions before you met with your grandfather, but I guess I can now," Devin said, as Arianna finally noticed he was holding onto her to calm her down. Arianna moved away from him too, still unable to trust him. "On the eve of a dearg-dul's sixteenth birthday, a celebration is held. It's held then because all dearg-duls complete their transformation on that day. We were all under the impression your birthday was tomorrow, and that's why there's a dinner and dance being held tonight. It's to honor you joining society beside your grandfather."

Arianna leaned back against the couch. She could see they weren't crazy, but it was still too much to take in.

"Wait," she said as a thought came to her. "My birthday isn't tomorrow, it's today."

"Correct," Devin replied.

"But I'm still me," she replied. "You guys must be mistaken about everything."

Molina picked up a mirror and handed it to Arianna. Arianna hesitantly took it from her. Arianna stared at her own face in the mirror. *No long teeth*, Arianna thought. Arianna quickly turned to Devin as she smelled the scent of his blood. Devin gently pushed her hand to position the mirror back in front of her face. Arianna dropped it when she saw the face staring back at her. Gently, she touched her own face. It was different. Her teeth were a bit longer and slightly pointed, her skin cleared to perfect peaches and cream coloring, and her features refined to that of almost perfection. She looked more like a supermodel version of herself, than her real self. The mirror was not lying. She physically changed. With the scent of blood fading, Arianna stared at the broken glass on the floor.

"But," she began, not knowing what to say.

"It's not a life I wish upon anyone," Molina said quietly. "Like us all, you are now trapped by the need for blood. Do you remember how sick you felt last night?" Arianna nodded. "Every time, when you need blood, you will feel that way."

"But vampires in the movies are always evil. They kill people for blood," Arianna complained. "I don't want to be that."

Molina smiled. "I only said the movies are based on truth, not that they are true. There's a lot we need to teach you, but we don't have time tonight. This is why Lilly and Dean brought you here to live."

"To live? So, I'm not going back?" Arianna asked. She already knew the answer to her question. There was no way she could now live amongst her friends in her hometown. She finally understood why Aunt Lilly wouldn't give her date of return.

"You need to stay here. For now, this is the best place for you. Everyone here, humans and not, know about night humans," Molina replied.

"There are more?" Arianna asked, now looking at Devin.

"I'm human," he replied, holding his hands up in surrender.

"I wish we had more time to explain everything, but we need to get you to the dance." Molina replied.

"She needs to feed first," Devin replied, digging in the winter coat Gabriel had draped over Arianna earlier. He tossed a plastic packet to Arianna. "Drink that before we leave," he ordered, all joking gone; he was serious again.

"What is it?" she asked.

"You don't want to know," he replied, knowing she would reject his order. Arianna stared at the packet in her hands unsure what to do with it. Devin took it from her and pulled at it until a flexible tube hung from it. He handed the packet back and disappeared into the additional room with Mori and Molina.

As Arianna pulled the top off the tube, she immediately knew what she had been handed to drink. Arianna recapped the tube and stared at it. The scent was similar to Devin's blood, yet somehow different. Dressed in a tux, Devin returned to the room to find Arianna still holding the full bag.

"Are you still having problems?" he asked.

"It's blood," she replied, disgusted.

"And?" he asked, impatiently.

"I'm not going to drink blood," she replied.

"You already have," he responded. "I'm sorry if this is strange to you. You can get blood from drinking it, or injecting it, but we don't have time to set up an IV." Arianna nodded, but still didn't uncap the blood. "Not this again…"

"Again?" she asked.

"You turned last night," he explained. "To stop the pain, I gave you my blood. You drank only enough to slightly stop the pain before you passed out. At the safe house we brought you to, you refused to take any blood given to you. I figured this should be okay since it's from your uncle," Devin continued to explain.

"It smells like your blood," Arianna agreed. "Why?"

"That would take more time than we have to explain. Please, just drink the blood," Devin begged. "We don't want anything to happen before you meet your grandfather." Arianna nodded, but still hesitated. In her hands, she was holding real blood. Arianna pinched herself to find she wasn't dreaming, but she still didn't feel like the situation was happening.

"Fine," Devin replied. "We will do this the easy way." Devin opened the cap on the bag in Arianna's hands. Reaching down to the table, Devin flicked open a knife, and pricked his finger. The blood began to bead up on the tip of his forefinger. Arianna felt her face go warm at the scent of his blood. Without thinking, she reached for his hand. Devin gently pushed the bag in her hand to her face. Arianna felt an urge inside her long for his blood, but she was satisfied with the blood from the bag. When she finished, Devin took the bag from her and recapped it.

"Thank you," he said. "Was that so difficult?" he added, quieter, almost for himself.

Arianna looked around the room. The sounds had become louder, and the colors more vibrant in the dimly-lit room. Arianna could feel her senses increase as she took in the newly-colored room. Closing her eyes, she listened to Mori click on the computer in the next room. Molina was pacing behind him. Outside the door, she could hear footsteps at the end of the hall. Beyond the hall, faint music was playing amongst the soft laughter and talking of people. Arianna opened her eyes as Devin finally stood.

"Everything is a bit clearer now?" he asked. Arianna nodded.

"Why?" she asked.

"Though Molina makes it sound like a curse to be a deargdul, there are some benefits. Your senses are much more acute than before. You see more colors, even in the dark. You hear sounds better than normal humans. Your senses of smell, sight, and taste increase tremendously, and your sense of touch..." he explained, reaching for her face as Molina returned. He quickly pulled his hand back.

"It's time," she said quietly.

SIX

Devin gently offered his arm to Arianna as they approached large, gold-and–white-trimmed double doors. Two large men dressed in matching navy blue coats greeted them as they passed. Arianna clung tightly to Devin as the array of colors twirled before her eyes. In the grand ballroom of the Randolph estate, over four hundred masked men and women had gathered to celebrate with Lord Randolph the birthday of his only surviving heir. The women, all dressed in brightly-colored, formal, floor-length dresses, were being led by tuxedo-clad gentlemen. Many people dotted the large open floor as they waltzed around the room. Arianna paused at the sight. Devin smiled as he waited. It would be the party of the year, and with their matching masks, no one would recognize Arianna on Devin's arm.

Arianna continued to gaze over the room as Devin kindly ushered her along the back wall. Their faces all concealed by masks, the beautiful women were dressed in their best for such a special occasion. Shifting her gaze from the dancing people on the ballroom main floor, Arianna looked around the ornate, gold-trimmed room. There was a balcony above her, on which people lounged, watching the floor below as they chatted, but the raised platform across the room caught her complete attention. Sitting in a plush chair was an old man. He immediately stood out against the male guests in his deep maroon suit with gold trim. His eagle eyes gazed over the crowd, obviously searching and observing his guests. His hair was gray from the years and his skin slightly wrinkled. She couldn't guess his age, but she knew instantly who he was.

"Correct," Devin whispered in her ear. With a brief nod from Devin to her grandfather, her grandfather's face lit up with a smile.

"It's been years since he's smiled so easily in a crowd," a large, red-bearded man said, approaching Devin. The man grinned as he shook Devin's hand. "You haven't been up to visit in a while."

"I've been a bit busy babysitting," Devin replied. Arianna pulled closer to Devin's arm as the young man who was standing behind the bearded man peered at her. Arianna could feel the young man's gaze past the mask.

"The old man must be proud," the fellow replied. "To finally have his granddaughter home." Devin nodded. "Now that you have returned as well, don't be a stranger. Come visit any time. You and Brenton have a lot of catching up to do."

"As long as there isn't more work to be done," Devin replied.

"I'll have to have a talk with James. He keeps you too busy. You're only seventeen. You should be enjoying your youth, not working." The man laughed as he walked away. The young man behind him didn't speak, but followed the older man as he walked on to talk with the next group of people.

"Who is he?" Arianna asked.

"Lord Winter," Devin replied. "He runs the Triclan City north of here, and he is a good friend of your grandfather's."

"Why did the young man with him keep staring at me?" Arianna asked. Devin didn't reply. "It seemed like he knew who I was."

"Don't worry about it," Devin replied. "If anyone suspected, it would be him. He probably does know."

"But we're wearing masks," she added. Devin shrugged again. "How come Lord Winter seems to know everyone even if they're disguised?"

"His sense of smell is great," Devin explained as the music changed. Arianna turned to the orchestra. She recognized the tune as the melody began. It was the same song the jewelry box was playing earlier in her room. Somewhere in her memory, she could recall hearing the song before.

"This song," Arianna began, as she looked across the room to her grandfather. "It has words, doesn't it?"

"Yes," Devin replied. "Would you like to dance?"

Arianna shook her head no. "I don't know how to dance like that." She pointed to the people on the floor waltzing to the song.

"If you can remember this song, you should remember how much you loved to dance to it," Devin replied. "Besides, it's easy for the girl. You just follow my lead." Arianna tried to protest more, but being unwilling to let go of Devin's arm in the large crowd of people, she had no choice but to dance with him.

Devin led her to the middle of the dance floor. He placed his hand lightly on Arianna waist. Arianna's heart began beating faster. Standing so close to a cute boy who had actually asked her to dance made her a bit dizzy. Hesitantly, Arianna responded by placing her hand on his shoulder. As he whispered directions in her ear and gently directed her with his grasp, Arianna began to slowly remember dancing to the same tune many years before. Devin easily maneuvered them between the people as they joined the large group twirling around the dance floor. Though only able to catch slight glimpses of her grandfather, the happiness within him seemed to overflow as he grinned at the pair dancing.

"You said my senses would increase," Arianna began, as they continued dancing. "But I also seem to feel what other people are feeling now." Devin remained silent. "Like the old man over there dancing with the woman in the tight red dress. He is overly happy to be dancing with her, and she's bored to death. Or the balding man across the room by the hors d'oeuvres table. He isn't hungry but trying to waste time. He is nervous about something." Arianna paused to wait for a reply Devin would not give. "Why do I feel these things?"

"That will take much longer to explain. Let's just say, for now, it was something you inherited from your father's side of the family," Devin replied. "Gabriel could probably tell you more." Arianna nodded, though she hadn't gotten the explanation she wanted.

At the end of the song, Arianna quickly turned to her grandfather who was beginning to stand. The rustle of fabric caught her attention as a girl, who could be Arianna's long-lost twin, rose and stood beside the older man.

"Look familiar?" Devin asked, as he stood next to Arianna, staring at the pair. Arianna didn't have time to reply as Lord Randolph stood on the edge of the platform, and rapped his walking stick three times on the top step. The room hushed at the sound, and everyone dancing moved closer to the platform, forcing Devin and Arianna into the crowd of people. Devin placed his hands around her waist to keep her from being pulled farther away from him. Arianna felt herself blushing, but didn't want to be separated from him either.

"I'd like to begin by welcoming everyone tonight to this special occasion. It has been ten, long years since my granddaughter was given to her adoptive parents to raise, but I've thought about her every day. I knew some day she would return, but I didn't know how happy it could make an old man like me to see her smile." Lord Randolph talked while the young lady next to him smiled brighter.

Arianna stared from her grandfather to the girl. Her grandfather was standing before everyone, truthfully telling everyone of his happiness, while the girl next to him was faking hers. Though Devin wouldn't explain why, as her five senses had increased the past two days, also had her perception of people's feelings. How could the girl appear to be so calm when she was impersonating someone? The girl slightly swayed out of fake happiness in a pink taffeta dress to Lord Randolph's words. Arianna smiled, secretly happy to not be wearing the awful dress.

"It is with great pride that I welcome our newest family member into the clan," Lord Randolph ended as applause began. Panic set into the girl's face as the crowd began to part.

The crowd began to murmur as a person covered in a white cape walked between the people. Arianna listened from person to person around her to try to understand in her confusion.

"But it isn't midnight," the lady in the peacock mask said to the short man beside her.

"What is he planning now?" another man asked his companion.

"It's too early," the curly-haired man said to the younger man with him.

Arianna slightly tapped the hand firmly holding her in place. Devin leaned nearer to Arianna.

"What's going on now?" she asked curiously.

"When a dearg-dul turns, they need a large amount of blood. So a sacrifice is chosen and presented to the person at their coming-out party. At midnight, when they turn, they drink from their sacrifice. The person coming now is the sacrifice for you," Devin explained.

Arianna looked around the room for a clock and found large, ornately-decorated clock across the room from the platform. 11:26. Arianna turned back to her grandfather, and he smiled as the girl next to him was beginning to panic so badly that her cool cover was breaking. She was as confused as the crowd.

"A dearg-dul turns at midnight, right?" Arianna asked, and Devin chuckled. "But that girl, if she's supposed to be me, won't turn for another thirty-four minutes." Devin gazed across the room to Molina, who nodded her reply to the situation.

"Everything must be set then," he explained, as Arianna followed his gaze. Devin released his grip on Arianna who instead took his arm.

Arianna watched as her sacrifice neared. "So, what happens to the sacrifice?" she asked Devin.

"They die," Devin replied.

"But what if you don't want to kill a person?" Arianna asked, not approving of the situation.

"The first time anyone turns, they black out like you did, and won't know the difference. In normal situations you can take blood from someone without killing them by just stopping when the heartbeat changes. But for the first time, most people can't stop because they are overcome with thirst," Devin explained.

"But you're not dead," Arianna replied pointing out that she had changed without a sacrifice.

"I was prepared to die, but for some reason you stopped," he added. "You don't need to worry about the person who sacrifices themself," he added, seeing Arianna's concern. "That person knows what will happen. They choose to be the sacrifice. I'd have gladly died for you."

Arianna turned to watch the hooded person passed nearby Arianna and Devin's location in the crowd. Arianna caught the faint scent of lilacs, which she vaguely recognized, as the person passed. When they slowly began to climb the stairs, the whispers in the crowd increased.

"Everyone seems a bit talkative today," Lord Randolph said loudly, as the sacrifice approached the top stairs. "I understand I'm causing a bit of confusion by beginning this early, but I figured that since my granddaughter actually turned last night, it would be alright." The crowd burst into more conversations. Arianna tried to listen to everyone, but the fear growing on the fake Arianna's face caught her attention. "Since she didn't finish the transformation last night, I figure we can finish it now." The impostor began to back away from Lord Randolph on the platform. "Don't be scared, dear," he said kindly, though Arianna could feel the wickedness in his voice. "Everything has been prepared, just how you asked." Lord Randolph stepped down to the hooded person and untied the cape around her neck.

At the same moment, as the sacrifice's face was finally revealed, Arianna finally knew where the scent was from. Breaking from Devin's grasp, Arianna pushed her way through the crowd to the staircase. Hurrying to her aunt at the top of the stairs, Arianna tried to climb two stairs at a time.

"Don't, Aunt Lilly!" Arianna called to the woman, who watched Arianna trip as she approached her.

Arianna felt the sting in her knee as it hit the edge of the stairs, but quickly stood to continue up the last few. Arianna desperately wanted to save her aunt. As she moved to continue, Devin appeared beside her, and offered her his hand. Arianna finally realized the crowd had become completely silent. Arianna turned to her grandfather as he nodded to Devin. Molina and the other guards removed several people from the crowd. Remembering her aunt, Arianna climbed the last few steps and hugged her.

"What do you think you are doing?" Arianna asked, pulling her mask off.

"Arianna?" Lilly questioned. "But why are there two of you?" Arianna hugged her aunt closer, protecting her from the fake Arianna who had just planned to kill her.

"I can explain that," Lord Randolph replied. "It's so nice to finally meet you, Arianna," he added, kissing his granddaughter's hand before returning to the platform next to the trembling impostor. "As everyone who isn't human here can tell from the scent of her blood, the girl on the steps is my real granddaughter, Arianna Caoimhe. There was a bit of trouble this morning, but it has all been sorted out now." In one fluid movement, Devin reached forward and grabbed the base of Lord Randolph's walking stick as he pulled the sword from its case. Before anyone could speak, Lord Randolph moved so quickly that only Arianna could watch his movements. With one swing, the frightened girl's head rolled to the floor behind her. Arianna shuddered at the sight.

As she stood in shock, Arianna held onto her aunt. Both were horrified by Lord Randolph's actions. Arianna had never seen anyone die before. The headless body remained lying on the top platform next to her grandfather as he handed the bloody sword to Devin. Confused, Arianna was disgusted by the scene in front of her, but the scent of blood was beginning to make her thirsty. Suppressing the thirst within, Arianna stared at her cold-hearted grandfather. Lord Randolph's evil expression softened as he looked kindly down at Arianna.

"I'm sorry about shedding blood at your party," he replied honestly. "It will be cleaned up in a moment." Lord Randolph waved a hand. Several people appeared on the steps and removed the body.

The crowd stood like stone below, watching the scene unfold. Unable to move or talk, everyone stood completely still waiting for some indication of what to do. It was obvious, by the scent of her blood, Arianna was a purebred, a rarity amongst most families, but expected of the Randolph family.

Arianna continued to hug her aunt to keep from shaking as Lord Randolph addressed the crowd. "With great pleasure, I'd like to introduce everyone to my granddaughter, heir to the Randolph family." Lord Randolph offered his hand to Arianna, but scared, she continued to hold onto her aunt. Lord Randolph smiled. "I guess she's a bit shy since this is our first meeting as well." Devin walked back down the stairs to Arianna.

"I'll stay beside you," he said only to her, knowing Arianna was afraid to let go of the only person in the room she knew. Hesitantly, with the urging of her aunt, Arianna took Devin's arm and walked up the last few stairs to the platform beside her grandfather. Lord Randolph beamed as she neared him. Arianna could feel his genuine happiness, yet she couldn't do anything but fear him. The applause began as she took her grandfather's outstretched hand.

Arianna began to feel her knees weaken. The scent of blood was becoming more overwhelming. The body of the dead girl was gone and the blood wiped away, but her scent was now mixing with the new scent of additional blood. The aroma was growing stronger, and, closing her eyes, Arianna felt her face flush. It wasn't the overpowering thirst she felt before when Devin had given her blood, but more of an automatic reaction to the large amount of blood she could smell. Arianna opened her eyes as she felt Devin place his hand softly on her back to steady her.

"A toast," Lord Randolph began. "To my beautiful granddaughter, Arianna."

"To Lady Arianna," the crowd cried in unison as they raised their red-liquid-filled glasses.

Lord Randolph nodded to Devin standing beside Arianna. He momentarily let go of her back, causing her to turn towards him. Quickly, he pricked the tip of his finger and Arianna stared at the blood. The scent of his blood was different than the blood in the glasses below and from the blood of the imposter. The slight sweetness in the smell made Arianna unable to keep her composure. A thirst began that hadn't been triggered by the scent of the blood below. Arianna felt the change come over her as she involuntarily began the transformation into a dearg-dul.

The scent of blood and the change of her body disorientated her. Arianna reached out her hand for Devin, and he smiled in response, bowing to Lord Randolph. Confused, Arianna turned to her grandfather. He smiled as the crowd began to whisper. Arianna listened from one conversation to the other.

"It can't be," an overweight woman with brown, curly hair proclaimed.

"It's true," a younger, well-dressed gentleman whispered in disbelief.

"But how can it be," an older, gray-haired man asked his wife.

Arianna turned back to her grandfather after she scanned the crowd, wondering why they were shocked.

"What's wrong?" she asked him.

"Nothing is wrong," he replied. "They are all just entranced by your beautiful blue eyes."

Arianna looked down below at all the transformed faces. She searched from dearg-dul face to dearg-dul face. Hidden behind colorful, feathered masks, she could not tell who each person was, but one thing was all the same. She could see only brown eyes staring back at her.

SEVEN

The dance continued once Arianna released her dearg-dul form, and the chatter died down. As she sat beside her grandfather and watched the crowd of richly colored dresses twirl before her, she could periodically hear someone asking their neighbor about Arianna. She sat and listened to several of the conversations, still unsure as to why she was any different from the people standing below her, or what it meant. Arianna was beginning to feel strangely relaxed sitting next to her grandfather. Love was pouring off of him, masking the murderous feeling she felt before.

"Grandfather," she hesitantly began. Lord Randolph nodded, as he stopped watching their guests, and turned to Arianna giving her his full attention. "Why am I different?"

Lord Randolph smiled and patted her hand. "You truly don't remember anything of your past, do you?" Arianna shook her head no. "We have a lot to tell you about, but don't worry about it tonight. We have plenty of time." Arianna tried to hide her disappointment from his loving stare.

Arianna returned to sitting in silence, and watched the people below enjoy themselves. She hadn't noticed when Aunt Lilly left, but the faint fragrance of her perfume was not in the room any more. Unable to concentrate any longer on the people whispering about her, but not having an answer to her question of why she was different, Arianna yawned as she looked at the clock: two in the morning. *Where's Gabriel*, she wondered, knowing he would answer her questions. Arianna closed her eyes and listened to the footsteps of the people dancing. She searched around the room. He wasn't in the ballroom. She focused her attention on the rest of the building. Outside on the patio, she could hear the faint, distinct steps of Gabriel. Arianna opened her eyes to find her grandfather watching her.

"Are you getting tired?" he asked. Arianna nodded, wondering how she could detour to the patio before heading to bed. Arianna looked below at the people dancing. To leave the room, she could go straight through the dance floor, or around either side. If she headed around the right side, she could walk near enough to see if Gabriel was outside.

"Did you want to say goodnight to Gabriel?" Lord Randolph asked, surprising Arianna. It was of no use lying to him. Arianna nodded. Lord Randolph stood and offered her his hand. "I'll take you to him."

Whispers and stares followed them as they walked. Arianna tried to stay shielded behind her grandfather's large, powerful arm as he led her around the right side of the room to the patio doors leading outside. Relieved to find that Devin was following close behind, Arianna tried to ignore the curious guests.

Outside, the cool spring air smelled wet, as if it had just rained. It perfectly hid the scent of her uncle as he stood outside, watching the stars. Gabriel only moved slightly to acknowledge he heard them near him. Arianna could feel the tension between the two older men, and Devin seemed to be anxiously waiting for something to happen.

"Nice night," Gabriel commented. "What do you think, old man?"

Lord Randolph chuckled. "If I'm an old man, what does that make you?" he replied. "Arianna was heading to bed, but I believe she wanted to talk to you first. We will be right inside the door," he said kindly to Arianna. Arianna nodded her head, thankful to be left alone with Gabriel.

"Not enjoying the party?" Gabriel asked. Removing his coat, he placed it around his tiny grandniece. "Too much to take in at one time, isn't it?" Arianna nodded as she realized it was still quite cold outside, and his warm coat felt good.

"Why do they stare and talk about me?" she asked. "I know I'm different than them, but I don't understand why."

"You mean your blue eyes?" Gabriel asked. "They make you very special to them. There has never been a dearg-dul born with blue eyes. If I remember right, there's some sort of legend that goes along with your eyes. Everyone is curious if you are truly the person of legend."

"A legend? That's a lot to live up to. What does the legend say? Do I have to do something?" she asked.

"I don't know the specifics." Gabriel could see her disappointment. "I'm not a dearg-dul. You should ask Devin. I'm sure he can explain it to you."

"But he's not a dearg-dul either," Arianna said.

"No, but he was raised by the most powerful dearg-dul alive today, so he has a very good understanding of dearg-duls," Gabriel explained.

"Who is that?" Arianna wondered.

"Your grandfather," Gabriel replied. "Most of the people, if not all of them, that are in that room there respect and fear him."

"Do you?" Arianna asked.

"No. To me, he will always be that short crybaby that was older than me by a few years, yet always acted five years younger," Gabriel responded. Arianna nodded her head as she stared into the room of dancing people. She had sensed the fear in the people in the room because they feared her grandfather.

"Why do I have blue eyes? Why am I, yet again, different than everyone?" she asked, not expecting a response. She had spent her life being different for as long as she could remember. She was an orphan. Though she loved her aunt and uncle dearly, they couldn't hide the fact they were not her parents.

"Because you are not just a dearg-dul," Gabriel replied.

"But Grandfather said I'm a purebred dearg-dul," Arianna explained, confused by Gabriel's comment.

"Purebred sounds like it means one-hundred percent, but really it's a measure of the strength of your dearg-dul genes," Gabriel explained. "You are also what we consider a purebred baku."

"Baku?" she repeated, unsure of the word.

"There are more types of creatures that live off of human

blood than just dearg-duls," he replied. "Humans are food to different types of creatures which some call demons. We prefer not to be called demons, but rather 'night humans.' This is yet another conversation you should have with Devin."

Arianna felt light-headed. Her day had been filled, non-stop, with new sights, sounds, tastes, and ideas. Now, Gabriel was adding in one more piece of the puzzle. Arianna felt strained from trying to understand everything. Gabriel ushered her to a bench to sit down. She would need time to sort out what she was being told. Arianna stared into the vast dark sky dotted by tiny stars. In the past twenty-four hours, her life had changed by leaps and bounds, not the baby steps she was used to. She had been content in her own little world, living with her aunt and uncle. Their life, while sometimes a bit hard, was happy and full of love. She had friends, a home, a school, a life, but now it was all being taken away. Arianna winced as she felt her previous life shatter.

"Can I just go back to normal?" she asked.

"I wish it was that easy," Gabriel replied. Gabriel put his arm around her and squeezed. "You should get some sleep. Things always seem better after the rain has passed." Gabriel waved to Devin who returned, removed the coat, passed it back to Gabriel, and escorted Arianna back to her room.

"She's more unbelievable than expected, right James?" Gabriel said, as Lord Randolph joined him on the patio, both men staring into the dark night. "She grew up too fast."

"Agreed," the older man added. "I thought it would take forever until she returned, but in the blink of an eye she was turning sixteen. She seems a bit stressed tonight. Did we do the right thing, sending her away to live with Lilly and Dean?"

"What choice did we have? Her parents were both murdered. Neither one of us could provide her with complete safety. We had to let her go. It was Travis and Tiffany's wish." Gabriel wrapped his coat around himself. "Though it would have been easier if Lilly or Dean had mentioned a bit about her past to her. She is in for quite a shock now."

"I could already see it in her eyes. She's confused, and it's only going to get worse," Lord Randolph added.

"Isn't that what Devin's for?" Gabriel asked as Lord Randolph sat beside him. "You trained him well."

"Thanks, but that wasn't my intention," Lord Randolph added. "He filled the void she left. He has always been such an eager young man, wanting to learn as much as he can, as quickly as he can."

"Then what happens now? Is it finally time to end this feud?" Gabriel replied.

"I hope it ends this easily, but it will take time. I wish it would have ended sixteen years ago, but it didn't. It has been so long that we've been on opposite sides. You've gotten old, friend." Lord Randolph stared at the graying man beside him.

"So have you," Gabriel added, chuckling. "Our time is almost up. Hopefully we can set everything straight for her before she takes over." Lord Randolph nodded, as they both stared into the star-filled sky in silence.

Arianna returned to the room in which she had awoken that morning. Though everything was how she left it, it didn't feel comforting since she had been kidnapped from the same room. After much reassurance from Devin that she was safe, Arianna tried to relax with a hot bath. As she soaked in the tub, she pondered everything that had happened since she had left home. It was all too unbelievable. Her uncle Gabriel, her grandfather, dearg-duls, personal guards, drinking blood, kidnappings, murder, and a new, extravagant lifestyle swirled through her head as the last of the bubbles faded away. Her life had changed drastically in just a short twenty-four hours. Every fact she knew to be true was being shattered, one after another. Her life, as she knew it, was a lie. Her aunt and uncle were not related to her. Her family, which she thought was dead, was not. Her birthday wasn't even on the day she thought.

After rinsing off the soap and putting on her pajamas, Arianna tried to go to sleep in the king–sized, four-post bed, but found it was too different from her normal, single bed at home. *Home*, Arianna thought. *Where is that?* Her life was now in disarray, and though she could still remember the small apartment above the diner, a part of her told her it was no longer home. *But this isn't home either.* The strange room, decorated for a five year-old, wasn't home. The pink fluffy comforter was not home. The six ruffled pillows now piled on the floor were not home.

Arianna lay still, listening to the room around her. Though she tried to only focus on the room, her ability to hear traveled down the corridors of the large estate to the ballroom. She could hear the laughing and talking of complete strangers as they enjoyed themselves. The click of high heels and formal shoes kept the beat to the faint music that continued to play. *Doesn't anyone sleep around here?* she wondered, as she stared at the clock flashing 3:43AM. Arianna sighed as she realized, they were dearg-duls, night humans. *Of course they don't sleep at night*, she told herself. Arianna began to ponder her new existence. She knew very little of dearg-duls. Would it be like the movies? Would they turn to ash at the slightest sunlight? Did they attack innocent people to feed? Would vampire hunters follow her, trying to put a wooden stake through her heart? What about garlic and holy water? Was she now immortal?

Arianna tossed and turned in her bed as she failed to fall asleep. The guests, enjoying the night, continued to talk and dance as time crawled on. Arianna tried to picture her bed at home: the soft, worn sheets, her favorite pillow she refused to give up, and the window that allowed her to see the moon as she fell asleep. It was no longer her home, but she longed to be there anyways. *This isn't going to work*, she thought. There was no way she could fall asleep with all the noises to distract her.

Silently, Arianna opened her bedroom door to peer into the sitting room. The fire in the fireplace crackled and slightly flickered as the air from her bedroom pushed past it to the chimney. On the couch, sitting with his back to her, Devin was reading papers. Without looking up, he stopped, and placed the papers on the coffee table.

"Having trouble sleeping?" he asked, as he picked up a new set of papers.

"Mm hmm," she replied, sitting next to him. "You know, it's almost four in the morning."

"Is it?" he asked.

"Don't you sleep?" she asked.

"I normally only sleep two to four hours a night," he responded.

"What are you doing so late?" she wondered.

"Going over the files from today," he explained. Arianna nodded as she curled her feet beneath her to keep her toes warm. "It's my job to keep you safe, so I need to make sure we didn't miss anything."

"Your job?" she asked. "But you're only seventeen, right?"

Devin smiled as he set down the paper and picked up the next. "Correct, but I'm still employed by your grandfather."

"But you're just a high-school student," she added.

"I graduated from high school three years ago," he replied. Shocked, Arianna stared at the young man beside her. Was he really so smart that he could graduate high school at fourteen? Devin kept reading.

"It's too noisy here, and the party is still going on," he hadn't asked, but she explained why she couldn't sleep anyways.

"It could be a few more hours yet, before everyone leaves," Devin replied. "Just ignore the noise."

"That's easy for you to say. You can't hear every little whisper about you," she sulked.

"Eventually they'll get used to you, and the gossiping should stop," he replied.

"Why is everyone making such a big deal about me?" she asked. "Gabriel said there's some legend about a dearg-dul with blue eyes, but he didn't know the details."

"Mm hmm," Devin replied, not elaborating.

Arianna was starting to get mad at his short replies. "Why won't anyone tell me anything?" she pleaded.

"They've told you quite enough for one day. Too much information at one time can be bad," he replied calmly. "You need to get some sleep. Tomorrow I'll answer all of your questions, okay?" Arianna nodded. He was always correct. She already had way too much to think about.

"Can I sit here a little longer until I feel sleepy?" she asked. Devin nodded without looking up from his papers. "Thanks."

Arianna sat and watched the fire flicker. The flames danced on the walls, captivating her attention, but she couldn't stop the sounds running through her head of the people talking below. Arianna sighed. She wanted to sleep, but being in such an unfamiliar place made it impossible to ignore all the new noises she heard. There was nothing she could do to block out the sounds. Out of the corner of his eye, Devin watched Arianna as she endlessly watched the fire. She was exhausted from her long day, but she wasn't showing any signs of falling asleep soon.

"You really need to go to sleep," he said, as he scooped her into his arms and carried her back to her room.

"But I can't fall asleep," she complained, struggling to get out of his grasp. "It's still too noisy in this house."

"You have to get used to it. Your sense of hearing has increased now, and it won't change," he added.

"But," she began to complain again.

Devin sat down on the bed beside her. Arianna stared in shock as he began to unbutton his shirt.

"What are you doing?" she asked, moving away from him.

"Come here," he directed in a serious tone. He patted the bed and patiently waited. She slowly crawled back to him, sitting on the edge of the bed. Devin took her hand and placed it on his bare chest. "There's something a dearg-dul can hear even better than voices."

Arianna felt his heart beating beneath her hand. Closing her eyes, she concentrated on the sound of the blood rushing through his body. Arianna began to feel the outside world dimming. She could no longer hear the guests at the party, or the maid down the hall. Everything was covered up by the gentle thumping of Devin's heart. Arianna felt her body being moved, but she didn't fight it. The urge to sleep was slowly drawing over her. Without the distracting noises around her, she could finally rest.

"Devin," she asked, as she drifted off to sleep. "Promise me that you will always take care of me."

"Of course," he replied as she slipped into unconsciousness.

EIGHT

Arianna lifted her head slightly and heard a rush of noises around her. The bird outside chirped loudly, the maids clicked as they walked down the marble hallways, and the clanking of dishes told her it was already daytime. Arianna felt the warmth of her pillow before realizing her pillow had a pulse. She opened her eyes, in the dim light, and to her surprise, she found she was lying on Devin's bare chest. Swiftly, she sat up and moved away from him to the other side of the bed.

"I knew you were tired, but thirteen hours is a long time to sleep," he stated, as he placed the paper he was reading on the nightstand.

"What…" she began to ask, but fumbled with her words. Here she was lying in a bed with a half-naked boy with absolutely no memory of the previous night.

Devin smiled. "You don't remember last night?" he asked, knowing it would be fun to tease her a bit more.

Arianna blushed from head to toe as she tried to look away from Devin. Arianna's experience with boys was rather limited. While many girls her age were allowed to date, Aunt Lilly and Uncle Dean had told her she would have to wait until she was older. For the most part, Arianna didn't care, as she was too busy helping with the diner. In reality though, she wanted to hang out with her friends more, and the prospects of dating were quite scary. Every boy she had ever had a crush on was impossible to talk to. When she finally liked a boy, she couldn't make complete sentences when alone with him, even if just in a hallway at school.

Devin cautiously reached for her hand as she obviously, for a reason unknown to him, became frightened by the situation. Arianna moved to stand, but instead felt her legs weaken, and she ended up back on the bed. Without looking up, her face continued to glow red. Devin tried to catch her gaze, but she avoided him.

"Have I done something to offend you?" he asked as he looked down at himself. Devin buttoned his shirt and smiled. "Are you feeling okay?"

"My legs feel a little weak," Arianna replied, grabbing a pillow to hide behind.

Devin moved to try to catch her gaze, but she still refused to look at him. "That's because you aren't completely transformed yet. You use up your blood too quickly."

Arianna peeked up at him. "Will it always be like this?" she asked.

"No. It will get better as you learn to control things, such as your sensitive hearing. Doing things that are beyond human ability uses the blood you drink. So the more you do, the more blood you will need," he explained.

"How did you make me go to sleep last night?" she asked. "I tried to sleep, but everything was too noisy."

"I read in one of my books that you'd be drawn to the sound the heart makes. Just by touching my skin, you can hear it, can't you?" He waited for her to understand. Arianna nodded. "It seems that's enough to block out all other sounds."

"Does that mean every time I want to sleep, you have to be there?" she asked, blushing again as she found herself wanting to add *half naked*.

"Are you afraid of me?" he replied with a question. Arianna shook her head no. There was nothing scary about

Devin. He had been kind to her since the first moment she talked to him. He was very quiet, which made her always wonder what he was thinking, but he wasn't scary. "You are doing your best to hide behind that pillow like I might jump over there and attack you." Arianna looked down at the pillow she was still hugging. "Like you think I'm a monster. Let me reassure you, I'm human. You should be able to tell."

"It's just that this is all a little weird," she replied. "I've never even dated a boy, and here I wake up in the same bed with a boy I've only known for two days. Aunt Lilly would kill me if she knew," Arianna accidentally blurted out before turning bright red again.

"Oh that's the problem?" he replied with a laugh. "Then don't worry. You've known me much longer than two days. In fact, we met over ten years ago." Arianna slightly dropped her defensive pillow. "You don't remember? You told me that you would marry me when we got older." Arianna began to blush.

"But I don't remember that," Arianna replied, trying to remember ever meeting Devin.

"I came here right after my family was killed. Your grandfather took me in. He felt bad for me because he was too late to stop my family from dying," Devin explained. Arianna concentrated on Devin's face as he spoke in the dimly-lit room. She could see the honesty in his crisp blue eyes. "I was only seven-years-old when I first met you. You were already asleep when we arrived back here, so your grandfather didn't want to wake you to introduce you to me. Instead, he just tucked me into the bed next to you, and told me to sleep. After losing my family in the middle of the night, I found comfort in this strange place where everyone slept during the day. When I woke, it was already evening again, and I began to panic until I realized I wasn't alone in the room. The girl who had been sleeping during the day was now awake, watching me. I was scared, so you offered to play with me." Devin paused as he thought of a childhood that Arianna couldn't remember. "You were only there a week because it was your last week living with us. Your grandfather had been picking up Lilly and Dean to bring them back to meet you when he saved me. At the end of the week, you told me that you were going on a long trip, but someday you would come back and marry me."

Arianna giggled. "Did I really say that?" she asked, mortified at her bold younger self.

"Yes, but I suppose it doesn't count if you don't remember. Oh yeah, not to mention the fact you told two of the butlers, three maids, and your favorite cook you wanted to marry them also," he added before breaking out into laughter. Arianna smiled as she watched him. Since she had first seen him in her math class, she had never heard him laugh. He was always so serious about everything. Even being with him almost constantly for two days, she had yet to see him honestly smile.

"You're a lot cuter when you smile," she added. It was Devin's turn to blush.

"I'm not your type," he replied, trying to cover up his embarrassment.

"And how would you know who is my type?" she asked.

"I know everything about you," he replied, looking out the nearest window to avoid her gaze.

"What?" Arianna replied. How could someone who sat in the back of the room know anything about her? They had only just first talked together two days ago. "Doubt it," she added.

"You love chocolate, but only if it's dark chocolate. You return home every day at 3:48 to help the cook chop vegetables for the evening meal. Your prized treasure is a small bracelet Lilly gave you that she told you came from your mother. On weekends you change clothes at least twice a day because you finally have freedom from your school uniform. You love daisies and hate roses. Should I go on?" he asked as her mouth dropped. He was correct. He knew her quite well. "Now, I promised you last night to give you answers after you had time to sleep. Do you have any questions?"

Arianna stared at him, unable to form a sentence. How could he know so much? Devin smiled and laughed at her confused face.

"I can leave then?" he asked as he stood up.

"No, wait," she called, reaching over the bed and grabbing his arm. Devin sat down beside her. "Why do you know so much about me?"

"It's my job," he replied. "Like you believed about yourself, I have no family. I owe everything in my life to your grandfather. He took me in, gave me a home, and raised me. This is the only way I know how to pay him back: taking care of the most precious person to him in the world, his granddaughter." Devin's sincerity brought back her questions.

"What is a baku?" Arianna asked, remembering the word Gabriel used the night before. "Gabriel said I'm a purebred dearg-dul, and a purebred baku."

"Like dearg-duls, baku are also night creatures that survive on blood. You met a group of them the first night I picked you up from Gabriel's house. Those men with long white hair and pale skin were all baku," Devin explained. "There are four types of night humans you will encounter: dearg-dul, lycan, baku, and tengu. You have met dearg-duls, as most of the people here last night were dearg-duls who are loyal to your grandfather. They are what you would call a vampire. Mixed in with the guests last night were also lycans, or what you'd picture as werewolves. Your uncle and cousin are both baku, a night human that's like a vampire but can also feed on dreams and feelings. Tengu are more like lycan because they feed on meat as well as blood, but instead of being a bit on the furry side, they grow large wings that can support their body weight and allow them to fly. There were no baku or tengu at last night's party. Night humans don't get along too well."

"Were my parents human like you?" Arianna wondered.

"No, your father was a baku and your mother a dearg-dul."

"And that's why my families don't like each other?" Arianna asked.

"For hundreds of years, baku and dearg-duls have been fighting for control of the night. Lycans and tengu, which don't necessarily need blood, but can eat raw meat to feed, each joined sides of the fight. Lycans allied themselves with dearg-dul and tengu with the baku, but it's really just a fight between both baku and dearg-duls who need human blood to survive. Your grandfather is the leader of the dearg-duls. He had been leading the fight since he was a teenager against Gabriel, the leader of the baku."

"My parents both came from different sides? Like Romeo and Juliet?" Arianna asked. Devin nodded. "And you are human. Do humans get involved in this also?"

"Mostly not by choice," Devin replied.

"Why would my grandfather take a human child home to this strange life?" Arianna asked.

"Because my family was murdered by a baku as they slept. Whether I want to or not, I'm involved in this. Now, though, I'm here by choice," Devin replied. "I can leave at any time if I wished. Your grandfather has told me, time and time again, he would get me out of here with a new identity and all, but I want to stay."

"So, you were raised here amongst night humans?" Arianna asked.

"Yes, but as you will find, there almost as many normal humans as night humans living here at your grandfather's estate," Devin replied.

"Then you *can* tell me about the blue eye legend," Arianna deduced.

"All that I'm allowed to say is what you already know. When a person turns into the dearg-dul form, whether their eyes are blue, green, or brown, they all turn a reddish brown color when they transform. Your eyes do not." Devin explained. "There's a legend that goes along with finding a dearg-dul with blue eyes, but your grandfather has forbid us to tell you it. He doesn't want you to feel added pressure to live up to some legend." Arianna nodded. She could understand her grandfather's reasoning, but she still wanted to know.

"Can you at least tell me the basics of dearg-duls? Are they like vampires in the movies?" Arianna asked only to be interrupted by the distinct clicking sound of Molina's boots. Arianna turned to the door, and Devin stood to open it.

"Lord Randolph wants to go over the reports with you," a startled Molina said to Devin as he stood at the door. Devin nodded as he hurried over to a door on the left side of the sitting room.

Arianna sat on the bed, staring out into the sitting room. Devin returned from the door he had entered, dressed in new clothes. He walked across the sitting room to another door. He paused briefly.

"Molina can answer your questions about dearg-duls," he added, before heading through the door.

Molina stood in the doorway to Arianna's bedroom.

"Why don't you get dressed for the day first," she suggested, shutting the door behind her as she left.

Arianna dressed and found Molina waiting in the sitting room patiently.

"So you have questions?" Molina asked. "First, you can look around the apartment if you'd like."

"Apartment?" Arianna asked. So far she had only seen the

sitting room and her bedroom. She hadn't realized she was in an apartment.

"The door on the left is Devin's bedroom, the door straight ahead leads into the rest of the estate, and the door on the right here leads to the rest of your quarters," Molina explained. Arianna nodded as she cautiously opened the door to her right.

Stepping into the large living room, Arianna looked around. The plush sofas were facing a large-screen TV to the left. Straight ahead were French doors leading outside. Arianna walked to the doors and looked through the glass panes.

"What floor are we on?" she asked, seeing that the balcony was several floors off the ground.

"The fourth floor, or rather, the top. Your grandfather's apartment is right below yours," Molina replied. "It's past two; you can go outside if you want."

"Past two?" Arianna asked.

"Along with a thirst for blood, your skin is now more sensitive to UV radiation. If you go outside between ten in the morning and two in the afternoon, the sun's rays will instantly cause severe burns on any skin exposed," Molina explained. Arianna hesitantly opened the doors and walked out onto the veranda.

"We can go outside, into sunlight, as long as it isn't between ten and two?" Arianna asked, as Molina followed her onto the balcony.

"Yes, but it's still dangerous to stay in direct sunlight at any time for too long," she added, as she tried to usher Arianna into the shadows.

"What else is now bad for me?" Arianna asked. "Garlic or crosses?"

"Rubbish, all that movie stuff is rubbish," Molina replied, still trying to move Arianna, who remained in the sunlight. Arianna sat down in the warmth.

"What about killing a dearg-dul then, no stake through the heart?"

"A stake through the heart would kill just about anyone," Molina replied, and Arianna laughed.

"I suppose that's true," Arianna replied.

"The most common way to kill a dearg-dul is to drain their blood, or prevent access to fresh blood. We need blood to survive. It gives us the non-human powers such as a good sense of hearing and makes us heal quicker. Without blood, any dearg-dul or night human would die," Molina explained. Arianna thought back to when she was sitting in the cell. The men who took her were planning to deprive her of blood until she died.

"How long can you go without new blood?" Arianna asked.

"For a new dearg-dul like you?" Molina asked, and Arianna nodded. "Only days. Once you get used to everything, and learn how to regulate the amount of blood you use, you'll be able to go weeks without needing fresh blood." Molina looked into the sky again. They were staying outside too long in direct sunlight.

"How do you get fresh blood?" Arianna asked. "Do you have to keep finding someone to drink from?"

"The fridge in the kitchen is filled with packs of fresh blood like the one Gabriel gave you yesterday. There are markets around dearg-dul towns that provide blood. Otherwise, dearg-duls can take a keeper or custodian. Normally a keeper is a human, but it could also be another dearg-dul or night human. There a bond is made between the person, or ward, and the custodian so that the custodian promises to provide blood to the ward."

"Oh, but isn't that a lot of responsibility for one person?" Arianna asked.

"For normal dearg-duls like me, we can only take one keeper, which is fine because I don't require much blood.

For you, and other purebred dearg-duls, you need a lot more blood, and therefore have the power to take multiple custodians," Molina explained, as she winced from the increased sunlight that peeked from behind the clouds. "We aren't the monsters you're picturing," she tried to reassure Arianna. "And, like you, we are not this way by choice. It's just what we are. The biggest difference between us and the movie versions of us is how we choose to live. It takes time to get used to, but this is your life now." Molina could feel the skin on her arm start to bubble. "We need to go in now," she said quietly. "Please come with me." Arianna finally noticed the blisters forming on Molina's exposed arms.

"What's this?" she asked pointing to Molina's arm.

"Even though it's later in the day, direct sunlight will easily burn our skin," Molina explained.

"This is my fault," Arianna complained, carefully looking at the blisters on the back of Molina's left arm.

"Don't worry. It's nothing a little blood won't heal," Molina replied, leading Arianna through the living room and adjoining dining room to the kitchen. Opening the refrigerator, Arianna peered inside as Molina grabbed several packets of blood from the bottom shelf. Her face changed suddenly as she bit into the packet. The bubbles stopped growing, and began to shrink. After Molina finished the second packet, the blisters still remained but were much smaller. "Dearg-dul is named for our undead properties. Day humans consider us undead because we don't die from normal things due to our intake of blood." Molina ran her hand over the blisters. "I guess they need a little time. I didn't realize they were so deep."

"So, blood heals your wounds?" Arianna asked.

"The same with yours," Molina replied.

"But why are they still there?" Arianna pointed to the remaining blisters.

"To heal you first need blood, and then you need some time for it to work," Molina replied.

"Is that night human blood?" Arianna asked. She could still smell the faint odor on Molina's breath. Molina nodded. "So, will it heal quicker with dearg-dul blood?"

"The stronger the blood, the quicker it heals," Molina replied.

"Then my blood should heal you quicker because I'm a purebred?" Arianna asked.

"Correct, but don't get any ideas. It's a crime to drink purebred blood," Molina answered.

"But what if I offer it?" Arianna asked, feeling guilty that she caused Molina to get burned. Arianna took the knife from the counter and sliced the palm of her hand. "You have to follow my orders, correct? I order you to take some of my blood to heal."

Molina was stuck. It was true she had to follow Arianna's orders, but it was also true that it was a crime to take it. Molina shook her head as Arianna held out her bleeding palm. Hesitantly she licked the blood off Arianna's hand, which had already healed itself. The blisters faded until nothing was left from the burn. Arianna smiled.

"My blood can heal that easily, even with just a drop?" she asked, surprised that it had actually worked.

"Just a drop of your blood could heal over fifty people. You know nothing of this world you are now a part of, but you are the strongest I've ever met, and you haven't even finished turning yet," Molina replied.

NINE

Arianna followed Devin and Molina downstairs from the dining room into the apartment below hers. From the lingering scent, she could tell that it was her grandfather's apartment. She curiously peered into the side rooms, beginning to remember only fragments of her childhood: the deep burgundy satin-covered pillows on the couch, the leather-bound books stacked near his desk, the little ship sitting on the fireplace mantel in a bottle. Lord Randolph sat quietly in the formal living room, watching his curious granddaughter. As soon as she realized he was there, she backed into Devin. Lord Randolph had the same glaring indifference from the night before as he looked to Molina, who was standing beside Arianna. Arianna quickly understood, as she could also still smell her own blood on Molina's breath.

"I ordered her to take my blood," Arianna began. "It was my fault she got burned while outside with me." Arianna waited for her grandfather's reply, but he said nothing. With a wave of his hand, Molina bowed and returned up the stairs. The fear in Molina didn't decrease even as she left. Lord Randolph was not a forgiving man.

"You seem to be fine," he commented, as his tone and facial expression changed.

Arianna looked at her own arms. It was true. She had been sitting in the sun longer than Molina, but nothing was burned. "I don't know why, but I'm fine. We were only outside for ten minutes or so."

"Please join Devin and me for dinner," Lord Randolph added, as he stood and walked to the set table.

Arianna stared at the elaborate elegance of the place settings. This wasn't a normal dinner in her eyes. From the delicate flower pattern around the edges of the expensive china, to the lace napkins at three place settings, everything indicated that it had been specifically arranged for Devin and Arianna to join him for his meal. Lord Randolph sat down at the head of the table as Arianna moved to the seat set next to him and across from Devin. Arianna's forehead wrinkled in confusion as food was brought to the table by a maid.

"Don't I need blood to survive? Isn't that my food now?" Arianna asked softly, afraid of her grandfather, who was still mad.

The loud laugh from the head of the table nearly made her jump. Lord Randolph's tone changed as he replied. "Yes, you will need blood to survive now, but you are not always a night human. There's a day human side to you too. So, for that we eat food as well as blood." Arianna nodded. The older man's eyes twinkled at his granddaughter. It had been ten years since she left, but he had thought of her every day. Once a year, he had traveled with Devin to check up on Arianna, but he never talked to her. Each time, he found delight in watching her do just about anything. Her mannerisms reminded him of his own daughter so much. It was hard, year after year, to leave her behind.

Arianna sat uncomfortably through the meal as she was waited upon by maids in black and white dresses. It was too extravagant for her, but Devin and her grandfather didn't seem to find it odd at all. Devin and her grandfather talked to great lengths about everything and nothing at the same time. There was a clear bond between them. As the meal finished, the maids returned with dessert. Arianna stared at the pie on the delicate plate. It was her favorite, lemon meringue pie.

"Was it made correctly?" Lord Randolph asked as Arianna took her first bite.

"It tastes just like Captain Lou's," Arianna replied. "I didn't know anyone could make it like him."

"Lou did teach our staff how to cook," Lord Randolph replied, and Arianna stopped eating.

"Is Lou," she began to ask, and Devin nodded a reply. "I didn't know." Arianna stared at the pie in front of her. Everything was so new to her; she didn't realize that it had always been happening around her. Just because she didn't know about it, didn't mean that it didn't exist. "Who else?" Arianna wondered.

"More than we can list right now," Devin replied.

"But then, why didn't anyone tell me about all of this?" she asked.

"Because I ordered them not to, and Gabriel did the same. Very few people knew who you were, and those who did could not say. We wanted you to have a childhood free from this world; the same world that killed both your mother and father, and would do the same to you if they knew about you," Lord Randolph replied.

"Are Aunt Lilly and Uncle Dean really not my family?" she asked earnestly.

"No. Lilly is a friend of your mother's and Dean is her older brother. Lilly was raised here at this estate beside your mother, and they were the best of friends, almost like sisters," Lord Randolph explained.

Arianna turned to the entering maid, who had the lingering scent of blood on her. Arianna's sharp eyes quickly glanced over the maid. She wasn't a night human; yet, she had the strong scent of blood all over her. Her blond curls bobbed as she near Lord Randolph and bowed to him before speaking.

"Excuse me, my Lord," she said quietly. Arianna guessed she was not much older than herself. "Would you like me to bring it in a glass or medical bag?"

"I don't think she will readily drink it," he replied. "Medical should be fine." The young girl curtsied again and left the room. Arianna stared from Devin to her grandfather unaware of what they were cryptically discussing. "We need to finish your transformation," Lord Randolph explained, as the maid returned with a bag of red liquid.

"I heard you were being very picky after you turned, and refused any blood but Devin's, but you need to take more blood to finish your transformation. Devin will take care of everything for you upstairs," he offered. "Devin, after you get Arianna settled, please send Molina back down here."

Unsure of what was happening; Arianna followed Devin upstairs to the sitting room outside her bedroom. They didn't explain how she would take the blood that smelled so unappealing. Arianna sat patiently on the couch as Devin and Molina put an IV in her. She knew immediately their plan to give her blood, and she was thankful she wouldn't have to drink it.

"Just sit here until it's empty," Devin instructed, as he and Molina left the room.

Alone in the fancy sitting room, Arianna studied the paintings on the wall as she drifted into peoples' conversations throughout the house: two maids talking down several hallways, a young man helping an older man with tools outside, the splash of water as an older woman washed clothes. Arianna focused to the room below hers as the scent of blood caught her attention. It was dearg-dul blood.

"I am sorry, my Lord," Molina repeated after Lord Randolph hit her across her face. "I didn't mean to disobey you."

"You were told that you are under her command on

everything but one issue. No one is to take even a drop of her blood," Lord Randolph growled. "No one includes you." Arianna winced as he slapped Molina again. Though she couldn't see him, Arianna could feel the anger in Lord Randolph's voice. Arianna listened as Devin helped Molina back to her feet. "The next time anyone takes her blood—I don't care if she offers or is forced, I'll kill them."

"Out of my sight," Lord Randolph ordered. "Just remember, next time I won't be as lenient."

"Yes, my Lord," Molina replied. Arianna listened as the click of Molina's shoes brought her upstairs and through the kitchen.

"She doesn't understand the value of her own blood," Devin said quietly to Lord Randolph.

"She needs to learn it soon. As soon as we let her out of this house, they will all come looking for her." Lord Randolph's tone of voice changed as he talked alone with Devin. "I have already received over fifty marriage proposals, and just as many custodian proposals."

"You expected that much," Devin replied. "Do any of them look promising?"

"I threw them all in the fire this morning. She's only sixteen. There's no way she's ready to be promised in marriage to someone. She doesn't even know the value in her own life," he complained. "As to custodians, she doesn't need to decide that for a few more years. Besides, she has you."

"Forever," Devin replied. "Is everything set with the school?"

"Yes, she can begin tomorrow. You and Molina will accompany her," Lord Randolph ordered. "I prefer to keep her here, but she might get suspicious if we never let her out of her apartment."

Arianna tried to continue listening, but realized the words were now starting to sound funny. Arianna giggled as

81

the last bit of blood drained into her arm. For some reason, she felt so warm and happy. Maybe the blood had something in it. The overly-decorated room became amusing to her as she looked from one corner of the room to the next. *So much stuff in such a little space*, she mused. Arianna giggled more. Everything she just heard sounded so scary, but she just had the urge to giggle. She now was a prisoner in her grandfather's home. He was going to arrange a marriage for her. Her life was now completely in his control, but for some reason, Arianna found herself not caring. The blood had to be spiked with alcohol.

Devin returned to find Arianna lying upside down, hanging off the couch.

"What are you doing?" he asked as he placed her right side up and took out the IV.

"Eww," she said plugging her nose as Devin picked up the IV bag and threw it in the fire. "That smells so gross." Devin turned to Arianna, and she smiled back at him before giggling. "You look better upside down." Arianna turned herself around and upside down off the couch again.

Devin sighed. "He really gave you his own blood didn't he?" Devin asked, knowing Arianna wouldn't know the difference.

"Grandfather's blood? Is that why it smelled so badly?" she asked poking his arm with her toes.

"Promise me, that from now on, you'll only drink my blood?" Devin demanded.

"Devin's blood is nummy," Arianna said while bouncing her feet off the back of the couch, refusing to sit up. As Devin made to move and sit her on the couch again, Arianna clumsily rolled off, and hit the floor with a thud. She burst into giggles.

Ignoring her, Devin picked up his papers from the coffee table and began to read over them.

"What'cha doing?" Arianna asked, as she crawled around

the couch and hung over the back behind Devin.

"Babysitting," he replied, not looking up from his papers. Lazily, for her own amusement, she blew the edges of his hair over his ears.

"Babysitting papers?" she asked, confused.

"Babysitting you," he responded, straightening his hair.

"But I'm not a baby," she stated. Devin rolled his eyes. "Did you say you would answer all my questions?" Devin nodded but still didn't look up. "How long have you been stalking me?" she asked, smiling politely.

"Three, maybe four years," he replied, not taking the bait to argue with her.

"So, that's how you know things about me. How much do you know about me?" she asked.

"You're not going to remember most of this conversation tomorrow, so why not save the questions until later?" he wondered.

"So, you don't know too much then," she replied as she flopped on the couch, upside down, again.

Devin looked over his papers to her face by his knee. "Though you tell everyone you hate the color pink, your favorite bra and panty set is the pink and white striped one Lilly gave you for Christmas last year."

Arianna's mouth dropped. How could he know that? She'd never told anyone. She'd never written it down or said it out loud, even. Arianna blushed as she searched her mind to figure out how he would know. There was no reason he should know such information. Arianna sat up and pulled the papers from his hand throwing them messily on the coffee table.

"Did you guys set up camera in my room or something? Isn't that invasion of privacy?" she asked, angry that they must have been watching her for a very long time.

Devin picked back up his papers and began to read again. "First of all, it's only invasion of privacy if it was not owned by your grandfather, but Lilly and Dean's apartment is one of the hundreds that Lord Randolph owns. Second, I wouldn't stoop so low as to use cameras to watch you. Cameras can be fooled. It's far better to watch over someone in person, even if they are annoyingly drunk off their grandfather's blood."

"I'm not drunk. I'm not old enough to drink," she laughed as she answered, no longer angry with Devin.

"You could save us all a lot of trouble if you'd just go to sleep until it wears off," Devin suggested, as he set his papers down and picked her up. Walking to her room, he gently placed her in her bed. Placing his hand gently on her cheek, Arianna could feel his pulse echo loudly in her ears. Arianna smiled up at Devin as she became sleepy.

"All this following me around, and learning every detail about me, do you love me?" she asked sweetly. Devin blushed, but didn't reply. Arianna smiled back as she could feel his answer. "Why?" she asked.

"Just get some sleep," he instructed, not answering the question. "We can talk more tomorrow."

Arianna pushed his hand off her face. "No, I want to talk now. You said you would answer every question I had today. I want answers now," she demanded. "I'm living in a strange place where I'm basically being kept captive. My aunt and uncle have left already. I've listened to the whole house. I know they're not here anymore. So, I've been basically abandoned by the only family I have. Then, I hear there are marriage proposals. Marriage! I'm only sixteen. Who asks for a sixteen-year-old's hand in marriage? I am beginning to feel like I'm in a nuthouse. Vampires exist, marriage at sixteen, killing without any remorse, my blood being valuable, I have family, an uncle that kidnaps me, strange men trying to kill me, oh, and did I mention that vampires are real? What does this all mean? Why am I here? Why didn't Aunt Lilly and Uncle Dean take me home with them?" Arianna began to sob. "Why did they leave me? Don't they love me anymore? Aunt Lilly always told me that even though she wasn't my real mother she always felt like she was meant to be my mom. Then why did she leave alone in this strange place? Doesn't she love me anymore?"

"She loves you more than you will ever know," Devin replied, gently stroking Arianna's head as she sobbed into his chest. "She didn't want to leave you here, but she knows that this is the best place for you."

"Why am I this way?" Arianna asked. "If I wasn't so different, then she would have kept me, right? Why did everything have to change? I feel so alone here. Everyone talks about me, but no one wants to talk to me. Everyone seems either in awe or a bit afraid of me. Am I always going to be alone?" Arianna pulled back and looked at Devin, her blue eyes still filled with tears.

Devin gently wiped the tears away. "I'll never leave you," he promised. "I'll always stay by your side." Tenderly he took her chin in his large hands and tilted her face to meet his. He pressed his lips briefly to hers.

TEN

Snuggling in close to the warm sensation beneath her face, Arianna opened her eyes to find that it was already morning. Outside, the birds were chirping to signal the beginning of a new day, but in the house, filled with people who slept through the morning and most of the day, there was silence. Arianna lifted her head to listen. Complete silence. No maids walking through the halls, no gardeners giving orders to the young boys that worked for them, nor were there any cooks clanking dishes. Arianna listened to the sounds around her. In the peacefulness of the morning, Arianna closed her eyes and lay back down on Devin's warm chest.

Aunt Lilly would kill me if she saw me now, Arianna thought. Devin's grip around her waist tightened as he continued to sleep. She wasn't allowed to date, let alone sleep in the same bed as an unrelated boy. Arianna didn't care that she was breaking Aunt Lilly's rules. In this strange place where she had been abandoned, he was the only thing constant. If it weren't for him, she would have turned, and attacked some unknown person, three nights ago, or she could still be sitting in the cell underground withering away from lack of blood. Devin had been by her side since she entered this strange, new, dreamlike reality. Of all the strange and scary people she was surrounded by, she did not fear Devin. He was safe—her protector. Smiling, Arianna compared her small hands to Devin's by placing her hand over his. His large hands were twice the size of hers. *These hands keep me safe*, she thought, as her heart began to beat a little faster. Arianna's gaze continued up the muscular arm that held onto her. She knew he was strong, yet he held onto her so gently. Arianna felt warm and safe within his grasp. Although he was serious most of the time, she knew his affection for her was real. She could see it in his eyes when he spoke. Arianna's gaze rested on his bare chest. Gently, she traced the muscles. His well-defined muscles were a sign that he had worked hard to get where he was today. Arianna blushed while he continued to sleep, unable to stop herself from touching the man sleeping beside her.

Arianna could vaguely remember the night before, as if it were a dream covered in fog. Exact words and conversations were not registering in her head, but she did remember one thing. *He kissed me*, she thought, staring at the sleeping Devin beside her. Arianna was entranced by the rhythm of his chest, rising with each breath he took. Analyzing his face, Arianna stared at each feature: golden eyelashes that fluttered slightly as he slept, the rosy color in his cheeks, his messy blond hair that hadn't been cut for months, and his light red lips. Arianna continued to stare at his lips. She had never been kissed by a boy before. Reaching up carefully, so as not to wake him, Arianna gently touched his lips. Though she still felt like she was in a dream, it was real: the boy lying beside her, the large, fancy room and house, and the blood. Arianna jerked up suddenly, looking around the room. She could smell blood. Was it in her room? Whose blood was it?

Devin rubbed his eyes as he released his grip on Arianna.

"Something wrong?" he asked.

"There's no one awake in the house, but I smell blood," she replied.

Devin lay back down. "Don't worry about it," he responded. "It's probably my blood you smell." Arianna thought for a moment. The scent was familiar, but she couldn't understand why. She glanced over Devin and couldn't see any exposed blood. "Now that your grandfather completed the transformation, blood you have tasted doesn't have to be showing for you to smell it. Purebloods tend to be really sensitive to blood, and can even smell blood within someone."

"Oh," she replied, lying back down on her own pillow.

"Are you finished sleeping?" he asked, noticing her shy away from him. Devin rubbed his eyes and grabbed his watch from the nightstand. "Seven o'clock," he read aloud. "I don't know too many night humans that like these early hours," he joked. Arianna continued to stare at him.

"Why?" she asked as she stared intently at him.

"Why what?" he replied, rolling to his side to face her while still lying down. Devin had grown accustomed to the life Lord Randolph led, and also did not normally wake early.

"All of this. Why? Why do you watch over me? Why do you do all of this? You are human, aren't you? Why get involved, especially with me?" she wondered.

"Do you remember any of last night?" he asked. Arianna shook her head no while beginning to blush from head to toe. "So, you at least remember that," he chuckled.

"But why me?" she asked. "I'm nothing special. I'm just some supposedly orphaned kid whose grandfather was kind to you. Just because he took you in doesn't mean you have to like me."

"No, I don't have to like you; I just do. I've watched over you for the past few years as a 'thank you' to your grandfather, but falling for you wasn't part of the job description. It just kind of happened," he replied. "I've had a crush on you since I first met you. It used to be a treat to go see you at Lilly and Dean's house. Your grandfather would promise me if I did well on my studies and training, I could go with him to see you. Year after year, we would stop by to visit Lilly and Dean without you knowing."

"Grandfather would visit also?" Arianna asked. Devin nodded. Arianna pictured her grandfather but couldn't recall ever meeting or seeing him at their home or restaurant.

"No matter what you say to me, you can never convince me that you are not special. You are the most important person to your grandfather and me, along with many people that have been waiting to see the legend about the blue eyes come true," he added.

"You still won't tell me about the legend though." She pouted.

"Nope, not even if you make a cute face like that. I respect your grandfather's decision. He will tell you when he feels you should know," Devin added.

"So, you really do like me?" she asked, feeling like she was in a dream. She had never had a boy tell her he liked her before, especially not a cute one. Her heart began to beat faster as she waited for his reply.

"Very much so," Devin replied seriously.

"But Aunt Lilly said I can't date until I am sixteen," Arianna automatically replied before quickly covering her own mouth.

Devin laughed. "And I suppose sleeping in the same bed with a boy night after night wouldn't be allowed either?" Arianna blushed as he climbed out from beneath the covers dressed only in boxers. "Besides, I'm not asking you to date me. I'm not even asking you to like me back. I just want to be your friend. I am satisfied just being beside you."

Arianna continued to blush, not knowing how to respond.

Devin walked to the door. "If you want, I can give you a tour of the house and grounds while everyone is asleep," he offered. Arianna nodded. "Take your time getting ready. No rush."

Arianna sat on the bed as Devin shut the door behind him. She finally realized she, too, was dressed in her pajamas. *When did I put these on*, she wondered, as she searched her hazy memory. *Nothing,* she thought. *I can't remember anything after the kiss last night.* Arianna fell back against the fluffy comforter and pillows and stared at the ceiling. Arianna laid still and listened as the soft dripping of Devin's shower began. Beyond the water, she could hear no sounds. Everyone in the house was still asleep.

"Molina was explaining how each dearg-dul has a keeper to drink blood from. Since I drink your blood, does that make you mine?" Arianna asked, as they walked around the estate gardens.

"It's a little more complicated than that," Devin replied, sitting on the edge of an empty fountain. "There are rituals involved in making someone your custodian."

"Like what?" Arianna asked.

"How about I explain that to you in a few years? Deargduls usually take four or five years or longer to choose their keeper. It's a big decision. Once you choose someone, it can't be undone," Devin replied.

"But Molina said I can have as many as I want," Arianna replied. "Couldn't I just choose someone new, if I make a bad choice?"

"She didn't explain it all to you. Once you make someone your custodian, they are obliged to follow your every order. They'll never be able to tell you no, and they will always know how to find you if you call for them. It's a bond formed between two people, and it's stronger than you can imagine." Devin watched the clouds drift overhead.

"Well, then, some day, when I finally get to choose one, can I choose you?" Arianna asked.

"You don't need to make me into a custodian to keep me close. I already live only to protect you," Devin replied, not looking at Arianna, who was staring at him. "You're sure the sun isn't bothering you at all? No blisters?" Devin took her face in his hands and scanned it over, looking for burns. "It must be the baku in you."

"What are baku?" Arianna asked. "I know Gabriel is one and you say I am also, but what exactly are they?"

"They are very similar to dearg-duls. They come out only at night and drink human blood. That's why I think baku and dearg-duls can't get along. They need the same food. The only difference is where dearg-duls are sensitive to sunlight; baku can sit in the sun all day long in their human form. On the other hand, dearg-duls can turn any time they choose, but baku can only change into their baku form at night time."

"What does a baku look like?" Arianna asked more specifically.

"You saw them when I picked you up at Gabriel's house: those men I fought with. Big, pigment free, long white haired guys? They always look like that," Devin replied. Arianna pictured the men that appeared out of nowhere to surround them that night.

"They all looked the same," Arianna complained. "With straggly hair, and very tall, muscular bodies. Eww. Will I look like that if I change into a baku?"

"I don't know," Devin replied. "I've never seen a female baku before."

"What?"

"I've only ever encountered male baku, never female," he repeated. "There are some females, children of purebreds that can partially transform, but never a full transformation. I'd guess, with being a purebred, it will be a full transformation for you."

"Eww," she repeated, imagining herself growing into a large, ugly, muscular man. "If dearg-duls change at sixteen, then when do baku change?"

"There's no special age. Baku change through a ceremony that I believe Gabriel, or the head of the clan, performs. I've never seen a baku changing," Devin admitted.

"I do my best to avoid them. They don't bring back too many fond memories for me."

"Right," Arianna replied, remembering the reason Devin was also an orphan. "Then what happens to me now? This isn't a life I ever dreamed of, or wanted."

"You learn to live this life and decide what you want now," Devin replied.

"And what if I want my old life back?" Arianna asked, picking at the stone beneath her.

"You can't go back," Devin replied. "Just forward." Arianna hung her head in defeat. She knew that she couldn't go back. There was no way to erase all that she knew. But that didn't mean she didn't want to go back.

"And how do I do that?" Arianna looked back up at him.

"By learning about who and what you are at our own school," Devin responded, offering her his hand to help her stand back up.

"When do I start?" Arianna asked.

"Tonight," Devin replied.

"Of course, night people have night school," Arianna deduced. Arianna took his hand and stood. "Great. More new people and another new place. How exciting," she added sarcastically.

"You'll be fine," he reassured her, leading her away from the fountain. "Besides, I'll be right there with you."

"Promise?" she asked. Devin nodded.

ELEVEN

Arianna walked into the neatly-organized classroom behind Molina. The blackboard was near the door that she entered from, and six long rows of tables were filled with students sitting before her. She didn't like how all the students eyed her over as the teacher talked. Devin moved to the back of the room and sat down as Arianna stood beside the teacher. Arianna had no problem being the center of attention in a group of people she knew, but strangers were a different matter. Arianna stood like a statue as the teacher talked.

"Everyone, we have a late arrival to the school term. This is Arianna Grace," the older, gray-haired woman introduced Arianna.

"Hello," Arianna replied, with a slight wave, before going back to curling the edges of her new uniform skirt between her thumb and forefinger.

"As everyone should be able to tell, she's a purebred dearg-dul. These are two of her PPU. Here, Miss Grace, we can make space right here for you, since you will have to catch up to the class," the teacher said, pointing to a seat already filled with a student. "Molly, move to the back please," the teacher added, smiling kindly at Arianna. Arianna could feel the distain behind the girl's eyes as she smiled sweetly back at the teacher.

"No problem, Miss Johnson," Molly said nicely.

"Don't worry about it," Arianna added, moving to stop the girl from standing. "I can just sit there. There are plenty of seats free back there."

"But," the teacher finally replied, getting frustrated as Arianna walked past the seated students to the empty last row of tables. "If that's what you wish."

Arianna sat through the first hour's lecture, and found herself daydreaming. She was completely lost on the material, and didn't care too much about it. Tuning out the lecture on the merits and quality of blood types, Arianna gazed out the large windows beside her rather than listen. The teacher didn't seem to notice, or mind, Arianna's lack of interest.

"Miss Grace," the teacher repeated to catch her attention. "Is any of this familiar?" she asked.

"Not really," Arianna replied, snapping out of her daydream.

"Have you gone over any of this with your guardians?" the teacher asked in front of the class.

"Nope," Arianna replied to the shock of all the students in the room. "They didn't think to tell me about anything, least of all that this was what I was." The students began to murmur. How could a purebred not be told about anything? The teacher looked to Devin sitting behind Arianna, and he nodded in agreement.

"Oh my," the teacher replied. "I guess we have a lot more catching up than I thought. We might need to have additional classes. Maybe some of the students can help you catch up as well," she suggested, but Arianna knew that wasn't going to happen. Without ever talking to the students, she could tell that they already disliked her.

"I can help her," a student said, entering the room late for class. Arianna stared at the boy. His shaggy, auburn hair hung past his collar, and he peeked from between his overgrown bangs. The boy quickly pulled his hair back as the teacher began to scold him.

"Late again, Mr. Winter?" she asked. "What was it this

time? Your shoes still missing?"

"No excuse," the boy replied. "I just couldn't wake up." The class laughed. The boy made his way through the rows of seated students and sat down beside Arianna. "I'm Turner Winter," he said, stretching out a hand and introducing himself.

"Arianna," she replied, shaking his hand while still staring at his eyes. Something about him seemed familiar, but she had never seen his face before.

"You may help her, on one condition," the teacher added. "You start showing up to class on time."

Turner glumly nodded. "I guess if that's what I need to do to work with such a beautiful young lady."

Arianna blushed to hear a stranger say something like that. The boys in the class all snickered in agreement as the girls continued to hide their hate and envy behind smiles beamed at Turner. Arianna began to watch out the window again as the teacher began her lecture. By the time she finished her second hour's lecture, Arianna was almost asleep. The students beginning to stand brought her attention back to the room.

"What's going on now?" Arianna asked Turner.

"Break time," he replied. "We have twenty minutes before the second half begins."

"There's more?" Arianna asked, staring out into the night sky.

Turner laughed. "Now you understand why I come late all the time," he replied. "Do you want to go for a walk outside? It seems more interesting to you than our class."

Arianna smiled. "Nothing she's said so far makes any sense to me, and even if I read more and tried to study it, it still wouldn't help." Arianna stood and followed Turner. "I've never been good at school, and all this is too new and confusing."

"Are they your PPU?" Turner asked about their

followers, Devin and Molina.

"Yep, the two I live with, at least," Arianna replied happy to be outside in the cool night air. With a deep breath she took in all the new scents around her. "You're neither human nor dearg-dul," she commented.

"Nope," he replied, directing her to the nearby empty table. Arianna turned and stared at a group of girls at a table across the yard as they began to snicker.

"She hasn't even been here one day, and she's already getting friendly with Turner," one of them said.

"It's because she is a purebred," the next on added.

"Purebreds are always like that. Thinking they're so much better than the rest of us," the first one complained more.

"Why would one even come to our school?" another replied.

"Show off," the first responded.

"To steal our prized Turner. Everyone knows purebreds can't stand to let us low lives have any good guys," someone added before Arianna turned away.

Arianna tried not to listen to them, but it was hard not to as all the girls sitting around had the same complaints. Arianna searched around the open courtyard and easily found Devin.

"Don't worry about it. Just ignore them," he spoke softly so that only she would hear him. Arianna nodded and turned her attention back to Turner.

"So, if you aren't a dearg-dul, then you must be a lycan," Arianna guessed.

"Correct," he replied as he glanced over at Devin. "Does he follow you everywhere?"

"Yep," Arianna smiled and waved to Devin.

"Don't you get sick of someone always watching over you?" Turner asked, smiling at Devin also. "He's so serious looking. Can't be much fun."

"Well, he is always serious, but I can't complain about him watching over me. If it weren't for him, I could be dead several times over," Arianna added.

"So, it's true you were kidnapped then?" Turner asked, and Arianna nodded. Turner stared at Arianna as she began to listen to other conversations again. He knew immediately that her sense of hearing was better than his. Amazed, he continued to watch.

Before Arianna realized it, the twenty minutes had passed, and they were headed back to the classroom. Disappointedly, Arianna returned to the drab room to listen, or rather, not listen, to the teacher drone on. As they neared the door to the classroom, Turner stopped.

"Do you really want to go back in there?" he asked. "I sure don't."

"But," Arianna started to complain, but he placed his hand over her mouth.

"Just go along with me," he instructed as he led the way back in but instead of going to their seat, he went to the teacher's desk.

"Miss Johnson," Turner began, and the older lady stared at him from beneath her glasses. "This is all a little too advanced for Arianna. I think it would be best if we could study in the library."

The teacher looked from Arianna to Turner. Apparently convinced, she nodded. "See if you can get her caught up by the end of the week. There's a practice test for our class on the library computers. If she can pass it, she should be fine." Turner turned Arianna around, and they both headed back outside the classroom.

"Where's the library?" Arianna asked.

"What?" Turner replied.

"The library?" Arianna repeated.

"Oh yeah, the library, back that way," he replied, pointing behind them.

"But I thought you just told the teacher we were going to the library." Arianna was confused.

"That was just to get her to let us leave. Now we have the rest of the night. We can do whatever we want," Turner replied.

"But if I head back to my grandfather's they'll know I am skipping school," Arianna replied. "And I guess I do need to learn about this stuff by the end of the week. At least enough to show I'm putting in an effort."

"Come on, can you really learn about being a dearg-dul from a book?" Turner asked. "It's best to learn first-hand. I can teach you that. I have a much easier method for learning all this stuff."

Arianna followed Turner as he left the school by the back door. He led her along the dimly-lit pathways to the nearest building. Arianna stared at the four-story, brick building in front of them.

"What is this?" she asked.

"The dorms," he replied, walking to the door and opening it for her. Arianna stared at the poster on the door. 'No girls allowed.'

"Male dorms?" Arianna questioned.

"Yep," Turner agreed.

"But it says no girls allowed," she replied, hesitant to follow him.

"Do you do everything you're told?" Turner asked, and Arianna nodded. "No one is here. Everyone is at class, so it doesn't matter. Besides, I need to change, and my room is up there. You can wait here if you want, but someone might come along and see you skipping class."

Arianna followed behind Turner closely. She didn't want to be caught alone skipping class. Turner led her to the stairwell and up three flights of stairs. Cautiously, Arianna followed him as he opened his room door. The room wasn't as she had expected, with everything neatly placed on the shelves. The desk on the wall was completely cleaned, with papers organized into stacks. The only thing out of place was the messy bed, which she knew he probably rushed out of to make it to class late after sleeping in.

"No roommate?" she asked, as she noticed only one bed in the room.

"Are you offering?" She blushed. Turner smiled at her reaction. "No. If I had a roommate I'd get in a lot more trouble, so my father insisted I have a room alone." Turner gave her a sly smile as he moved to his dresser and began to dig through his clothes. Finding a shirt, he swiftly removed his school uniform top. Arianna blushed again, trying not to stare at him. Turner smiled as he noticed her peaking at him shirtless.

"Here," he said, throwing a sweatshirt at her. "If you walk around in your uniform, someone will know we're skipping class." Arianna nodded as she pulled the large sweatshirt over her top.

"It's a little big," she commented, giggling as she stood and the sweatshirt covered more than half her skirt. Turner laughed as well.

"That's because you're so tiny," he replied, comparing his height to hers.

"Am not," Arianna pouted, as she hated to be called small.

"Okay, fine," he replied patting her head. "It's because I'm so large." Arianna smiled and nodded in agreement, though she knew the latter was not the case.

"So, how will skipping school teach me enough to pass the test?" she asked.

Turner opened his desk drawer and pulled out a set of keys. Arianna followed Turner as he led her back out the door they came in. Stopping in the nearby parking lot, Turner handed Arianna a helmet. Hopping on the only motorcycle in the lot, Turner put his keys in the ignition and started it.

"But," Arianna complained.

"We aren't breaking any laws. Just skipping a class. I do this all the time. Hop on," he directed. Arianna stared at Turner. "I'm seventeen. This is my bike, really." Turner extended his hand to Arianna, and she hesitantly climbed on the back of his seat. "Hold on tight," he instructed. Arianna placed her arms around his waist. "You might want to hold a little tighter. I want to see if your PPU can keep up with us."

Arianna adjusted her grip as he peeled out of the parking lot. Arianna left the school, and the Randolph estate, behind. She hadn't been allowed to leave her grandfather's home since she arrived. She didn't even know where she was living except that it was beside some mountains. Arianna closed her eyes as she clung to her new friend. The wind whipped by as he sped up. *Free*, Arianna thought. Turner checked behind him as he maneuvered between two cars. Arianna turned and noticed Jackson and Nixon in a car not too far behind, also making the same turns as they had. Arianna could feel Turner's happiness increase as he sped up. Her security guards kept pace with them. Surprised, they entered back into the city. Driving down the streets, it looked just like a normal city. Her sense of smell confirmed it was mainly made up of day humans. Reaching their destination, Turner hopped off his bike first, and then helped Arianna.

"Your grandfather sure knows how to pick good ones," Turner said, as Nixon exited the car next to them.

"Where are we?" she asked, as Turner began walking down the sidewalk.

"In town," he replied. "I come into town to get away from all that school and Randolph estate crap."

"How will this help me learn?" she wondered, watching the humans around her walk by without even noticing them. It felt different to be around normal people again. No one was afraid of her, and no one stared. This was the life she was beginning to miss.

Turner opened the bright blue door of one of the shops. Arianna followed him with Nixon and Jackson close behind. Neither man said a word to her as they followed. Arianna peeked around the corner of the room they just entered. Actual videos lined the shelves. It was an old-fashioned video store like she had seen in movies. She didn't recognize any titles by looking at the pictures on each nor even knew how or what you played them in. Turner waved to the lady behind the counter as he walked around. Stopping periodically, he checked movies that they passed. When he finally was satisfied, he walked to the counter with Arianna behind.

"Skipping again?" the lady asked. Turner nodded. "You spend more time out of school than in." Arianna stared at her bright red lips as she spoke. "Oh my, you're not alone. Hi dear. Don't let this delinquent rub off on you." *Too late*, Arianna thought, as she nodded in agreement.

"Movies?" she asked as they left the store.

"In six hours I can teach you everything you need to know to pass that test," Turner replied, tapping the four videos in his hand.

"This can teach me?" she asked, dubiously staring at the old, tattered videos. "Molina said the movies are not true."

"Oh yes, the Hollywood movies are pretty bad," Turner agreed. "That's why we came here. Trust me; this is all you need to know to pass any of the tests." Turner led her back to his bike to drive her home.

Arianna was disappointed that her only trip away from her grandfather's house ended so quickly. Sadly, she climbed off Turner's bike in the school parking lot to find that students were returning from their classes. Students didn't seem to notice them as they walked by. Listening to the students chatter about her being alone with Turner easily ended her day on a bad note.

"I had better head back so that my grandfather doesn't worry." Arianna spun an excuse. Turner looked over at the girls approaching.

"I'll walk you back," he offered. Arianna quickly shook her head no.

"Devin and Molina are right over there," Arianna pointed to a group of trees. She turned, and began to walk away.

"Don't listen to what they're saying," Turner replied, catching up and walking beside her. "Those petty girls are only jealous." Arianna kept walking, not responding. "Besides, we still need to watch these movies," he replied.

"Hanging out with me is just going to make it worse," Arianna replied. She knew how these games were played.

"Can we watch the movies at your place?" Turner suggested. "Then no one will know we're hanging out together." Arianna turned and stared at him. She could almost feel a hint of desperation in his voice.

"I suppose I do need to pass that test at the end of the week," she replied, and felt the tension in Turner ease. "Okay." Happily, Turner followed Arianna back to her grandfather's house.

TWELVE

"Devin, do we have popcorn?" Arianna asked, sticking her head in the sitting room where Devin was working.

"Second shelf on the right, by the window," Devin replied, still staring at the papers in front of him.

Arianna hurried to the kitchen and found the popcorn as Turner set up the TV. Though she was beginning to feel Turner had a motive behind offering to help her catch up in her school work, Arianna didn't care. He was different from anyone she'd ever met. He was so free. He didn't care what his peers, or the teachers thought of him. He wasn't afraid of disappointing anyone like Arianna was. Arianna stared into the living room as Turner forwarded through the previews. His loud laugh, and twinkling eyes, which seemed to always be looking for trouble, were such a stark contrast to the composed, quiet, thinker, Devin.

"Which one first?" Arianna asked, returning to the living room with popcorn.

"Here," Turner replied, tossing the empty film sleeve to Arianna. Arianna wrinkled her nose as she read over the back of the cover. "Come on, it's a classic. Besides, the real reason this one is good is because the lead actor really is one of us." Arianna stared at the cover more. The actor looked human to her.

After it was over, and as Turner was popping the second movie into the old VCR machine they dug up in the manor's electronics room, Arianna couldn't wait to start asking questions.

"The main guy wasn't a dearg-dul was he?" she asked.

"No, the writers combined dearg-duls and baku to make the character," Turner replied. "When you turn, your features only slightly change, but when someone turns into a baku, they look just like that guy."

"Then the ugly, white, muscle guys are baku," she began and Turner nodded his head. "They feed on dreams, right?"

"More so on emotions," Turner explained.

"Then why do they drink blood?" Arianna asked. "I can feel emotion off of people without drinking their blood. Wouldn't it be easier to creep around feeling out people's emotions than waiting for them to fall asleep to drink their blood?"

"The energy they get from feeling the emotion is ten times more than they'd get from drinking blood," Turner replied. "And most of them don't need people to fall asleep. They have methods to make people go to sleep."

"Like hypnosis?" Arianna asked.

"Correct," Turner replied. "Next movie?"

Arianna nodded, and watched the second movie. Turner added his own comments every now and then. This time they stopped half way through.

"That's enough of that one," Turner replied. "The rest of the movie is pretty bad."

"Awwww," Arianna teased. "Nice puppy." She reached over and petted Turner's head.

"I'm not a dog," Turner replied with a playful growl. "That's the one thing I've always hated about that one. They used dogs and not wolves."

"So, do I get to see your lycan form?" she asked innocently.

"Not now," Turner replied. "One more movie to go."

"But I'm a little cold," she replied. "I could use a doggy to keep warm." She smiled as she got another growl from him. Turner stood and started the last movie.

During the last movie, Arianna often took the time to steal glances at Turner as he explained everything. By the time they made it through it, things were getting clearer. Given the extent of his knowledge, there was no reason for him to be at the school taking classes.

"Why are you here if you know so much?" Arianna asked.

"To meet you," he replied mischievously. He changed the subject as Arianna became uncomfortable with his reply. "I really wish I could take you back to where I grew up. Everyone in the city knows, or is, a night human. It's completely different than here. Most stores are open all day long to serve both humans and night humans. We are free to be ourselves, and never worry that some bystander might figure out what we are."

"You miss it, don't you?" Arianna asked, noticing the sadness in his voice as he explained everything.

"A bit," he replied.

"How long have you been here?" she asked.

"Since August, so about eight months." Turner stood and collected the movies. "Seems like forever. I've been home twice since I moved into the dorms, but only for a weekend."

"Doesn't your family miss you?" she wondered.

"My father does," Turner replied. "My brother, not so much, I think. We haven't always gotten along so good. I'm the younger brother after all. No responsibility. I think he's jealous, but there's nothing I can do about it. He's the heir to the family whether he wants to be or not."

"Like me?" Arianna asked, and Turner nodded.

"Do you have a boyfriend?" Turner suddenly asked. Arianna tried to look away to hide her embarrassment, but he was sitting right next her. Turner caught her face as she tried to turn. Arianna had surprisingly found that being with Turner felt easy. Every other boy she had met, and liked, in her life was always hard to talk to. Even though she was picking up his intentions, she still felt at ease with him.

Arianna listened in on the room next door, knowing that Devin stood on the other side of the doorway. "Well," she replied, unsure how to answer. Turner quickly leaned forward and gently kissed her before she could reply.

"I hope everything makes a little more sense now," Turner said, standing. "Tonight was fun. We should do it again sometime. I had better get back, it's already past curfew." Flustered, Arianna could not reply as he left.

Arianna sat on the couch, staring at the blank TV screen. *He just kissed me*, she thought. In her almost sixteen years alive before moving to her grandfather's home, she had never kissed a boy before, and now, she had been kissed by two. Arianna closed her eyes and leaned back. What was she supposed to do? Two very different boys had kissed her in the past three days. *Stop*, she thought. *Why can't life just stop for a moment, and let me catch up?* Everything was moving fast past her. It was all new; night humans, boys, family, life, everything. *Devin or Turner?* she asked herself. *Which one should I choose?* Arianna listened to the people walking around the house. Everyone was heading off to bed. Down a long corridor, a clock was chiming. The door to her sitting room opened softly.

"You should get some rest," Devin recommended. Arianna jerked her eyes open, and looked at him. He seemed unaffected by what had just happened, even though she knew he was listening to everything. He was as neutral as always. Slowly, tears began to drip from the corners of her eyes. Everything was just too confusing. *Why isn't Devin mad or jealous?* Devin moved around the couch, gently picking her up.

"Are you hungry?" he asked, and she shook her head *no* as she laid against his chest, wanting to fight back, but finding herself lulled by the beat of his heart. "You should get some sleep." Arianna nodded as the tears continued to dribble down her cheeks.

The next day, Arianna arrived at school minutes before class was to start. She had overslept and didn't have enough time to get ready. Closely following behind Molina, Arianna dreaded returning to the classroom where all the people snickered at her behind her back. Surprisingly, her classmates were no longer filled with contempt and hatred of her but now with curiosity and some with fear. Arianna looked around as she moved to the back of the classroom, trying to understand the change.

The girl up front from the day before tried to offer Arianna her seat now. Arianna quietly shook her head *no* and headed to the back of the room to sit next to Turner.

"Someone told their parents about the new student, and they all now know who you are," Turner explained while Arianna sat beside him. He acted as if the kiss had never happened. Arianna looked around the room. The atmosphere had changed, but Arianna wondered if it was for the better or not. "I found one more movie to watch," Turner explained as he stood up. "If you can find everything wrong in this one, then you are ready for the test."

Arianna glanced at him. "Already?" she asked, and he nodded as he offered to take her bag. Arianna followed him into the hallway. Behind her, she listened to the students talking as they shut the door.

"She really is Lord Randolph's granddaughter," a boy replied. "I've seen her guards before. The female one tested out of the training at the age of fourteen. They say she's the best non-purebreed to ever come along."

"And the guy. I've seen him often with Lord Randolph," a quiet girl said. "My mom works in the Randolph estate."

"I suppose it can't be helped then," the girl from the day before replied to her friends. "I was really hoping Turner would ask me to the next dance."

"I wouldn't count on it now," her friend answered.

Arianna was surprised as Turner walked towards the library at the end of the hallway.

"You just don't seem like the library type," Arianna replied, hurrying to catch up with him.

"I'm not, but the head of the boy's dorm is in his room sick today. If I take you back to the dorms, you will get in trouble with your grandfather," Turner replied.

Arianna spent the first half of her school day watching the terrible horror film that Turner had brought with him in the library. Arianna expected things to be awkward between her and Turner after he had kissed her, but it was like nothing happened. He was the same happy-go-lucky guy she had met the day before.

"There wasn't anything correct in this movie," she complained after they finished it.

"So?" Turner replied. "Seeing the blood spurt like it was streaming out of a fountain was worth it."

"That was horrible," she replied, laughing at the scene replying in her mind. "Why are you here at this school?" she asked a second time. "You already seem to know everything." Turner smiled but didn't reply.

Arianna sat down at the computer at the back of the room. Turner had pulled up the exam, and convinced her she was ready to try it. As she started to read the questions on the screen, Arianna was amazed that she could actually answer them. She had jumped into this new world without any idea of what it meant, but with the help of Turner, things were now starting to become clear. By the time she finally finished the last question, Arianna was surprised to find it was already time to leave school for the day.

"So, was it as hard as you thought it would be?" Turner asked from the doorway. Arianna turned to him. She hadn't heard him enter the library test room, nor did she know that he spent most of the time sitting with Devin, watching her.

"Nope," she smiled as she replied. Walking to the printer, she took the sheet that had just printed. "Only one question wrong," she added handing the sheet to Turner.

"See, you kept complaining that this was too confusing and so unrealistic," Turner teased.

"Turner," a boy yelled as he entered the library. "Are you coming or not?" Arianna looked to find Turner was no longer wearing his school uniform.

"I'll be there in a minute," Turner yelled back. "As a reward, I'll take you on a date," he offered.

"But-" Arianna started to turn him down.

"Tomorrow after school," Turner said, before kissing her forehead, and running out the door behind the other student.

"But," Arianna said, as he left her without waiting for an answer. Arianna turned to Devin who was uninterested in their conversation.

Huffing, Arianna ignored Devin, too. She walked back home with Devin and Molina in silence. *What am I supposed to do?* she wondered. It wasn't that she disliked Turner, she just didn't know about her relationship with Devin. She felt something for Devin each night as she lay down to sleep, her heart beat uncontrollably, and the butterflies in her stomach tumbled and twirled. Devin had told her he liked her, and yet, the night Turner kissed her, Devin had no reaction. Not anger, not jealousy, nothing. Arianna hurried to her room and changed out of her school uniform while pondering her new predicament. *Does Devin really like me?* she thought. Arianna lay on her fluffy bed and tried to sort everything out. Devin was always caring, and treated her like she came before everything, but was that because he liked her, or was it just his job? *He did kiss me.* She didn't notice the time passing as she was stuck in thoughts about the day.

"You should get some sleep," Devin suggested, opening

her bedroom door and interrupting her silence. Arianna nodded as he sat down on the edge of the bed next to her.

"Doesn't it bother you Turner asked me on a date?" Arianna asked, lying down in bed to avoid his eyes.

"No," Devin replied, lying down next to her.

"But didn't you say you like me?" she asked, still trying not to look at him.

"Yes."

"Then, shouldn't it bother you?" she pondered, sitting up to finally judge his reaction. "Did I misunderstand?"

"You are not an object I can own and do with as I please. I have no right to decide your life for you," he explained. "And I promise, I'll never ask to be your boyfriend. So you may kiss anyone you please."

"Then you don't like me?" Arianna asked, confused by his response.

"No, I like you very much," he replied.

"Then why don't you ask me out?"

"No reason," he replied. His serious face didn't flinch as he replied. Through his voice sounded like he was telling the truth, his hand, placed on top of hers, told another story. Arianna felt his heartbeat slightly increase as she inquisitively stared at him, wondering whether to believe him or not. He had been truthful with her all along, but now she got the feeling that he was lying.

Arianna laid her head down, and listened to the soft pounding of the heart beneath her head. *He likes me, but doesn't want to be my boyfriend*, she thought. *How can that make sense?* Arianna looked up to find Devin watching her as her eyes became heavy, and she fell asleep.

Arianna quietly sat up as the first rays of the sun beamed through her bedroom window. Devin, still asleep on the bed, did not move as she climbed out from under the covers. Silently, she walked around to the nightstand that was still holding the papers he had been reading the night before.

Curiosity overcame her as she picked them up. Without waking Devin, Arianna looked through the folders. Arianna read the names at the top of each before realizing they were all files on her classmates at school. She slowly looked from one paper to the next. The details of each student were written in Devin's handwriting. He knew everything about each. As she neared the end of the pile, she found Turner's page.

Brenton Turner Winter, she read. Arianna tried to remember. She had heard the last name Winter before. *Lord Winter,* she reminded herself. Arianna thought back, and finally remembered the red-bearded man she had met at her party. Arianna finished reading the paper on Turner, and flipped it into the pile with the rest. There was nothing new on him. Lazy and rebellious were both accurate descriptions of him. Devin was keeping close tabs on her, so it was not surprising her knew about everyone in her class. Arianna picked up the novel placed under the file. *He's reading a novel,* she mused, unable to picture Devin reading anything but the files he was constantly going over. As she turned to the page with the book mark, Arianna stopped in shock. Two young boys stared back at her from the old tattered photo that was being using as the bookmark. Arianna looked closely at the faces. The young blond-haired boy was Devin and the dark-haired boy was Turner.

Arianna put the book back carefully, and hurried to get dressed. *Turner and Devin are friends,* she thought. *Is that why Devin doesn't mind Turner asking me out on a date? Maybe Turner asked Devin for permission? No, Turner isn't the type to ask permission for anything. Devin would have said something if he really cared. Does Devin really care, or am I just his assignment?* Arianna pondered her options, but none made sense. *I can't ask Devin,* she thought, knowing he would lie to her again. *Lies, they all lie,* Arianna thought. Devin watched over her carefully, but now he was withholding information. Arianna grew angry as she thought more about it. Everyone was keeping secrets from her, and now Devin even lied to her.

Arianna quietly snuck out of her apartment. It was still too early for anyone to be awake. Arianna walked the wooded path from her home to the school dorms. Though no one was up yet, she was determined to wait until Turner woke for the day to ask him her questions. It was the first time since she had come to her grandfather's that she was truly alone. No one was following her. Arianna paused in the woods and listened to the animals waking up for the day: the nest of squirrels rummaging in the leaves, the birds chirping to wake their neighbors, and the small rabbit munching on his morning meal. *No humans, night or otherwise, around,* she thought. Arianna sat down, leaned against a tree, and watched the sun shine through the budding branches overhead. It was peaceful to get away from everything. Closing her eyes, Arianna listened to the sounds around her. She could hear someone approach, but she wasn't startled by his presence.

"Running away from home?" Turner asked.

"I wish," she replied. "This place is a fortress. I managed to get out of the house, but I doubt I could leave the grounds without anyone knowing."

"Something bothering you?" Turner replied, sitting beside her.

Arianna glanced around the forest, searching for anyone else. They were alone. "This is all a bit overwhelming," she replied, not directly answering. "I feel like everyone knows a secret that no one is telling me. I thought Devin was honest and would answer all my questions, but I'm pretty sure he was lying to me last night. It's weird, I am constantly surrounded by people, but I feel all alone."

"Do you want to run away? I haven't been home in a while. We could ditch school and go visit my father."

Turner offered seriously.

Arianna quickly shook her head no. There was no way her grandfather would let her leave.

Almost sensing her dilemma, he offered, seeing her hesitation, "I know a way out where no one would be able to stop us," Arianna paused. "We can just take a long weekend. I'm sure my father would like to meet you."

"But grandfather would be so mad if he knew," Arianna replied.

"Do you always do what everyone else wants you to do?" Turner asked. "What about what you want?"

Arianna felt her heart beat faster as he talked. Turner was the first person she'd met in her new life that had even asked her what she wanted. She hadn't really ever thought about it.

THIRTEEN

Arianna sat next to the window in their private room on the train. Turner was right. He had easily snuck them off of the Randolph estate and to the train station without anyone stopping them. Guilt tugged at Arianna as she stared into the busy train station. Arianna was hesitant to leave without telling anyone, but her anger easily made her follow Turner. Turner sat next to her, watching out the window as well.

"How long before they know?" Arianna asked.

"It shouldn't take them too long. We left your phone in my room. Once they find that you're not there, they'll know we left," Turner explained as his phone rang. He looked at the caller ID and smiled. "It seems like Devin figured it out already."

Arianna took the phone and stared at Devin's name. She carefully opened the phone.

"What the hell are you doing? Where are you?" Devin yelled through the phone. Arianna dropped the cell. She had never heard Devin get mad before. He was always so quiet and composed, Arianna hadn't even been sure that he could get mad.

Turner picked up the phone. "Well, hello, Honey," Turner said, smiling to Arianna as he talked. "It's so nice of you to finally return my call. What has it been, almost three or four days since I called you and you never returned my call? That's a bit rude. I was beginning to think you didn't like me anymore."

"Is she with you?" Devin desperately asked, a little calmer.

"Of course," Turner replied. "She would never had made it off the estate without me. You seem to keep her caged in well."

"Stay where you are," Devin ordered.

"Well, we would, but I have a feeling we will be moving, not of our own accord, really soon," Turner replied before shutting his phone and turning it off. "They'll be here soon. Should be fun to see if they make it on time." Turner looked over to Arianna who was still staring, shocked, at the phone.

"Never heard him yell before, I suppose," Turner added. "It's good for him. He's always too serious. Keeping emotions bottled up inside is never good for anyone. Besides, we should do things like this to keep him on his toes." Turner easily relaxed her. Arianna smiled and nodded. Turner was right. Devin was always too serious, but was it okay for her to leave without telling anyone? Arianna was starting to regret her decision after hearing the genuine panic and concern in Devin's voice.

Arianna stared at Turner, finally remembering her questions. "Are you friends with Devin?"

"We were very close at one time. We kind of grew up together. Your grandfather and my father are friends and visit each other often. We just kind of ended up together all the time," Turner explained.

Arianna listened to the whistle blow, signaling that the train was closing the doors, and she disappointedly watched as six people hopped out of a car and ran to stop the train. Arianna waited to be escorted off the train, but to her surprise it began to move. Arianna glanced to Turner, who also knew who had just boarded the train.

"Are you ready for our lecture?" he jokingly asked, as the group neared the compartment where Turner and Arianna sat. Arianna held her breath as the door slid open.

His face flushed, but in his normal, serious composure, Devin entered the room and sat down across from Arianna and Turner. Arianna listened as the other five entered the rooms on either side.

"Are you still mad?" Arianna asked curiously. Devin sat there without saying anything.

"If you want to leave, all you have to do is tell me, and we can make safer arrangements," Devin explained. Arianna nodded. "Please think before you act in the future. If your grandfather knew, he would have been completely lost. We only care for your safety."

"She did think," Turner defended Arianna. "She thought she needed to get away from being followed around all the time." Devin glared at Turner, knowing it was true.

"Ari, you need to feed," Devin said, ignoring Turner. "Come here," he directed. Arianna wanted to refuse, but knew it was true. Just sitting across from him made her hungry.

Arianna moved to sit next to Devin as he unbuttoned the top few buttons on his shirt. Though she was aware that he wasn't telling her everything, Arianna knew Devin was always conscious of what she needed. He seemed to understand the new night human side of her better than she did, even though he wasn't even one of them.

"Can't we do the IV thingy?" she asked, blushing from embarrassment.

"We could at home, but someone decided to run away this morning, so we were a bit rushed getting here," Devin replied.

"But I still don't know how to," she complained as he picked up her hand and placed it on his bare chest. With a rush of overpowering sound, Arianna felt his heart beating and slowly the scent of his blood was beginning to pull her near. Kneeling beside him, Arianna closed her eyes and continued to listen. Brushing his shirt away from his neck,

Arianna neared close enough for Devin to feel her breath. Arianna slowly bit down, trying to not touch anything except the vein that was throbbing. As she released her bite, she tasted his blood. It definitely tasted better than either her grandfather's or uncle's blood. With her hand still resting on his chest, and listening to his heartbeat, Arianna drank until she felt the beat slightly change. Licking the holes she had made, Arianna slowly pulled back and watched them close before her eyes.

"Was that enough?" Devin asked.

Arianna pulled her hand back at his voice and turned to face him as he spoke. Realizing she was mere inches from his face, Arianna tried to quickly move, but was dizzy from the blood. Devin held onto her waist to keep her from tipping over.

"You'll get used to that feeling eventually," he explained. "But for now it would probably be best if you just sleep it off." Devin picked up her hand and placed it back on his chest. "It's a four and a half hour train ride, so you have plenty of time to rest."

Arianna couldn't complain. She nodded as the sound of his heartbeat filled her mind again. Arianna could hear clearer than she had before she took his blood. Everything in the small compartment seemed to be amplified. Arianna looked around the compact space as colors vividly swirled in her mind. Turner stared at the crystal-blue eyes scanning the room. He had been at her coming-out party, but he hadn't been close enough to be as in awe as he was now, watching her. Slowly, she curled up on Devin's lap, placing her head against his bare chest, and she instantly fell asleep.

Devin lightly placed his hand over her other ear. "I don't need her ability to feel emotions to see the jealously written all over your face," he teased. Turner tried not to pout, knowing Devin was correct.

"If you ever try this stunt again, I won't promise that I'll be able to keep Lord Randolph from coming personally to take her back," Devin continued. "Are you stupid? You know there are many people that want to get a hold of her."

"Does it make a difference? She was taken from her own bedroom upon arriving here," Turner replied.

"True, but she was safe the entire time. Her uncle makes it a point to personally see that she doesn't get into trouble," Devin explained.

"Is that how you knew so fast that we were gone?" Turner asked.

"Yes, he called as soon as you stopped at the station and bought tickets," Devin replied.

"But I was so safe. No one was following us. I am sure," Turner complained, racking his brain to try to recall any little detail that would have indicated that someone was following them.

"You'd never notice he was there. It's his specialty, or rather should I say, he was meant to be a spy who goes unnoticed. That's what his *kind* are good at," Devin replied.

"You mean he's baku?" Turner asked.

"The best," Devin replied, moving Arianna slightly to prop his legs up on the rest of the seat.

"Are you saying that her uncle is Gabriel?" Turner responded in awe, still staring at the sleeping Arianna. "The best?" Turner repeated, raising his eyebrow at the thought. "Then is he here now, on this train?" Turner asked.

"Correct again," Devin replied, shutting his own eyes. "Purebred baku and purebred dearg-dul."

"She really is both?"

"Yes, I wouldn't doubt it. He doesn't exactly trust us to watch over her yet, and I doubt it's for her dearg-dul qualities," Devin said, yawning. "But you wouldn't find him even if you went door to door looking in each room. You don't live as long as he or Lord Randolph have, in the middle of an ongoing war between the two races, no less, unless you are the best."

Turner spent the rest of the ride alternating between looking out the window and watching Arianna peacefully sleep on Devin. Devin was right. Turner couldn't sense the presence of a baku on the train at all, but he knew Gabriel must be somewhere. Gabriel obviously didn't trust Devin and his team alone to protect Arianna. He had to be close, but Turner couldn't even guess where.

When the train finally stopped, Devin gently placed Arianna on the seat and joined Molina in the room to the right of their compartment. Turner could hear them talking. It was 1:30 in the afternoon, still too soon for any dearg-duls to be out in the sunlight. They would have to wait on the train. Turner listened to them debate their options as two large, black cars with tinted windows arrived at the station. Turner knew immediately his father had sent an escort for him and Arianna.

Arianna stretched as she yawned. "Why does he always have to be right?" she asked.

"Who?" Turner replied.

"Devin," Arianna responded.

Turner laughed. "I wouldn't say he's always right, but concerning your health, he is the best person to trust. Your grandfather has trained him well."

Arianna peered out the window into the train station. "What are we waiting for?" she asked. "Is this our exit?"

"Yes, but it's 1:30," Turner replied. "Molina and Devin are deciding what to do."

Arianna listened to the next room, then looked at the train station blocking her view. "You said the train goes right into your city. So, we don't have to travel farther do we?" she asked.

"No, it's only about a ten minute drive to my father's house from here," Turner replied.

"Then why can't we leave now? Molina, Nelson, and

Mica can catch up after two," Arianna replied. "I've traveled around with just Devin before, and they considered that safe. Besides, my uncle is nearby."

"You know where your uncle is?" Turner asked.

"Yeah, I can smell his blood," Arianna replied, standing and walking to the door.

Turner closed his eyes and searched for the baku scent. Again, he found nothing. "How can you smell his blood, he must be quite a ways away from us right now 'cause I don't smell any baku blood."

"No, he's just four rooms down," Arianna replied. "It's like Devin. I can smell his blood anywhere he goes," Arianna explained. "The same with my uncle."

"You've drunk his blood before?" Turner asked, dubious that such an important baku would share his blood.

"Mm hmm," Arianna opened the compartment door. "Are you going to stay behind?" Arianna asked as Turner remained seated.

"It still isn't two yet," he replied.

"So what?" Arianna tied up her hair, ready to go.

"Do you want to be burned?"

Arianna laughed. "You're worried about me? Don't be." Turner followed as Arianna opened the door to the room with Devin and Molina in it. "Can we leave now?" she asked boldly, still running on the elation that freedom gave her.

Devin and Molina looked to Arianna.

"I mean, can I leave with Devin, Jackson, and Nixon as my guards and then you guys can catch up later?" Arianna rephrased her question, trying to be nicer.

"If you leave now, people will know your secret," Molina replied.

"Who cares?" Arianna shot back. "I'm sick of all the secrets. They'll eventually find out anyways." Molina gave Devin a look, but he just shook his head *no*.

"Fine," Molina replied hesitatingly. "You can leave here,

but only go straight to Lord Winter's compound. Wait there for us to catch up." Arianna nodded.

"Right boss," she replied with a salute and then a giggle as she noticed Turner's complete shock.

FOURTEEN

Arianna and Turner arrived at his home and threw the whole estate into chaos. Lord Winter sent them to town to get clothing and supplies for the weekend, as they had left Lord Randolph's estate without a single packed item. Once the shock wore off, Lord Winter had promptly decided a formal dinner was required for Arianna, his son's unannounced guest, and the plans were off and running. Arianna and Turner happily ran back into town to avoid the chaos that always pursued Arianna. It took five stores, but they had found everything they needed for the weekend, and regretfully knew they would have to return to Lord Winter's home.

Arianna sighed as she took the last bag from the cashier. "That should be enough to get through the weekend," she commented, counting the bags between Turner and herself. "I still think that hat suited you. It completes your look," she pointed to the small, multicolored beanie hat Turner was wearing around the last store.

"One more stop," Turner added as they walked out of the store.

"But I have enough," Arianna counted the number of outfits she had bought in her head.

"Nope, you need something for tomorrow night," Turner replied.

"I thought your dad was just being generous, offering to throw a party in my honor," Arianna complained. "I didn't know he was serious."

"Oh, he sure was," Turner replied. "It's important to people like my father to show their connections in the world, and what better connection than his son being friends with Lord Randolph's granddaughter?" Turner explained with a shrug. "I thought he might do something like this, but I didn't think he'd do it the first time I brought you here. The old man is a little eccentric when it comes to these things. This way," Turner directed, grabbing Arianna's arm and pulling her across the street. Arianna smiled. *First time,* she pondered.

Her smile instantly faded. Arianna wrinkled her nose as Turner pulled her into a nearby dress shop. Lining one wall were various-styled wedding gowns and on the other side were formal dresses.

"Pick anything you like," Turner responded. "No dress codes for the guest of honor."

Arianna looked behind Turner to Molina standing outside the shop. Arianna waved her inside.

"I need help," she whispered. "I don't do the formal girly things that well. It's easier to just wear what someone else picks out." Molina smiled. Arianna's boldness at the train station was only temporary. She had changed back into the shy girl that needed an older sister's help. Obliged to follow her orders, but more so amused by the sudden change in Arianna, Molina began picking through the racks of dresses.

"Try these three," she said, handing three deep blue colored dressed to Arianna. Arianna nodded thankfully.

Following the sales lady to the dressing room, Arianna sighed again as she plopped down in the seat in the waiting room. So far, she had found the town was more normal than she expected. No one walked around in night human form. People weren't drinking human blood as they walked down the street. In fact, it could be anyone's hometown. As she listened to the random conversations outside, it was what you might expect in any town: a group of teenage girls talking about their latest crush, a middle-aged man in the hardware store asking how best to install a new kitchen sink, and a little child asking his mother to be picked up.

Reluctantly, Arianna stood and picked up the first dress. She wasn't looking forward to another dinner in her honor. Whether the guests realized it or not at the last one, she could hear everything anyone said about her. She didn't like being made the centerpiece for an evening, but even more dreaded wearing a formal gown again. *At least it's not pink with lace*, she reassured herself with a giggle as she slipped into the first dress. It wasn't something Arianna could be seen in public in, so she changed to the second dress. The second dress was fine, except it was too long for Arianna's short size. And the last dress, Arianna knew her grandfather wouldn't approve of. Changing back into the second dress, Arianna exited the dressing room for Molina's approval.

"That looks good," Molina said, as she walked into the dressing room hallway. "It's a little too long though. Eight-inch heels should do the trick," she teased. Pulling her hand from behind her back, she offered up a pair of heels. "But I thought these would probably look best with any of the dresses."

Arianna put the shoes on, but the dress was still too long.

"Not a problem," the saleslady said, joining them. "We can alter that for you and have it to Lord Winter's place by tomorrow afternoon."

Arianna returned to the dressing room. Pausing in the room, she tapped on the wall between her room and the next.

"Gabriel?" she asked quietly, trying not to be heard by Turner standing in the store.

"Put your hand under here," Gabriel directed, waving to her from beneath the wall between the two rooms. Arianna followed his direction, squatting down by the wall and

124

placing her hand under the partial wall. "Just hold still one second, and we can finish talking." Arianna felt him take her hand gently and prick the tip of her finger. Quickly he grasped her finger in his hand, but Arianna could already hear Turner and Molina hurrying to the dressing room.

"Arianna, are you okay?" Turner asked, worried as he had momentarily smelled her blood.

"I'm fine," Arianna replied. "I just pricked myself on one of these pins," she lied.

"Okay," Turner said, leaving the room.

'Good lie,' Gabriel replied. Arianna stared around the room. She was sure she heard him clearly, as though he was standing next to her and not through a wall.

"I don't understand," Arianna replied.

'Don't talk out loud,' Gabriel explained. *'Turner will hear you'* Puzzled, Arianna continued to sit on the floor, wondering how he was talking to her without talking out loud. *'This is a method baku can use to communicate without talking. Blood to blood allows us to communicate with any other night human. All you have to do is think what you want to say, and I'll hear it.'*

'Just think?' she pondered. Immediately imagines flashed to mind of Devin and Turner.

'Yes, just think but not about those boys. I don't need to know what you think of them,' Gabriel replied.

Arianna blushed, realizing her thoughts had just been conveyed to him.

'Why don't you just talk to me normally?' she asked.

'Because this isn't a safe place for our kind,' he explained.

'But Devin and Molina are fine with you, now that you helped them,' Arianna tried to reason.

'They may be, but your friend out there, and all the people of this city, wouldn't be,' he replied. *'I wanted to talk to you before I left. I need to get home and deal with some business, so I won't be following you around until you*

return to your grandfather's home. I need you to promise me, no more of this running-away-without-Devin business. That boy knows how to better protect you than anyone. It's just not safe for you to be running around. You don't know what kind of world is waiting to get a hold of you.'

'That's the same thing Grandfather said,' Arianna added.

'For once, I agree with him. Promise me, until I return, you will keep two guards with you at all times,' Gabriel begged.

'I promise, but I only have one with me right now,' Arianna replied.

'Turner counts as a guard,' Gabriel explained. *'He is as strong as most purebred dearg-duls.'*

'Oh,' Arianna added, still unsure why they worried so much about her.

'Please follow anything Devin tells you to do. He is watching out for you, and trying to keep you safe. I know you get frustrated because you don't like to be lied to, but cut him some slack. He is a seventeen-year-old taking on the responsibility of protecting the rarest night human to ever come along,' Gabriel explained.

'I know,' Arianna replied. Gabriel was right. Devin was holding a great responsibility to take care of her and from what she could tell, he was getting nothing in return. *'I'll be a good girl until you return. Then can I be a bad girl again?'* Arianna teased.

'Of course,' Gabriel replied. How could one keep a teenager from not acting out and testing the rules? She needed to find her own place in the world. Gabriel let go of his niece's hand and quietly slipped out of the store, unnoticed by everyone.

"Now that we have bought clothes and a dress for tomorrow night, is anything else left?" Arianna asked Turner as they left the store. Arianna listened as Gabriel continued to move father away from her. She had known all along he was following them on the train. Like Devin, Gabriel had become a constant in her new life.

"I figured we can stop and get something to eat before we head back," Turner suggested. "Your choice."

Arianna grabbed his arm to turn him back the way they just walked. She stopped before a store window and smiled. "This is what I want," she said, pointing at the large ice cream cones displayed in the candy store window. "I'd always had ice cream on a mid-summer's day when the sun was the hottest. That was my old life. Since I'm getting used to a new life, how about ice cream at," she glanced at her watch, "11:37?"

"I was thinking more like real food," Turner replied, and she pulled him into the candy store.

"Last time I checked, this is all real," she said. "Besides, I can find all the food groups here. See, here are your fruits and vegetables." Arianna pointed to the wide assortment of jelly beans lining the wall in clear canisters. "Grape, strawberry, banana, orange, carrot," she read the labels. "Carrot?" she repeated while scrunching up her forehead. "Eww."

"What about grains and meat?" Turner asked.

"Well obviously this is meat," she said, picking up a hotdog-shaped bubble gum. "Looks like a hot dog to me." She laughed, and Turner reluctantly nodded. "And grain along with dairy is over here in the ice cream cone." Arianna posed in front of the row of cones that came in multiple shapes and sizes.

"Fine, you win," Turner said, giving up his protest. "Just as long as I get to pick out your jewelry from these for tomorrow night." Turner pointed to the candy rings, bracelets and necklaces.

"Mmmm, looks good," Arianna joked.

"That way, when you get bored, you can just eat some candy and get a good sugar high. I'll be able to tell how bored you are from how many pieces are missing," Turner laughed.

After hours shopping and walking around, Arianna was actually ready to go back to Turner's home and rest. As she entered her room to put her bags away, Arianna found Devin sitting with his laptop, typing away.

"Do you want to see what we bought shopping?" she asked, and he didn't reply. "Your scent is different," she commented, as she moved closer and looked at the computer screen. "Your blood doesn't smell as strong as normal."

Devin nodded without meeting her eyes as he continued to type. Arianna sat down and stared at him. He was back to being the same as he was the first time she met him, almost like he didn't even notice she was in the same room as him.

"Are you not interested at all in what we did today?" she asked, wanting to grab his computer and demand his attention like a child.

Devin stopped typing and finally looked up from the computer screen. "No," he replied, and then continued to type. "I can read Molina's report tonight."

"You're no fun," she teased. Devin continued to ignore her. Arianna leaned closer and stared at him as he typed. Arianna tried to read his emotions like she had accidentally done before.

"Do you need something?" Devin asked, and she shook her head *no*. Arianna continued to stare at him. His cool exterior seemed to extend to his core. He was not sad or happy; he was completely indifferent to Arianna sitting beside him.

"Why do you get this way?" she asked. Devin continued to type and ignore her. Arianna waited, but he didn't reply. Arianna could feel herself beginning to get angry. He was the one who told her he liked her, and now he was completely uninterested. She knew he was keeping secrets from her, like everyone else, but she was trying her best to forgive him. His apathetic attitude wasn't helping her at all.

Devin closed his computer and stood up. "We should head to bed," he suggested. "Do you need to feed?" he asked.

"I'm fine," she lied. Arianna stood and glared at him. *He's treating me like a child again*, she thought. She could feel the hunger in the pit of her stomach, but ignored it. Devin shrugged and walked over to the bed. "I need to get some fresh air." Arianna turned and left the room. She closed the door hard and stood outside the room. *Boys are too confusing*, she thought, as she slid to the floor outside her room door.

He says he likes me, and then acts like he doesn't, she thought. *How am I to know if he is lying or not? Am I just another assignment?* Arianna sat on the floor as tears began to trickle down her face. Her new life wasn't anything she wanted: a strange new home, strange people, strange customs, and blood. Arianna ignored the strange scent of Devin's blood inside the room. She heard him as he lay down on the bed. He really was going to go to sleep. He didn't even seem to mind that she was just left alone. Gabriel had warned her not to go out by herself, but Devin didn't seem to care. *Does he really care less for me than Gabriel?*

"Do you want to go for a walk?" Turner asked, kneeling beside Arianna. Startled, Arianna looked up at Turner expecting to see Devin.

"Sure," Arianna replied, as he offered her his hand to help her stand.

Dashing to his room, Turner returned and placed his coat around Arianna. Taking his arm, Turner led Arianna down the hallway, stopping at the last room.

"We're going out," Turner said, peeking his head into the room.

"Who are you telling?" Arianna asked as her question

was quickly answered by Jackson and Nixon exiting the room. Silently, they followed behind Turner and Arianna as they walked through the house. As they reached the garage, Turner threw keys to both Jackson and Nelson.

"I thought we were going for a walk?" Arianna asked.

"I know a great place to go for a walk, but we have to get there first," Turner explained, smiling slyly like he was up to something.

"Why do I always get the feeling you are always two steps ahead of me?" Arianna asked, and Turner winked.

"The two red ones over there are mine," he called back to Jackson and Nelson as he hopped on the nearest bike. "Are you coming?" Turner asked, extending his hand to Arianna. Arianna listened inside the house. Devin was still in bed, probably asleep by now. He wasn't coming to apologize to her like she expected. Taking Turner's extended hand, Arianna hopped on behind him and grasped him around his waist.

FIFTEEN

"I was only twelve, when my mother died," Turner explained, as Arianna snuggled into the coat Turner had given her. Arianna stared at the bright sky filled with stars. Turner was right; it was the perfect place to take a walk. When they stopped outside a forest with just a small dirt path entering it, Arianna was as hesitant as her two guards, but Turner reassured her that they were still safe. Climbing the last hill, to the large stone she was now lying on, she understood why Turner would choose such a place. Below them was the city, with lights twinkling, and around them were the tall, snow-capped mountains.

"I'm sorry," Arianna replied.

"There's nothing to be sorry about. She struggled to live for three years after her diagnosis. Death was the kindest thing for her," Turner stared into the sky. "It's taken me a long time to realize that much. She was always in so much pain."

"What was she like?" Arianna asked, often wondering the same thing about her own mother.

Turner pondered the question. "It's been five years now. I feel like my memory of her is fading somewhat. Most of my memories are from after she was diagnosed. Dad always said she became a much different person after that, trying to fit a lifetime into as much time as she had left. She would often talk about what sort of men she wanted my brother and me to grow into. Her expectations were high, and hopefully, someday, I can achieve them."

"Was she human?" Arianna asked, knowing it was a strange question.

"Yep," Turner replied. "She grew up here in town and knew about everything. Dad always said his in-laws were more than happy to have her marry a night human, but I guess they expected her to have at least one child like her. Since both my brother and I were not what they expected, they drifted away from us after she died."

"But you still have your dad and brother," Arianna added.

"My dad is great, Eric, not so much," Turner replied. "Don't get me wrong. He's my brother, and I'll always love him. I just don't plan to stay around here forever and have to deal with him. The greatest thing about moving to go to school was getting away from him. My dad says Eric treats me the way he does because of jealously, but I think it's because he's an immature brat."

"He wasn't that bad," Arianna added, thinking back to the only meeting she had with his father and brother after they arrived in town.

"Why does everyone call you Turner?" she asked, changing the subject. "I saw Devin's files on all the students in our class, and it had your real name on it."

"Well, technically, Turner is my real name," he corrected. "It's just my middle name. I stopped going by Brenton after my mother died. She was really the only one who called me that anyways."

"Do you miss her?" Arianna asked, turning to watch his expression as he responded, expecting him to try to lie and cover up.

"No," he replied honestly. "I wish she were here with me, but I don't miss her. One morning two weeks before she died, we talked for such long period of time that it was almost morning before we realized how much time had passed. Together we watched the sunrise. She told me that that was where she was going to be. If I ever missed her or needed to talk, she would be waiting in the sunrise."

"Is that why you always go for a run before you go to bed in the morning?"

"Yep. I know she's somewhere out there, listening to me," he replied. "How can you miss someone who isn't completely gone?" Arianna smiled.

"She sounds like she was a good mom," Arianna replied.

"The best." Arianna and Turner sat in silence for a while as they both gazed at the night sky. "Arianna," Turner began, turning to face her as he talked. Shocked by his serious tone, Arianna faced him as well. "What do you think of me?" he asked.

"What do you mean?" she asked back. Arianna blushed as she thought of how he had kissed her.

"That's exactly what I mean," he replied watching her blush more. "This probably isn't the best time to ask, with you fighting with Devin and all, but I want to know what you think of me."

Arianna blushed more. She'd never met anyone as direct and carefree as Turner. He lived life to the fullest, and on his own terms. Arianna didn't know how to respond. She tried to turn onto her back, and continue looking at the stars, but he was even quicker as he caught her and made her face him.

"At a loss for words?" he asked, waiting. Arianna nodded. "Then how about this. Do you hate me?" he asked, and she shook her head no. "Do you find me attractive?" Arianna closed her eyes, and, embarrassed, nodded her head yes. Turner chuckled. "Do you enjoy being with me?" Keeping her eyes shut, Arianna nodded yes again. "Would you object if I leaned over and kissed you right now?"

"Wait a second," she said, opening her eyes to find him laughing. "You're teasing me again."

"Correct," he said, continuing to hold her face. "But I'm serious about knowing what you think of me."

"How am I supposed to answer that?" she asked. "It's such a complicated question. Let's turn it around first. Turner, what do you think of me?" she asked.

"You're more than I ever imagined you would be," he replied honestly.

"But you just met me," she questioned his answer.

"No, I met you a long time ago. Devin had always talked about this beautiful angel he was going to marry. She lived very far away, but he had met her briefly when he came to live with Lord Randolph. I begged and begged to be able to see this girl he was talking about, and one time he took me with him and Lord Randolph on a visit. He was right. The girl he was in love with was a beautiful angel, just as he had described," Turner explained.

"Me?" Arianna questioned.

"You. I knew at that moment, you were the only girl I could ever love. You were so beautiful and focused, playing with your friends. You didn't even notice the strangers at the park watching you," Turner continued.

"You were that boy," Arianna said, suddenly remembering Turner's face.

"I couldn't help it," Turner blushed. "We were told we couldn't speak to you, just watch. As soon as Lord Randolph stepped away for a moment, I hurried to the swings. I just had to tell you." Arianna remembered the red headed boy that told her, when she was younger, that he loved her. She had never met the boy before, and yet as she played with her friends, there he was, confessing. At an age where boys had cooties, Arianna spent weeks being teased by Mary Ellen and Tish for the boy who told her he loved her. He wasn't from their school, and they never saw him again.

"Arianna, please let me..." He hesitated, and Arianna closed her eyes again. She knew what he was going to ask, and she didn't have an answer for him. "Be your keeper."

Arianna's eyes jerked open, and she stared at him. It

wasn't the question she was expecting. "I don't understand. You just told me you liked me. Shouldn't the question be about being my boyfriend?"

"That's not something I would ever ask of you," Turner replied.

Arianna sat up. "I hate boys. They are so confusing. You sound just like Devin, now," she complained as she moved to get out of the coat she was wrapped in.

"Wait," he begged, taking her hands in his own. "I can explain." Arianna stopped moving and turned to him. He had just said exactly what she had been waiting to hear from Devin. "I'd love to ask you to be my girlfriend, but I wouldn't want to put you through that."

"Through what?" she asked.

"The stares and snickering," he said. "You've not lived in this world long enough to see. If you said yes, to be my girlfriend, everything said about you, and behind your back, would amplify. You already have to deal with enough."

"Deal with?" Arianna questioned. "My parents were outcasts because one was a dearg-dul and the other a baku, but I thought we were allies."

"They are, and there are no problems between our kinds dating. The problem people would see isn't that you are a dearg-dul but that you are a purebred dearg-dul. Purebreds only marry other purebreds, or people with purebred ancestry. Needless to say, my family line is only lycan and human, so people wouldn't accept me being with you. I want to be beside you forever. I've been in love with you since the day we first met. By asking to be your keeper, it would be acceptable to society for me to be at your side constantly just like a boyfriend would," he explained.

"So, I can only marry someone of pureblood ancestry?" she asked. "The only difference I see between purebreds and other dearg-duls is power. But then I don't understand. Gabriel just said you were more powerful than half the purebreds out there."

Turner laughed. "When did you see Gabriel?" Turner had tried endlessly to sense the baku.

"At the last store we shopped in," Arianna replied.

"I thought something was strange when I smelled your blood," Turner smiled. "He sure is good. I didn't sense a baku around any time I was with you today, and yet, there he was." He sighed and then shrugged his shoulders. "In reality, you can marry anyone you like," Turner replied, answering her original question. "I don't think anyone would be stupid enough to tell you no, but you would have to deal with the ridicule that goes along with not following tradition. There are few purebred dearg-duls. Of the thirty-seven clans, only twenty-two have a purebred leading them. The purebred gene is passed from generation to generation. If you were to marry someone not of pureblood descent, such as me, even though they may be powerful, your pureblood gene could be lost in the next generation. Most wouldn't be happy with that possibility."

"Oh," Arianna couldn't think of another reply. The situation was so new to her. She could understand the problems her parents caused marrying between feuding clans, but she didn't know there were more traditions to follow. "This is all so strange. Don't people around here marry for love?"

Turner smiled. "Yes, most of the people marry for love, but they only look for love within the bounds of tradition. I personally don't care for all of the traditions, but I don't want to make things worse for you. You'll have a hard enough time when people find out that you're both baku and dearg-dul," Turner explained. "I'm not expecting an answer from you right now. It's a big decision, to choose a keeper. But since you are a purebred, just think of it this way, you can always say yes, and when you get sick of me, just get a new one."

"That's what I said, but everyone tells me to make good decisions the first time, and then not have to worry about it in the future," Arianna agreed.

Arianna lay down in silence as Turner continued to hold her hand. She watched the stars above, and unconsciously began to listen as the blood within Turner pumped through his body. The slight swish of blood as it flowed through him sounded different than Devin. Everything about the two was different. How could she choose between them? She knew already that she liked Devin, and in a way he was already acting as her keeper, but when she had asked if he would become her keeper, he had said no. *What does it all mean?* she pondered. Arianna moved Turner's hand to her face and listened as the sound of his heartbeat grew louder. Arianna felt her eyes become heavy as she listened to the rhythmic beat. Arianna didn't say anything as she felt herself drifting off to sleep. She was so confused; her head hurt from thinking so much about the situation. Sleep was welcome.

Turner put his other hand gently on her face. Arianna instantly drifted off to sleep. Turner gently brushed her hair from her eyes. She was so small and delicate. He thought back to his first meeting with her. She hadn't changed much over the last few years. She still was smiley and bubbly, but he could see the strain behind her smile. This whole situation that she had been flung into was hard on her. Turner looked down the pathway where Nelson and Jackson were sitting quietly. There was no way he could take her away from everything as much as he wanted to. Turner silently held onto Arianna and watched her sleep as the sun began to rise in the east.

"Mother," he said quietly, as the first rays appeared over the mountains. "I really wanted you to meet her." Turner squinted into the sun. "I finally asked her. I don't know if she will say yes, but I asked her anyway. You always told me I'd know what love was when I finally found the right girl. I know now, Mom." His mother would have been proud of his decision. Turner closed his eyes, drifting off to sleep too, as he didn't want to return home. His father and brother would object to his decision to stay by Arianna, but he didn't care. Neither found prestige in choosing to be someone's servant and dinner. However, the only opinion that mattered was his mother's, and she would be proud that he was following his heart in living his life.

SIXTEEN

"Time to get ready." Molina was tapping at Arianna's head.

Arianna groggily opened her eyes. She had actually been awake for several hours after she was placed in her bed—alone—but she didn't feel like moving. There was too much to consider. Devin wasn't there when they finally returned. She'd looked all over the house, but he wasn't anywhere. Giving up, Arianna lost herself in her thoughts until Molina entered the room.

"Where did he go?" Arianna asked, sitting up and rubbing her eyes.

"Devin had some business for Lord Randolph," Molina replied. Arianna turned her head sideways as she stared at Molina. Closing her eyes, Arianna sensed the blood beating through Molina's body. The beat remained constant. Molina wasn't lying.

"How did you choose your keeper?" Arianna asked Molina, moving on to the second subject clouding her mind.

"I haven't yet," Molina replied. "Normally, we choose one around our twentieth birthday. Mine just passed, but I've been too busy to even worry about it. My parents pressured me to choose before Lord Randolph hired me, but now they've backed off. I think they're actually hoping that I'll ask Nixon or Jackson."

"Oh," Arianna replied, still not finding the answer she wanted to hear.

"Are you trying to decide on a keeper?" Molina asked,

picking up on Arianna's dissatisfaction with the answer. Arianna didn't reply. "Well, I'll give you the advice my mother gave me. The relationship between a custodian and a dearg-dul is a unique one. Unlike any other relationship ever formed, there's a bond made that can never be broken. You must choose wisely, but not be afraid to choose at all."

"I understand that. I just don't know how to tell if it would be right—forever," Arianna nodded.

"I know you're afraid to choose someone, and then have complete control over them. So just ask yourself, even if you didn't make them into a keeper, would this person, at any rate, always put you first? Follow your heart, and you should know the answer." Molina patted Arianna's hand before leaving the room. Molina felt like the big sister Arianna never had.

By the time Arianna finally dressed and was ready, they were going to be late. "Sorry," she said, as she took Turner's extended arm to lead her to the waiting car.

"Actually, I was hoping you would take more time," Turner replied. "The later we are, the less time I have to wear this silly tux." Turner fidgeted with his black bowtie. He was uncomfortable dressed up. "Maybe we should just ditch it and find somewhere else to go."

"If we skip it altogether, your dad would be mad," Arianna replied. "He's just a proud father. Let him have his little happy moment."

"But..." Turner tried to protest.

"Come on," she said, dragging Turner to the open door and car outside.

Turner fidgeted with the bowtie and cufflinks the whole ride to the banquet hall. Arianna tried to read his mood. He seemed to be a mixture of everything: excitement, fear, laziness, happiness, irritation, and shyness. Arianna wondered how one person could feel so much at one time. As the car door opened, Turner exited and helped Arianna from the car. With people arriving to the dinner alongside them, Turner became the model date. Arianna giggled at the sudden transformation.

"Hey, no giggling," he whispered.

"I didn't know you had it in you," she replied, as they began to walk up the grand staircase and past all of the stares of the people milling around, waiting for her arrival. Arianna felt the wonder in the people.

"Is it really her?" a young lady asked her father.

"She's so tiny," an older lady commented to her gray-haired friend.

"It can't be her, she doesn't look sixteen," a man said quietly to his wife.

"But she's with the younger of Lord Winter's sons," his wife replied. "It must be her."

Arianna felt Turner pull her closer. "I know you can hear everything being said. Ignore them. They all like to gossip too much." Arianna nodded. No one knew how well she could hear, otherwise they'd all be quiet.

"Welcome," Lord Winter called from across the room, as they entered, and he hurried towards them. "For a moment, I wondered if Turner was just going to whisk you away, especially after you didn't return last night."

Arianna poked Turner's side, giving him an 'I told you' look. She could feel the genuine relief in Lord Winter's voice that they actually arrived. Turner wasn't just disobedient in school, obviously.

"Come this way, my dear." Lord Winter took Arianna from Turner and led her to the large table on the platform in the front of the room. Lord Winter pulled out a seat and offered it to Arianna. "I'd like you to sit here, next to me. It's such an honor to have you visit us. I want to learn more about you, and how you came to meet my son." Arianna nodded as she sat down. Lord Winter remained standing as the guests around the room hurried to their seats. After everyone was seated, he greeted the crowd, and the wait staff began to bring out drinks and food.

Arianna felt a slight pain in the pit of her stomach as the servers began bringing drinks to the table. The overwhelming smell of blood easily caught her attention. They carefully placed glasses before specific guests. Watching each, she began to see that each guest with a glass of blood was a night human. As the waiter neared her, Arianna pondered how to decline without insulting Lord Winter. To her surprise, Turner stopped the waiter before she could say a word.

"Just water for Arianna," Turner said, and the waiter quickly placed a glass of water in front of Arianna instead of the blood-filled glass. "She's not to drink any blood unless it comes from Devin," Turner explained to his confused father.

"How did you know that?" Arianna whispered.

"I got my orders from Devin yesterday on the train while you slept. Man, can he be strict," Turner replied. Relieved, Arianna watched as the food began being served. As a raw piece of meat was placed before Turner, Arianna wrinkled her nose at him.

"You like blood, I like raw meat," he replied, cutting a piece and holding it to her. "Want to try?"

"I don't think so," she responded, and he laughed. As she sat through dinner, she couldn't help but periodically giggle between answering Lord Winter's questions while Turner constantly added his piece to every answer or question. Even though he had been so serious the night before, no matter what her answer to his question, nothing would change. As the meal finished, and the tables moved, a small orchestra began to set up in the corner of the room. Arianna tried not to move, as she could feel the dull pain beginning in the pit of her stomach. How long would it take before she got sick?

"Are you feeling okay?" Turner asked quietly. With a

strained smile, Arianna nodded her head yes.

"I'm just a little tired," she lied, though Turner wasn't about to believe her.

Turner crossed the room to Molina, who was standing watch over Arianna at the party. Devin was nowhere around. Arianna already knew that much, but his absence made her a bit sad. Arianna strained to listen to the conversation between Turner and Molina, but her increased hearing was slowly fading. She easily picked up the conversations of the people seated between her and Turner, but she couldn't focus to his conversation.

Arianna resolved to sit and watch his movements. His large hands gently messing with his hair as he talked. *He's upset about something*, Arianna thought. He impatiently turned his face from Arianna so that she couldn't see his expression as he continued to talk. Molina gave no clue to the discussion, as her own expression didn't change. Turner finished talking and returned to Arianna's side. All his worry was carefully hidden.

"How about I have the first dance with you, then?" Turner asked, as he offered her his hand.

"I dunno. Is it safe to dance with you?" she shot back.

"I guess you'll just have to test your luck and see," Turner grinned. "I think you lead. Right?"

Standing in the middle of the dance floor, Arianna heard the soft music begin. A bit self-conscious as everyone in the room stared at her with Turner. Arianna could feel her face flush. Turner gently placed his hand around her waist while taking her other hand in his. Pulling her close to him, he whispered in her ear.

"Since they are already staring, let's give them a show." Turner winked at Arianna as he stood back tall.

"Easy for you to say," Arianna complained, as he began to lead her around the dance floor. "You grew up going to these parties." Arianna followed his lead, happy to find he could actually dance as well as Devin. Arianna felt the pain return as she thought of Devin momentarily.

"I sent Molina to find him, but no one knows where he is," Turner explained as the song finished, and he led her back to her seat.

"He wasn't in town anymore, the last time I found him," Arianna explained. "I'm fine. I just need to rest a little bit," she tried to reassure the worried man beside her. Arianna patted his hand. "Really," she added, and he gave a weak smile. Turner relaxed a little bit as he watched her carefully. To him, Arianna was the most important person in the world. Sitting helplessly and watching her in pain, was hard to do.

"Do you know everyone here?" Arianna asked, trying to change the subject, and relieve her mind from thinking about the growing pain.

"Unfortunately," Turner replied, looking over the crowd. "When you grow up in a family like this, you're often at these parties." Two young boys weaved in an out of the dance floor. "You just kind of get used to it." Turner nonchalantly put his arm on the back of Arianna's chair. Arianna tried to ignore it as her heart beat faster.

Arianna studied Turner as he talked. She could see the distant look as he remembered his past. His gray eyes blurred over, not noticing her staring. Arianna easily compared Turner to Devin. He was much more open and outgoing. He never weighed the consequences of his actions, he just acted. The past few days, Arianna felt as though everything was so much more exciting in her new life. The more she learned about him, the more she was intrigued. How could he always be so happy when he had such a sad past? It didn't take any extra ability to know he was very close to his mother. Arianna never knew her own parents, so she had no memories. *It must be bittersweet*, she thought, *to have known your parents and then no longer have them beside you.* Though he often broke rules, and tested everyone's limits, Turner was a good man.

"Devin made things easier, being a kid in this world. That was us ten years ago," he explained, pointing to the two boys. Turner sat calmly beside her as they continued to watch the people dance. Every so often, he would smile as the two boys played. Turner didn't explain more, but just watched.

"Yes," she said, leaning near Turner and whispering in his ear. Molina was right. No matter if Turner was her keeper or not, he was always trying to protect her, just like Devin. Stunned at the realization to what she was saying, Turner sat still. "The answer to your question last night is *yes*," Arianna explained. "Sometime in the future," she quickly added. "I want to get used to this world first before I make anyone into one officially."

Turner smiled as he tipped his head onto her shoulder. "I didn't think you would actually say yes." Relieved, he sat with his eyes closed, leaning on her shoulder.

"And what could you have done to make my son so happy?" Lord Winter asked, approaching Arianna and Turner. Arianna smiled as Turner's smiled faded into hesitation.

"I told him I'd like him to become my custodian some day," Arianna replied before Turner could stop her. Turner waited in silence for his father to become angry, but was surprised to find the man heartily laughing.

"I knew he was up to something when he begged to go to school. Everyone knew he didn't need to go to any school," Lord Winter wiped the tears from the corners of his eyes. Even with her senses dulled, Arianna felt how proud Lord Winter was.

"You're not disappointed?" Turner asked quietly. "You always said it was beneath our family." Arianna hadn't ever seen him be so quiet and reserved.

"Disappointed?" Lord Winter asked. "That you want to devote your life to this precious girl sitting beside you? I'd have thought you a fool if you didn't want to, after meeting her. Contrary to what some people say, there's nothing wrong in dedicating your life to someone, especially someone as significant as Miss Arianna. More importantly, I should wish Arianna good luck with you. I've put up with this child for seventeen years. You see all the white hairs I have? They are all due to him." Arianna laughed at Lord Winters head of almost white hair.

"But he just keeps life interesting," Arianna replied.

"Interesting? That's a good way of putting it," Lord Winter stood, scanning the crowd. Turner moved closer to Arianna as she cringed from the pain.

"We need to find Devin for you," he said only to her. Lord Winter waved to Turner, and Turner hurried to him, his eyes darting around the room looking for Molina.

Lord Winter tapped his glass to get the attention of the crowd milling around the dance floor. Everyone turned to the head table and quieted down.

"I just wanted to give everyone the great news. My youngest son here, whom we have worried about for years over what he would do with his life, has finally decided to become a man and make a decision." Turner's cheeks reddened at his father's words. "Turner had decided to become Miss Arianna's custodian." Cheers erupted from the crowd, and everyone happily yelled their congratulations. Turner was the youngest of the Winter children, and therefore, was not in line to follow his father in running the city. He was much stronger and cunning than his older brother, but tradition made it clear, his brother was the next in line to the position.

Surprised by the reaction of everyone attending the party, Turner joined his father in shaking hands and receiving congratulations from the people individually. As a new face appeared before him to tell his own story of how proud he was of Turner, Turner continued to steal glances at Arianna, who sat alone, distracted by the pain. Not waiting for Molina to return to Arianna's side, Turner quickly moved to the head table only moments before her.

"We can't find him," Molina said. "He must have turned off all his electronics, and no one knows where he went. Lord Randolph said he should have returned by now from his assignment. We need to get you some blood soon."

"But he said not to take any blood from anyone. He made me promise," Arianna replied as her eyes began to haze over. Around her, people were beginning to smell enticing. "Can you take me back to my room?" Arianna asked, as Turner neared them. "It smells like blood everywhere."

"Turner, we need to move her now," Molina ordered. Molina could see Arianna was slowly changing, not by her own will. Any person in the room would gladly give their blood to Arianna, but Arianna didn't want to attack anyone. "Is your uncle around?" Molina asked, as Turner helped Arianna stand.

"No, he left yesterday for some reason," Arianna replied, taking Turner's arm, trying not to show the pain she was feeling.

As they finally reached her room, Turner carefully placed her on the couch. Touching her face gently, he winced; it was hard to watch her in pain.

"She needs to feed," Turner angrily told Molina.

"We can't go against Devin's decision. His orders come from Lord Randolph," Molina said. Arianna curled up in pain. "Right now, we need to wait. She still has enough blood for the time being. It would take hours, if not days, to die from lack of blood at this point."

"But she's in pain," Turner replied. "We can't just let her suffer like this."

Arianna sat back up as she caught her breath in a low moment of pain. "It's fine." Turner sat down beside her.

"Take my blood," he offered, pulling his bowtie off and exposing his neck.

"I can't," she replied, watching the vein in his neck throb.

"Part of being your custodian is that you can have my blood whenever you want," Turner explained. "If you take even just a little, the pain will stop." Arianna closed her eyes as the pain shot through her body. Opening them as it subsided again, she shook her head *no*. "Then how about this, take some blood so that you can find Devin. You said you can smell him no matter where he goes. Then, take a little, tell us where to find him, and I'll personally drag his butt back here." Arianna smiled slightly at Turner's agitation.

"He does have a point," Molina added, thinking over Turner's plan. Molina knew that going against Devin's word was as good as going against Lord Randolph, but if Arianna took the blood to locate Devin, he might overlook it this time.

"But I promised," Arianna added, sulking that Molina was now agreeing with Turner. Turner gently picked up Arianna's hand and placed it on his chest. Her sense of hearing was beginning to return to day human level, but the skin-to-skin contact brought the sound of Turner's blood swishing through his veins loud into her ears.

"Take a little bit," he begged. "Please."

SEVENTEEN

Turner sat, begging Arianna with his eyes. Molina was sitting behind him nodding her head. Arianna was in a predicament. It would be safe to take Turner's blood, but she'd promised Devin she wouldn't take any blood unless he said it was okay. Arianna instinctively closed her eyes as the pain began again. In the dark, she could hear Turner's heart beat louder. Arianna sighed as she caught her breath. "When you do find Devin, tell him I'm sorry for breaking my promise."

"Why can't you tell him yourself? I promise that I'll bring him right back here," Turner replied, confused.

"If you are as powerful as Gabriel says, I don't think he'll believe me, even if I mean it," Arianna responded, gently moving the collar of his shirt to expose the vein in his neck. "Brenton," she said quietly. "I'm sorry if this hurts."

Arianna moved to kneel beside Turner. Feeling the pain increasing again, she leaned against him and shuddered. Turner gently helped her balance beside him, waiting for the bite. He'd never been bit by a night human before, but it was too late to change his mind. Arianna needed blood to stop the pain, and Turner was willing to do anything to help her. Closing his eyes, Turner felt her teeth pierce the skin. After the slight pinch, he could barely move as a strange feeling came over his body. Surprisingly, it wasn't painful. After only a few moments, Arianna pulled away. Molina moved the computer screen in front of Arianna and her eyes glazed over, deep in thought. Moments later, Arianna pointed to a street on the screen.

"He is moving this way," Arianna said, tracing the street with her finger.

"Oak Street, heading east," Molina said rapidly into her phone.

"I can go help," Turner offered, trying to stand, but Arianna clung to his arm.

"Turner tastes like chocolate," Arianna said giggling. She had held on to her senses as long as she could, but now everything around her seemed funny. She was drunk on blood again.

"Stay with her," Molina ordered Turner as she left the room.

Pulling Turner back onto the couch, Arianna climbed onto his lap.

"More please?" she asked sweetly. Turner was unable to respond as Arianna picked up his hand and licked his wrist. Arianna looked up at Turner waiting for a reply.

"I think I understand why he doesn't want you drinking other blood now," Turner replied. "Did the pain stop?"

"Pain," she asked, distracted from taking more blood. Arianna pondered the question. "Pain?" she repeated.

"I guess you aren't feeling much of anything right now," Turner replied.

"I'm feeling happy," she responded, flopping over his lap to lay on the couch. She scrambled up and pulled his face near hers. "I have a secret," she said, pulling his ear close. "Turner likes me," she said whispering.

"Yes, he does," Turner replied, putting her close enough to hear his heart beating again, just as Devin had done to make her sleep on the train.

Arianna quickly pushed herself away. "I'm not sleepy, silly." Arianna sat up and looked around the room. She could hear Devin coming near. Arianna smiled as she lay down across Turner's lap and closed her eyes.

Bursting through the door, Devin hurried over to Arianna, kneeling beside her to pick up her limp arm.

"How long has she been like this?" Devin asked Turner.

"A whole five seconds," Turner replied, answering the question. Devin's face fell as he assumed he was too late. "I doubt there's anything to worry about," Turner reassured him.

"Hey," Arianna said, sitting up and startling Devin. "You ruined my surprise." Arianna pouted.

Relief spread across Devin's face. "How much did she take?" he asked as Arianna began to giggle at Devin's sudden change in emotions.

"Not much," Turner replied. "She told me before she took it to tell you she's sorry for breaking her promise. Now I see why you made her promise."

"Come here, you," Devin said, picking Arianna up. Arianna wiggled in his arms.

"No, Devin is a meanie," she replied.

"Are you still hungry?" Devin asked, knocking his head against hers to get her attention.

"Mm hmm," she replied, licking her lips.

"Thanks," Devin called over his shoulder to Turner as he walked away with Arianna. As Devin gently placed her on the bed, Turner and Molina left the room.

"What have you been doing to use up your blood so fast?" Devin asked.

"I dunno," she replied with a giggle. "How do you use up blood?"

Devin sighed. It was difficult to deal with her as she was, but he wanted to get an answer. "Were you listening to anyone?"

"Like you when you didn't come out to get me after you were a jerk?" she asked. "Or when Gabriel left me all alone?"

"You knew he was gone?" Devin asked.

"He told me to be a good girl and listen to you, but why should I listen to a meanie?" Arianna crawled away to the opposite side of the bed. "You're just a meanie, keeping me here in the world locked away with my scary grandfather. I want to go home. Back with my aunt. At least she loves me."

"Come here," Devin said gently to Arianna, who stared at him from across the bed.

"No," she replied with a pout. "You're going to be nice to me now, and then later you'll just be mean again. I'm sick of being confused by all of this. I want to go back home to Aunt Lilly and Uncle Dean where everything is less confusing. Where I can be a normal teenager."

"I'm sorry," Devin replied quietly. "I don't mean to confuse you. I just don't know how to handle it myself."

"I can tell Turner is as confused as you are at times, but he's never mean to me," Arianna responded. "Why are you?"

"I wasn't trying to hurt your feelings, but I needed you to get closer to Turner," Devin replied.

"If you like me, why do you want me to like Turner? Most guys aren't in the habit of wanting the girl they like to like other guys."

"It's not something I want to happen, but it's something that must happen for you to achieve what everyone is expecting," Devin cryptically replied.

"Again with the puzzles. Why can't you just tell me the truth?" Arianna sighed, determined to stay on her side of the bed.

"The legend states that for the blue-eyed one to reach full power, he or she must take five companions: each of a differnt race. The guys told me that you agreed to take Turner as your custodian." Arianna nodded her head. She already knew that nothing got past Devin. He'd always watched her every move. "I'm sorry I was mean to you last night, but this is what I was hoping would happen. Granted, I didn't think he'd act as fast as this, to ask you to allow him to be your custodian."

"But why? Did you ever like me? Or was this all a game to get me to trust Turner?" Arianna felt tears begin to well up in her eyes.

Devin moved across the bed and took her hands in his own. "My feelings have never been a lie. I'll love you until the day we die."

"Then why did you push me to Turner. Now I have feelings for him, too. This is way too confusing," Arianna complained.

"If I told you last night, I wanted you all to myself, and didn't want you to ever speak to Turner again, what would you have done?" Devin asked. Arianna didn't reply as she thought the answer. "You would have never gotten close to him. I've known all along that I won't be the only man beside you. For the legend to come true, and I truly believe you are the one to make it come true, you need to take on five keepers. I know I could have told you earlier, and you would have listened. You've always been good at obeying orders. But that wouldn't have been enough. Do you know why you like the taste of my blood so much?"

"'Cause you were bit by a baku?" Arianna guessed.

"That's only part of it. The main part is because blood tastes differently when the person loves you," Devin explained. "I love you, your uncle loves you, Turner loves you, and in his own way, your grandfather loves you."

"But his blood tasted sour," she complained.

"Sorry. He's a bad example. He does love you, but I won't lie when I say, your grandfather is an evil man. He's had to do things that have hardened his soul, and he no longer feels emotions like you and I do. I'm sure he loves you, but his blood will never show it," Devin explained.

"But why do you only love me sometimes, and not at

other times. I can tell."

"First and foremost, I have a job to do. I was hired by your grandfather to make sure you stay safe. That's my main concern, and my first priority. When we're safe and alone, I can let that part go and just be beside you. Like now. Otherwise, I have to do my job. My feelings for you don't just disappear, but my priorities of love versus safety have to interchange depending on the moment. Outside of these walls, I can never be that boyfriend you always wanted."

Arianna rested her head against Devin. She was beginning to see how complicated everything was. Devin really did love her after all. But now it was even more baffling.

"This is too confusing," she complained. "It's almost like I have two boyfriends now. And that's just wrong."

Devin laughed. "Think of it this way. Not two boyfriends, but two boys you're dating. It's just that we'll never make you choose between us." Devin softly stroked her head. "Now, you really do need to feed more."

"Uh huh," she replied, listening to his heartbeat. The sound filled her ears as she began to get lightheaded and dizzy. Without trying, she could smell the scent of his blood. It was intoxicating. Arianna carefully pushed his shirt away from his neck and watched the blood she had been listening to flow through his body. Devin sat still, waiting for her to bite. He was only a child the first time he was bit. The emotions he felt then were completely different from those he felt now. Filled with terror, he had pretended to sleep silently as a man entered his room. The man had viciously attacked Devin's older brother in the bed next to him before he turned to Devin. He could remember the pain as the teeth pierced into his neck. It was nothing like the sensation he felt as Arianna began to gently lick the same spot now. Careful not to touch anything other than the vein she was aiming for, Arianna bit down tenderly.

EIGHTEEN

Arianna glanced across the private compartment she was sharing on the train ride home with Devin and Turner. Devin was explaining the contents of the box he had just handed Turner. Arianna looked from one to the other. She could see the friendship between them as they talked about each item.

"When alone with Arianna, it's best to turn one of these on," Devin picked up a small cylinder with a clip. Turning the cap, the bottom blinked red. "Mori can then track you and send someone to your location, if needed. His blood readout from last night should be enough for him to really know where you are, but these are to be on the safe side."

"Why doesn't he track Ari based on her blood readout?" Turner asked. "Wouldn't that be easier?"

"He tried, but because she is both baku and dearg-dul, there seems to be a problem with it," Devin replied.

"Here," Devin said, picking up the ring in the box. "Everyone wears one of these at the Randolph estate." Turner put the ring on, and the stone changed from red to white.

"Wait a second," Turner said, and it caught Arianna's attention.

"Why did it change colors?" Arianna asked.

"A blood stone," Turner replied. "I've never seen one before in person."

"For night humans, it changes to be the color of the

family member you are loyal to. Since you are loyal to Arianna it's white, just like everyone on her security team," Devin explained.

"Except yours," Arianna added, pointing at Devin's ring.

"For humans, the color doesn't change," Devin replied.

"What does blue mean?" Arianna questioned.

"Blue was the color of people loyal to your mother. Red is for your grandfather. As far as I know, I'm the only person with a blue ring. It was given to me by the head of your mother's security team. Your grandfather went and changed the rest of the rings the non-night humans were given, since it doesn't change color on its own when we wear them," Devin replied.

Arianna went back to staring out the window. As the train bounced on the tracks, the scenery passed outside. They sped by farm after farm before heading back into a tunnel again.

"I didn't realize there were so many tunnels on the way," Arianna commented.

"That would be because you slept through the ride here," Turner added, moving to sit beside Arianna. "Are you feeling better?" he asked.

After Devin returned, Arianna had fed and slept through the rest of the weekend. Turner stopped by several times to check on her, but she had been sleeping.

"Mm hmm," she said, nodding her reply. "Good as new." Arianna tipped her head and rested it on his shoulder. "I guess not quite good as new. I'm still a little tired."

"Are you hungry?" he asked, concerned.

"No, just tired," she replied, still watching outside. The scenery stopped as they entered another tunnel.

"You can take a nap," Turner suggested, putting his arm around Arianna.

"But I slept on the way here. I want to watch outside," she answered. "This sure is a long tunnel," she added, as the windows were still dark.

"This is one of the longer ones," Turner added. "It's a few miles long I think."

Arianna quickly sat up and looked around. She was sure she heard several thumps on the tops of the cars.

"What's wrong?" Devin asked, instantly putting his earphone on.

"It sounded like several thumps on the ceiling," she said. "Up at the front end of the train." Turner closed his eyes and listened. He opened his eyes and put his earphone in just as fast.

Arianna heard the front door to the train open. Listening carefully, she counted the set of footsteps.

"It sounds like there are two groups," she said. "One is moving down the cars this way and the other is staying in place."

"How many?" Devin asked, repeating Mori's question, as Molina entered the room.

"Eight in each group," Arianna replied. Arianna ignored the conversation between Mori and Devin while she listened to the group approaching.

"It's a purebred vamp," Turner said, suddenly pulling Arianna's attention back to the people around her. The group had moved close enough for Turner to find them. "Six cars ahead."

"How much further is the other group?" Devin asked Arianna.

"I'm not sure how many cars, but it's about the same distance as the first group is to us right now," Arianna explained. Devin nodded with a quick, reassuring smile as he relayed the information to Mori.

"Can you tell who it is?" Devin asked Turner and Mori at the same time.

"No," Turner replied. "He's still too far away for me to be certain."

"Are you sure?" Devin asked Mori. Quickly searching in his pocket, Devin removed a small vial. Popping the lid, Arianna immediately recognized the scent: her grandfather's blood. "Arianna, can you give Turner a small drop of your blood?" Devin asked.

"But grandfather said..." Arianna replied staring at Molina.

"He won't do anything to Turner now. You've already announced he was going to be your custodian," Devin replied.

"I'll be gentle," he promised.

Turner gently picked up Arianna's hand. Pulling her finger to his mouth, he partially changed forms. Arianna watched curiously, as she hadn't seen his lycan form before. His reddish brown hair slightly lengthened and small hairs began to grow on the back of his neck. Arianna felt a slight prick as he bit the tip of her finger. He changed back as soon as he let go of her hand.

"Thank you," he said softly, feeling the strength of her blood rush through his.

"Turner, sit down beside Arianna," Devin directed. "Arianna, sit between Turner and the window and lean against him. Close your eyes and pretend to be sleeping." Arianna followed his instructions. "It's Michael Seeger," Devin said to Turner.

"But if he's here, then that means..." Turner trailed off.

Arianna lifted her head from his shoulder and looked at the two exchanging glances.

"Arianna, pretend to sleep, or we'll have to make you actually sleep," Devin replied.

Arianna pouted as she closed her eyes again. She didn't want to be left out of the conversation, but Devin was serious. Placing her hand on Turner's chest, Arianna suddenly had a plan to be part of the conversation. Using her nail, Arianna cut her own finger and Turner's chest.

Placing her bit finger over the cut on Turner's chest, she connected.

'Can you hear me?' Arianna asked Turner.

Turner smiled. "When did you learn how to do that?" he asked. Devin stared at Arianna and Turner. Devin nodded, as he understood.

"When Gabriel visited me," she replied, lifting her head and getting a stern look from Devin. "Okay, I got it. Sleep." Arianna laid her head back down and listened to the group walking through the train cars toward the one she was in. As the footsteps neared, she tried to relax and picture everything without seeing it. Arianna listened to the slight clicking of Molina's shoes as she met up with the second group that was waiting several cars away. Devin stood and opened the door.

"Welcome," he said, bowing his head slightly to the young man standing in the hallway.

'Why is he being so nice?' Arianna asked.

'Because even Devin has to behave in front of purebreds,' Turner replied.

Arianna listened as the man entered and sat down next to Turner.

"Been a while since I last saw you, Michael," Turner said, he moved Arianna just enough to stand and bow to the men. "You didn't make it down for her party."

"No, father was too busy," the young man replied.

Arianna listened to Molina near the room. As the door opened, Arianna wanted to open her eyes. She could smell the same scent she had smelled on her grandfather on the man that was with Molina.

"You found me," the older gentleman said, laughing as he entered. "Seems your skills are as good as normal," he added sitting beside Devin. "I didn't expect to find you guys all on the train today."

'He's lying,' Arianna said to Turner.

"I thought you were at school," he added.

'More lies,' she said. *'Who is he?'*

'Paul Seeger, head of the Seeger family,' Turner replied. *'One of few dearg-duls that like to cause problems for your grandfather. He often times starts trouble, which he leaves for Lord Randolph to clean up. Of all the dearg-dul clans, he's always the one voicing dissent to every choice your grandfather makes.'*

'He smells like grandfather,' Arianna added. *'Sour.'*

'But he is nowhere near as powerful,' Turner explained. *'He's probably hoping to set his son up with you so that he can finally get the power he wants.'*

'Too bad grandfather said he would rather marry me himself than give me to any of the purebreds alive,' Arianna added. *'He's already received proposals and threw them out.'*

Turner chuckled accidentally causing everyone to look at him.

"And this sleeping beauty must be Miss Arianna," Paul said examining Arianna like a prized specimen. "So peaceful."

'If he comes near me, I'll bite him,' Arianna threatened. *'Arrrgh.'* Turner chuckled more and tried to cover it with a cough.

"It seems you found yourself quite a good position." Paul was staring at Turner, who kept coughing.

"I suppose, but she can be such a handful," he added, as Arianna pinched him.

"You would talk that way about the heir to the Randolph name, and your new charge?" Paul replied.

"Why not? At least I don't lie every time I open my mouth," Turner added. The man sat down across from him, glaring, but Turner didn't even flinch.

"You're just a wolf. What would you know about being able to tell if someone was lying?" Paul replied.

Devin smiled. He enjoyed seeing Lord Seeger, the famed

'stone man' who never got angry, but he knew things had to be calmed down for Arianna's safety.

"Ari," Devin said kneeling beside her. "Can you please go to sleep now for real?"

Arianna opened her eyes and looked at Devin. "But I'm not tired." Arianna looked over Devin's shoulder at the older man. His keen eyes bore holes into her as he stared. She could feel the delight he was feeling from just being near her. Devin turned her face back towards him.

"Please," Devin added.

"Fine," she replied laying her head back against Turner's chest. Arianna looked up at Turner as he placed his hand over her other ear.

'Don't worry,' he added. *'We will protect you.'*

Arianna smiled as she drifted off to sleep.

NINETEEN

The wind on the windows sounded different as Arianna opened her eyes. Arianna woke to find herself no longer in the train but in the rear seat of a car as it hurried toward the Randolph estate. Devin and Turner were talking together facing her.

"That was great," Turner added. "Did you see his face as I carried Arianna out into the sunlight, and he had to sit in the train?"

"I couldn't tell if he doubted we would take her into sunlight, or that it wouldn't matter," Devin added with a chuckle. Arianna could see the pain shoot over Devin's face as he began coughing. Concerned, she reached for his hand but was too dizzy to make contact.

"Are you finally awake?" Turner asked, as the car pulled into the driveway. Arianna nodded.

"Are you okay?" she asked Devin. Arianna touched his skin. It felt cold, but he nodded his head yes.

Arianna, Devin, and Turner exited in front of Randolph Manor. Arianna hurried to follow Devin and Turner. They weaved their way between staff through the long hallways. As they approached Lord Randolph's study, Arianna began to worry slightly about Turner as well. She could still smell the scent of her own blood on Turner's breath. Without knocking, Devin opened the door.

"Uncle," he called into the dimly-lit room.

Lord Randolph placed his papers down behind the large

grand desk. Looking at Devin, Lord Randolph only needed a moment before hurrying to the young man.

"You should have gone straight to the infirmary," he said, catching Devin as he fell to his knees.

"I'm fine," Devin replied, steadying himself on Lord Randolph.

"What did you do?" Lord Randolph asked, escorting Devin to a chair. Arianna had never seen her grandfather be so nice to someone before.

"I thought I'd be fine until we made it back here, but we had some unexpected guests," Devin explained. "We left them on the train to get back here before them. Paul Seeger and his son Michael are on their way to visit and discuss matters with you."

Lord Randolph strained a smile. "That old fox thinks he can corner me into handing away my granddaughter now, does he?" Devin nodded.

"I tried to explain to him that you were not interested in taking proposals, but he didn't seem to care," Devin replied. "We left them at the train. I thought you might want to see Arianna safe in her apartment before he arrived."

"That's for sure," Lord Randolph added. "Arianna, take Turner with you, and return to your apartment."

"What's going on?" she asked, looking from Devin to her grandfather.

"Don't worry about Devin; I'll take him down to the infirmary," Lord Randolph replied.

"But why is he sick?" Arianna asked. Before she had fallen asleep, Devin seemed to be perfectly healthy.

"This is what happens, when he uses up too much blood," Lord Randolph replied as Devin's cheeks became red. Obviously, Devin wasn't about to tell Arianna the blunt truth.

"So, this is my fault?" Arianna asked.

"No, he would have been fine getting home if it was just

you feeding," Lord Randolph added. "But he used some of my blood. Humans can drink night human blood and gain extraordinary powers. But to do so, the night human blood feeds on his own blood. Since he was already low on blood from feeding you, he shouldn't have used my blood on top of it."

"What choice did I have?" Devin tried to defend himself. "We know his intent."

Lord Randolph nodded, but he didn't elaborate further. "Turner, your things have been moved from your dorm room to the apartment. Once you get upstairs, Mori will set the security, so don't leave your apartment until Devin or I come for you." Turner nodded. "Jackson, Nixon," Lord Randolph called into the hallway. "We will be in complete lockdown mode." Both men nodded also. Arianna wanted to ask more questions, but her grandfather hugged her and turned her around to leave the room.

"What's going on?" Arianna asked, as they walked into her apartment.

"She's in, Mori," Nixon said into his headphone. "Don't try to leave here, please." Nixon said, as he shut the door behind him.

Arianna listened as the sound of grinding metal brought her attention to the windows, where they were slowly being covered. Outside the front door, she could hear the same metal noise grinding.

"We're locked in a box," she commented, walking to the stairs that led to her grandfather's apartment, only to find the entrance was also covered with a metal plate. Arianna listened through the barriers. The clicking of heels and shuffling of feet told her everyone was working as normal. Arianna sat in the living room and waited.

"It seems so. I'm going to get some sleep," Turner said, turning to walk away. Pausing, he turned back. "Are you tired?" Arianna replied with a head shake. She continued to sit and listen to the house around her. "If you get tired or hungry, just come wake me up. Don't worry about everything so much. Devin will be fine." Arianna nodded as she continued to search the house for him.

Listening through the entire house Arianna heard Paul and Michael Seeger finally show up. Her grandfather greeted them as he would an old friend though Arianna knew differently from his emotions.

"Please come this come this way to the dining room. After such a long trip, you must be hungry," Lord Randolph said, as they began to walk down the hallway.

"Will your granddaughter be joining us?" Paul asked.

"She was still tired from her exciting weekend, choosing a custodian and all," Lord Randolph added with a smirk.

"And what a good choice. The Winter boy is from such a prestigious family. You must be proud," Paul added. Arianna listened as his heartbeat changed. He was lying again. Arianna heard the moving of chairs as they all sat down at the table. "So, out of all the proposals she must have received, her first choice was Turner?"

"Oh no, I didn't give her any of the proposals. Turner goes to school with her. It seems he proposed himself over the weekend," Lord Randolph explained. "I don't think she should be bothered with such things right now. She only just turned. She has plenty of time to make decisions about such a large commitment."

"That is true. She does have plenty of time," Paul added.

As the meal finished, Lord Randolph stood and finally asked the question Arianna wanted to know. "What brings you here so early? The council meeting isn't for another two weeks."

"I've been thinking of enrolling Michael here in school," Paul lied. "I think it would give him the opportunity to broaden his learning, since we spend so much focus on purebred teachings."

"Then, you are not here to propose a merging of our two families?" Lord Randolph added.

"Shouldn't we leave that to the kids?" Paul added. "Although, I wouldn't be opposed to the idea," he said, finally telling the truth.

"Actually, I don't think Arianna should marry anyone for at least ten or sixteen years. She will have enough pressure learning everything she needs to know to run the clans." The anger was building in her grandfather.

"I agree completely, but you have to remember, you won't be around forever. And there are always traditions to keep. Wouldn't you rather know she's going to be taken care of?" Paul added.

"She has her PPU and Turner. They will make sure she's happy. Also, I don't think her father's family will let her be unhappy, even if I'm not here." Lord Randolph was on the brink of snapping at his guests.

"About that, you've never said who her father is. Rumor has it, he isn't a dearg-dul," Paul added, trying his luck to get an answer. He had watched with his own PPU as Arianna was carried out of the train into the sunlight without a problem.

"Well, he isn't much of anything anymore," Lord Randolph replied.

Paul waited, but there was no explanation. "Well, we should head to bed. It was a long trip down, and we had so much to discuss with Devin. Thank you for the wonderful meal." Arianna listened to Paul and his son talking quietly as they walked away down the hallway.

The rustling in the adjacent room caught Arianna's attention. She knew immediately who it was. Shuffling into the room, pulling something on wheels, Devin joined Lord Randolph.

"Seems he's being a bit more cautious than I expected," Lord Randolph said to Devin. "You must have given him a stern lecture."

"I just told him the truth. Maybe a bit bluntly," Devin replied. Arianna could sense the humor in Devin's voice. Though he his heartbeat was weak, he was better than when she had left him downstairs. "Are they still talking nicely?" Devin asked.

"They are out of range of my hearing," Lord Randolph replied. "As are we."

Arianna turned her attention back to Paul and Michael. Still talking in hushed tones, the conversation had changed.

"You should have said more," Paul scolded Michael. "You need to sound as if you are really interested in her."

"Why? Don't you just want to get her blood?" Michael asked.

"Stupid child," he replied, slapping Michael. "Don't you see how Lord Randolph is playing? He's neither allowing anyone near her, nor is he going to make her marry anyone. The old man has finally lost it. He's letting a sixteen-year-old make decisions about her own life. How stupid can he get? It'll be so much easier to convince her to like you than it would be to get his permission." Michael didn't reply.

Arianna caught herself yawning as she listened. She was using too much blood by listening at such lengths, but it was now a little clearer as to why they were being so cautious. As the metal panel between the rooms began to move, Arianna quickly turned to find Molina walking up the staircase with Lord Randolph close behind.

"Still awake?" he asked nicely, as if the dinner had just been a great evening between friends.

"I slept most of the way home, and have been sleeping most of the past two days. How much sleep can one person get?" she asked. She carefully assessed her grandfather, trying to see a hint of the frustration she just heard.

"Quite a lot until you get used to your new life," Molina replied. "Is Turner asleep now?"

"Yes," Arianna replied. Lord Randolph didn't seem worried at the least.

"Don't wake him until you are all ready to leave," Lord Randolph added.

"Leave?" Arianna questioned.

"Yes," Lord Randolph replied. "Devin said you're a bit homesick. I didn't think it through too much when I brought you here. I should have known you would miss your home. So, we figured out a schedule that will hopefully work. When everyone heads to bed here at the manor on Sunday night, you and your team will fly back to Lilly and Dean's place. You then can stay there Monday through Wednesday before coming back here. I've arranged for you to have your classes there as well. There are two private tutors that will teach you at school while your classmates take their normal classes."

Arianna hugged her grandfather. He had thought of everything.

"Don't thank me," he added. "This was Devin's plan. I just agreed with him."

"Either way," Arianna added, hugging him again. "I get to go home."

TWENTY

Not waiting for the car to stop, Arianna bolted from her ride as it pulled in front of the diner. She walked around back, into the alley, and through the only open door to the diner. She stopped in the kitchen surprised to find Dean cleaning and cutting vegetables so early in the morning. Surprised at seeing Arianna, Dean immediately put down everything and hurried over to her.

"Where's Auntie?" Arianna asked, as he hugged her tight. "Doesn't she do the morning prep?"

"Not since we returned," Dean replied, finally putting Arianna down. "What are you doing here, kiddo?"

"Devin talked to Grandpa, and he said I can spend Monday through Wednesday with you and Aunt Lilly, if you still want me," Arianna quickly added.

"Of course we do," Dean patted her head like always. "Maybe this will help Lilly."

"Help her?" Arianna questioned.

"She should be up by now," he replied. "You better go say hello. If she finds you down here without greeting her, she'll be mad at me." Arianna nodded, and ran back out the door to the stairway.

Arianna hurried to climb the stairs to the second floor. She wanted to surprise her aunt. It was only 5:30 in the morning, so she opened the door quietly. Arianna walked into the living room of her old apartment. The light in the kitchen caught her attention. Slowly, she crept into the kitchen doorway. Aunt Lilly sat at the table, still in her pajamas, staring off to the other side of the room. Tears trickled down her cheeks.

"What's wrong?" Arianna asked, concerned, no longer wanting to surprise her.

"Ari?" Lilly replied, turning to Arianna in the doorway. "Is it really you?"

"Who else would it be, silly," Arianna hurried over and hugged Lilly. Lilly relaxed into her arms. "Uncle Dean said if I didn't get up here now he'd be in trouble." Lilly grasped Arianna, still unsure if her eyes were correct.

"But you should be with your grandfather," Lilly responded.

"It's okay. I get to come home now from Monday to Wednesday. I was getting a bit homesick, and this was the solution," Arianna replied, wanting to let go, but knowing Lilly would not.

Lilly continued to hold onto Arianna. Her tears gradually turned from sadness to happiness. "You didn't run away," Lilly prodded, finally letting Arianna back a few inches.

"No, she didn't," Devin replied from the doorway. "She tried to last week, but her uncle keeps pretty good tabs on her."

Lilly looked over to Devin. "This is really real? She can stay here part of the week, every week?" She questioned Devin as if he had the authority to say no.

"Yes, Lord Randolph only wants to see Arianna happy," Devin replied. "She can stay here three days a week, as long as we stay with her." Devin pointed to himself and Turner standing behind him.

"Of course, anything," Lilly replied.

Arianna yawned, and stretched after her aunt let go of her. "I think I should get a nap in before I go to school."

"Of course. You flew here just this morning?" Lilly asked, her chipper self slowly returning.

"Yep, on a private plane," Arianna replied. She knew that everyone flew on the same plane to get to her grandfather's home the first time, but Arianna wasn't awake and had no memory of it. Arianna walked to her bedroom door, which was closed. Arianna carefully opened the door and found her room exactly as she had left it, her closet empty.

"It's good to be home," she said, as she plopped down on her bed. It even smelled like home.

"I didn't move anything," Lilly explained from the doorway. "I guess a part of me was hoping you'd come home." Arianna grinned. "I'm sorry we only have one couch," Lilly said to the two boys standing behind her. "I hate to make one of you sleep on the floor."

"That's okay," Arianna said cutting her aunt off. "I normally sleep with one of them every night."

Lilly's mouth hung open in shock. "I raised you better than…" she began to get angry, but Devin cut her off.

"She means she literally sleeps with one of us. Since she changed, her hearing has increased tremendously. Night humans are attracted to the sound of a beating heart." Devin explained from behind her. Lilly cringed at the word. "We found the only way she can sleep is by listening to a heart beating to block out additional sounds."

"Oh," Lilly replied, her anger subsiding slightly.

"What did you think I meant?" Arianna asked.

"Well, you said you were sleeping with them," Lilly replied, blushing.

Arianna playfully hit her aunt. "You think I'm that type of girl?"

"Turner, you stay here with her," Devin directed. "I need to go talk to Molina about all the arrangements."

Turner remained frozen in the doorway. Arianna hurried over to him and grabbed his hand, dragging him into the room while Devin headed back to the open apartment doorway where Molina stood.

"Aunt Lilly, you've already met Devin, but I don't know if you've met Turner. This is Turner Winter," Arianna introduced him. "He goes to my school back at grandfather's place."

Lilly eyed the tall, good-looking boy. Nodding, she replied, "I can see it. You're Lord Winter's son, correct?"

"Yes, I am his youngest son," Turner replied. Arianna smiled as Turner sat uncomfortably under Aunt Lilly's gaze. There weren't many places he could go without people knowing his father and older brother.

"Well, you better get to sleep," Lilly said, turning from Arianna and Turner to leave the room. "You don't have much time, since school starts in a few hours."

"Actually, she's going to take private lessons at school. We've arranged it so that she doesn't have to be there until the ten o'clock class," Devin explained, stepping into the room in time to follow Lilly out of it. Turner motioned for Arianna to join him and she complied while easily falling instantly to sleep.

Waking from her peaceful dream, Arianna reluctantly sat up and rubbed her eyes. She was happy to be home, but now she was beginning to worry. *What will I tell my friends? What private classes will I have? Who is my new teacher? Who was the man I left at Grandfather's estate? Would he be safe there alone with him?* Automatically, Arianna closed her eyes and began to search. Her senses passing over the hundreds of miles between her and her grandfather, she found what she was listening for: the steady beat of grandfather's heart as he sat in his office. He was fine. Arianna opened her eyes and sighed.

"Ari?" Turner repeated, as he tapped her face.

"What?" she asked, swatting as he continued to tap.

"What were you doing?" he asked, knowing the answer.

"I just wanted to make sure everything was alright with my grandfather," she replied, looking on the floor for her shoes.

"You listened all the way to Randolph Manor?" Arianna nodded, and Turner sighed.

"That's what phones are for," he replied, picking up one of her shoes.

"I suppose," she thought, grabbing the second shoe on the bed. "I didn't think of that. It just comes natural to hear everything."

"How much blood did you use up?" he asked, knowing she couldn't answer.

"I'm fine," she replied, trying to move her legs over the side of the bed to stand. Arianna stared down at her legs that would not move.

Turner instinctively picked her up and placed her on his lap. "You need to feed."

"But," Arianna resisted, but it would make no difference. Turner and Devin knew more about her new body than she did.

Arianna complied and bit down gently on Turner's neck. By taking only a little blood, she was able to move again. She hurried to get dressed, and make it outside to the waiting car before Devin could yell at her for being late. As the door opened to the tinted-window car, Arianna smiled, moving to sit beside her uncle.

"You were listening to your grandfather?" he asked. Arianna nodded, ready to be scolded again. "That's a pretty good range," he added with a smile, as Devin and Turner sat in the front of the vehicle. Gabriel lifted her chin and looked into her eyes. "You need to feed more," he said quietly. "Take as much as you need," he said setting his own wrist on her lap. "I can always get more blood. I'm not picky."

Devin grunted up front to cover his laugh.

As predicted by Devin, they were late. Walking into the empty hallways, Arianna smiled. She really was home. Though she disagreed with all the strict rules of her private school, it was still home.

"Your lessons will be in the auditorium," Devin said, directing Arianna across the empty school common room.

"Don't I need to tell them I'm here?" Arianna asked as they walked past the front office windows. No one rose to stop them or ask for a late note.

"No," Molina replied. "Your tutor is waiting."

Arianna opened the large doors and stood in shock in the doorway. "Mr. Wallace?" she asked.

Mr. Wallace, one of the youngest teachers in the school, sat on the stage dressed in his normal plaid sweater vest and wire-rimmed glasses. When he noticed Arianna, he quickly stood up and hopped off the stage.

"Hello, Miss Arianna," he replied with a slight bow. "And Turner."

Arianna turned around and stared at Turner. "You know him, too?" she asked both men. Arianna turned back to Mr. Wallace. She could faintly smell the scent of dearg-dul blood. "You're a dearg-dul?" she asked. Arianna hadn't returned to school since she had changed. Closing her eyes, she looked around the school. Mr. Wallace wasn't the only night human. "And there's more?"

"I'm glad you have at least figured out how to tell people apart," Mr. Wallace commented. "So, should we begin today's lesson?"

For two hours, Arianna sat in the dimly-lit auditorium with Mr. Wallace and Turner. Carefully they explained how to tell how powerful a night human was. Arianna found all their lengthy explanations useless, as she still couldn't understand. As her lesson was finishing, Mr. Wallace made one last attempt.

"Why don't we make this very simple? Let's just compare Turner and I," he explained. "You already know which one of us is more powerful, but is there any other way you can tell the difference? They don't have to be the same ways we see things. I'm beginning to see you have your own way of doing what the rest of us do."

Arianna stared at Turner, seated on her right, and Mr. Wallace, on her left. There were many differences she knew immediately: dearg-dul or wolf, younger or older, brown hair or blond, glasses or no glasses. Arianna closed her eyes. They were not trying to have her find an outward difference, but rather, some sort of internal difference. *Who is more powerful?* Arianna continued to keep her eyes closed as she thought. Dearg-dul and lycan were different based on the scent of the blood. Arianna concentrated harder and compared the blood.

The ringing bell easily brought her back to reality.

"Well, we will continue this tomorrow," Mr. Wallace added.

"But don't I have another lesson this afternoon?" she asked.

"Not with me. I was told you have a second tutor coming after lunch," Mr. Wallace replied.

As Arianna followed Turner back down the auditorium rows, she stopped and turned around, searching for a very soft sound she heard near the stage door. Glancing around the room one last time before leaving, she couldn't find the person she thought she just heard enter. All the doors were shut, but Arianna was sure of what she heard.

Outside the auditorium, the commons room was beginning to fill with students heading to lunch. Arianna hurried over to her two best friends. Standing beside Tish, Arianna sighed. It was good to be home. Tish reached up and hugged her friend, sighing herself at finally getting the third wheel back to their trio.

"I thought your aunt was finally going delusional. Well, what is the scoop?" Mary Ellen asked. "Your aunt said you weren't returning, and then calls us not even a week later to say you are home and coming back to school today." They had already been called earlier in the morning by Lilly explaining that she was back. Mary Ellen reached up and pulled Arianna beside her in a hug. All three girls hugged and giggled to finally be back together.

"Devin talked to my grandfather and arranged for me to come back here three days a week, and spend four days a week with him," Arianna replied.

"You look beat," Tish replied, patting her friend's head. "You need a nap."

"We flew in this morning," Arianna sighed. *And I drank too much blood*, she wanted to add.

"Are you going to tell us all about those two cute boys we saw with you?" Mary Ellen pointed to Devin and Turner, who were sitting on the edge of the room, glancing over the students filling the room.

Arianna yawned and nodded. "Where should I start?" she asked, laying her head on the table.

"Are they available?" Tish asked, smiling and waving to Turner as he approached.

"Ari?" Turner asked quietly. "You should get some sleep before your next lesson," he suggested. Tish and Mary Ellen stared at Turner, who was bent over Arianna whispering closely into her ear.

"But I want to stay here with my friends," Arianna complained. "It's been weeks since I've seen them."

"Ari," Devin whispered, and she nodded as she stood. Unfortunately, Devin was always right.

"You guys have to come back with me after school. Maybe then I can answer your questions," she said, as she was dragged away by Turner, down the hallway to the choir and band rooms. Tish and Mary Ellen just winked and smiled at Arianna, who began to blush at their reactions.

"But why the music room?" Arianna asked, as Devin opened the door for her.

Arianna peered in the room. She hadn't taken any music

classes, and had never actually entered either the choir or band rooms before. In the corner of the room, four boys sat quietly talking. Scowls crossed their faces at the sight of Devin, who didn't seem to care or notice. As soon as Arianna followed behind him, their faces changed from anger to curiosity. Arianna hurried to follow Devin, turning past the director's office and into a dim hallway.

"Soundproof rooms," Devin explained, opening the door to a practice room and pushing Arianna and her newly appointed keeper inside the room. It was safer for him to keep watch with his experience around baku being greater than Turner's experience. "Of course they won't be soundproof to you, but it should help some. I'll be outside the main doors. You should be safe here. Molina and I will stand guard outside the rooms. I don't exactly trust all the students here. Get some rest. You're tired."

TWENTY-ONE

Turner softly closed his eyes and lowered his heart rate. In the choir room outside, the four boys that they had passed were still sitting and waiting. One was a purebred baku, and the other three his guards. Turner kept the information to himself as he didn't want Arianna to be unable to get some rest. His heartbeat slowed until it was near the rate of a sleeping person. Turner had only been successful twice before in being able to fool people into believing he was asleep, but Arianna didn't need to be fooled, just comforted. Arianna relaxed and was instantly asleep. Turner tried to relax along with her but was intent on listening to the choir boys.

With a slight creak, the door to the practice room opened. Turner kept his eyes closed and relaxed as the person neared. Turner could barely hear the boy move. Suddenly, Turner reached in front of his own face. The air had been broken.

Covering Arianna's ear to keep her asleep, Turner held her in his arms as he glared at the student standing, leaning against the wall, just out of Turners grasp.

"What do you want?" Turner whispered. "Isn't it taboo to feed on a sleeping baku?"

"Oh, you know your lessons. Glad they still teach about my kind in your private schools," he replied. "I only want the same as you, to touch and hold such a beautiful creature. She's absolutely magnificent."

"Arianna isn't a creature- she's a person," Turner replied. "And she's not for you to touch."

"You're pretty good," the boy said, moving from one side of the small room to the other in the blink of an eye. "So calm. I suppose one little yell, and her guard will come running. The question is, do you think you could get a yell out before I get you?" the young man taunted Turner.

"If all you wanted to do was mock me, save it for later. Arianna needs to get some sleep." Turner closed his eyes again, ignoring the boy standing in the room. The school was neutral grounds. The baku wouldn't start anything here.

"Do you feel it?" he asked. "Even at your level?"

Turner opened one eye and looked at the student. Although the boy's dark, curly hair flopped over his face, Turner could see the expression of awe across it.

"She's truly amazing. I didn't know that after she became a dearg-dul that her power would increase so much. I wonder what will happen when she becomes baku?" The boy moved closer and squatted in front of Arianna, who was still sleeping. He was now close enough for Turner to touch, but Turner ignored him. Turner kept his arm around Arianna. The boy wasn't going to harm her. "We have all been anxious to meet her."

"Well, your kind and our kind don't mix too well, so I hope you won't be disappointed," Turner replied.

"You think you can keep her to yourself?" the boy asked, instantly bouncing back to the door. He moved as silently as Gabriel. "You know, I also do a little dearg-dul studies on the side. Doesn't the blue-eyed legend state she must have five companions: each a different race?" Turner tried to not pay attention him, but it was true. "Oh, so you do know. Someday, whether you like it or not, she will choose someone of my race to stay beside her. And even worse, she'll have to choose a tengu also. Can you handle that, wolf? Your sworn enemy as a friend to your precious savior?

Her doing to him what you wish she'd do to you?" Turner couldn't stop the anger starting to rise in him.

Arianna's finger's slightly tickled Turner, subsiding his anger. Yawning, she opened her eyes. "Is nap time over?" she asked Turner, ignoring the boy standing in the corner. Turner looked at his watch.

"I guess so," he replied. Arianna sat and stretched, cracking several spots in her back. "I guess I was more tired than I knew." Turner quickly buttoned his shirt as Arianna continued to ignore the third person in the room.

"It's not polite to stare," she finally said to the boy. "If you keep following people around, staring at them, they might get the wrong impression." His quiet steps were the same as she had heard in the auditorium. Arianna turned to the dark, curly-haired boy whose name she didn't know. He smiled as he knelt.

"It's so great to finally meet you," he said, as he continued his bow.

Arianna turned to Turner for an explanation, and he shrugged.

"Um, thanks," she replied, following Turner as he led her out of the room. Arianna stopped in the doorway as she turned back to the boy. Smiling, she instantly changed into her dearg-dul form. "This is what you wanted to confirm, right?" she asked, as he smiled back at her and nodded. "And the answer is yes."

"What?" Turner asked, as they walked down the hallway into the choir room.

"He wanted to know if I really was a dearg-dul. He can tell I'm a baku, but he couldn't believe I was a dearg-dul," Arianna explained as she led the way out of the practice rooms.

"How did you-" Turner began. They could barely get her to understand that night humans were all different in strength, yet she could easily read the boy's mind.

"I dunno. I just knew," Arianna replied. Arianna followed Turner and Devin across the empty hallway to the auditorium. The bell had already rung for the beginning of class, thus Arianna didn't have the chance to see her friends before her next lesson.

"Why is Gabriel hiding?" Arianna asked Turner. Turner glanced around the room. He couldn't find anyone else besides Arianna's guards.

"Where?" Turner asked.

"Next to you," Gabriel replied, appearing next to Arianna and Turner, just inside the doorway.

"How-" Turner began to ask, but quickly stopped. Gabriel was the enemy in the eyes of everyone Turner had ever known. He had never seen Gabriel until he had shown up this morning to escort Arianna to school.

"Who is my tutor for these lessons?" Arianna asked, leading the way into the room.

"No one for today. We can't have baku lessons until you are a baku," Gabriel ushered Arianna to the front row of seats so that he could sit on the stage and face her as they talked. "You seemed to have trouble with your lesson earlier this morning, yet you had no trouble finding me, or even Andrew, as he watched your lesson."

"Andrew? The rude, curly-hair guy in the choir room?" Arianna asked. Gabriel nodded. "The whole power thing is so confusing," Arianna complained. "They all said it's best to compare other night humans to your own strength. But my strength is never constant. Sometimes it seems like Turner is almost equal to me and sometimes it feels like I'm ten times stronger. Besides, how am I supposed to compare when I haven't found anyone stronger than me?"

"I understand," Gabriel said. "Then how about comparing everyone to Turner? If we were to put Turner on a scale one through ten, he would fall just about a nine. Where would Molina fall?"

Arianna glanced across the room and then looked back to Turner. "A six?" she guessed.

"That would be about right. Strength wise, Molina is only a little stronger than average, but her speed and quick thinking are well above all of us," Gabriel explained. Molina nodded at the compliment. She was growing more used to the old baku.

"So, power isn't the only thing to judge someone by," Arianna observed.

"No, this lesson was more or less to get you to see how your power is fluctuating. Since you are a purebred, you are able to regulate the power coming out of you. Turner and Molina are always at the power you see now, but you, like me, can change it if you choose." Gabriel sat and waited for Arianna to understand. "That's how I can get by Turner without him noticing. Some of us can actually turn our power down to zero."

Arianna nodded. "You're saying it's better to be lower?"

"Sometimes," Gabriel replied. "Other times it's better to show your strength and scare off an opponent." Arianna jumped as Gabriel increased his power to full strength.

"You are as strong as Grandfather," she replied in awe.

"That old man doesn't feel it's necessary to lower his power." Gabriel stopped and returned to normal. Smiling, he replied, "And you are stronger. Try it once. Just let go of everything. Don't get distracted by the slight noises you constantly hear. Close your eyes," he directed. "Relax. Take a few deep breaths and forget you're sitting here."

Arianna followed her uncle's directions. Ignoring the sounds that seemed louder with her eyes shut, Arianna focused on listening to her own breath. Calming down, she felt a warm sensation growing inside her. Arianna waited as it grew larger and larger. *Is this really my power?* she wondered, as it continued to grow. *It's not stopping*, she worried, opening her eyes to find Turner and Gabriel intently watching her, while Molina, Nelson, and Mica stood in shock nearby.

"I see the problem," Gabriel replied. "You are already repressing your power greatly."

"What do you mean?" she asked.

"Well if Turner is a nine on the scale and your grandfather and I are a ten, you would be a twenty-five," Gabriel explained.

"What?" Arianna asked in shock.

"I'd put her more at a thirty," Turner added. "She didn't get up to full strength before she stopped." Arianna looked from Turner to Gabriel. He nodded in agreement.

"Well, the best we can hope, then, is for you to try to keep matched to Turner," Gabriel replied. "It would be nice if you could stay below Molina to keep people away from hunting you before you can defend yourself, but if you can match Turner it will help more than it does now when you fluctuate and get stronger than him. Night humans will sense your power and want to catch you, even if they do not know who you are."

"I'll try," Arianna replied, knowing that everyone in the room was concerned about her safety.

"Good," Gabriel responded as he stood and walked to her. "I need to get going for now. Tonight, I need you to come over to my house at around nine o'clock. There will be a formal dinner to meet the rest of our family and the leaders of the baku community."

"Is this a dinner like the one Grandfather threw for me, or Lord Winter?" Arianna asked.

Gabriel smiled. "I prefer the one your grandfather threw, if you are up to it." Arianna nodded. It wasn't like she was given a choice the first time around. "Since you deserve some sense of normalcy, Devin arranged for you to still have your foods class at the end of the day with Mary Ellen." Arianna nodded, and Gabriel vanished just as the bell rang to end class.

Turner and Devin escorted Arianna through the crowded hallways to her classroom. Passing person after person, Arianna was surprised when she noticed that every other person she passed was a night human. Arianna stopped when Turner and Devin didn't enter the room behind her.

"We need to go take care of something," Devin explained, grabbing Turner's arm. "Stay here with Jackson and Molina, and don't go outside until after two."

Arianna nodded as the bell rang again and people began hurrying down the hallways to their classes. Arianna casually moved to her cooking station where Mary Ellen was waiting, all while listening to Turner and Devin as they walked down the hallway. They stopped not too far away and turned into the math quad.

"Wait here," Devin told Turner as he entered a room.

"I need to borrow Susan," Devin said to the teacher, who seemed to easily agree. "Here," Devin added, as he returned to Turner. "They don't keep blood in school because it would make it a target, but there are several students here that offer to feed dearg-dul and lycan who are in need of blood. Turner, this is Susan. Susan, Turner," Devin introduced them.

Arianna was beginning to get angry. She took a lot of blood from Turner, but she didn't think it would lead to him feeding on another girl. Though they were not dating, she still was angry that he would be doing such a thing with another girl.

"Earth to Ari," Mary Ellen repeated. "Your nap must have been good. You're still in a daze."

"Sorry," Arianna replied. "What's on the menu today?" Arianna wanted to keep listening to Devin and Turner, but she found that baking was a good distraction.

"Lemon cake," Mary Ellen replied.

"Mmm," Arianna added, looking at the recipe. "Do we

need anything from the store room?" Arianna asked.

"We're low on sugar," Mary Ellen held out the jar to Arianna.

Arianna hurried to the small hallway between the two rooms. She easily found the sugar and her mind drifted to find Turner and Devin. Turner was in the neighboring room. Arianna peeked into the office to look through the glass windows. Turner was in the far corner with his head down on the desk sleeping. Looking around, she noticed Devin was not in the room. She found him sitting outside the room with Molina, both immersed in their own work.

Though she still was mad at Turner and Devin, Arianna relaxed a little; after all, she was home and at school with her friends. Baking the cake with Mary Ellen reminded her of how much she had missed everything back at home. Arianna joked with her friend as they finished cleaning their station. Even though so much had changed, it still felt completely normal to be with her best friend.

"Don't you want to give some to your friends?" Mary Ellen asked, as they cut the cake they had just made.

"Not really," Arianna replied. "I'm mad at them right now."

"Well, fine," Mary Ellen took several pieces. "I'm not, and they're cute." Mary Ellen hurried away before Arianna could stop her. When Mary Ellen returned, she was triumphant. "The cute blond said to stay here with spiky hair girl, and she will take you home."

Arianna checked the room next door. Turner was gone and so was Devin. *What are they doing now?* she wondered.

"Are you helping with the diner tonight?" Mary Ellen asked.

"I don't think so," Arianna replied, as they stepped into the crowded hallway, filled with students leaving for the day. "I think I have to go to a formal dinner at nine. You and Tish should come over now before they take me away. Who knows when they'll let me back again?"

"We do need to catch up, especially about the two cute boys that follow you around like puppy dogs," Mary Ellen replied, winking at her friend and giving a little play bark. Arianna blushed. There was really no easy way to explain Devin and Turner without telling her everything about her time at her grandfather's house.

"Arianna," a male voice yelled from behind as Arianna and Mary Ellen walked to their lockers. Both stopped in surprise to find Chris Sherwood pushing his way through the crowd of students while yelling Arianna's name. Arianna had never talked to the captain of the basketball team before.

Mary Ellen giggled at the shock in Arianna face.

"Are you guys coming to our game tonight?" he asked, finally making it close enough to them to talk in a normal voice without shouting.

"I don't know. I just got back from a trip. I don't know what my aunt and uncle will say," Arianna replied.

"Well, we would love to have you there," he said, as more team members joined him. "What about the guy with the red hair that was with you today? Does he play?" Chris looked around for Turner.

"He had to leave a little early," Arianna explained.

"Talk to your aunt and uncle," Chris added, turning to the person who was yelling his name down the hall. "We definitely would win if you were there." Chris grinned and weaved his way back through the students.

"Uh huh," Mary Ellen replied, watching him walk away with a dreamy expression on her face.

TWENTY-TWO

Arianna sat in silence as Molina drove the three girls back to her aunt and uncle's diner. She listened to her friends talk about boys, mainly, and being invited to the basketball game by the captain of the team. Everything seemed so normal; it was like the last week had never happened. As her friends ran upstairs, Arianna went to the kitchen to get snacks.

"Lou?" Arianna asked cautiously, smelling the distinct smell of night humans all over the kitchen.

"Little one," Arianna heard Lou's hearty voice deep within the kitchen. Arianna weaved between everyone set on their tasks, preparing for the evening rush. The middle-aged man with the long, dark ponytail and mustache was at his normal position in the middle of the chaos. "You couldn't survive without me, could ya' now?"

Arianna felt her hesitation melt away as a smile crept over her face. So much had changed, but everything in the kitchen was the same. Captain Lou reached down and gave Arianna a bear hug.

"I was contemplating moving, but I figured, what would Dean and Lilly do without me? Are they at least feeding you right at Lord Randolph's?" he asked.

Arianna nodded. *In more ways than one*, she wanted to say, but remained silent. It was still too awkward to discuss her new life with everyone that was so familiar with her old life. The kitchen staff must have all known who she was all along, but she just didn't want the old familiar feelings to change.

"Chili cheese fries then?" Lou asked. "Mary Ellen and Tish are with you, right?"

"Yep," Arianna replied, remembering her friends. She hadn't even found a way to tell them what was going on, and they were waiting upstairs to bombard her with questions.

"We'll have those ready in a minute." Lou smiled and patted Arianna's head as he had done since she was a small child. Only Lou could get away with still treating her like a kid. Arianna looked one more time around the kitchen. Her better senses could pick up the subtle differences in the people shifting from one work station to another. As much as she wanted everything to stay the same, it was now different.

"You better get up to the girls," Lou commented as Arianna paused.

"But," Arianna didn't know how to explain her dilemma to Lou.

"Everything is back to normal now, right?" Lou asked. He always read Arianna's expressions perfectly.

"If you don't count the people that now constantly follow me around. How do I explain them to my friends?"

"It's probably easier than you think. You like to overanalyze everything. Do you honestly think Mary Ellen and Tish will ever see you as anything other than their best friend?" Lou began to push Arianna towards the staircase.

"But," Arianna wanted to complain more.

"They know more than you think," Lou added, as they reached the door.

Arianna turned quickly, and only caught the back of Lou weaving between cooks and orchestrating the mess in the kitchen. Turning back to the staircase, Arianna stood face to face with Molina. Molina didn't speak, she just waited for Arianna to climb the stairs in front of her. Arianna didn't move but just stared back.

"What did he mean by that?" she asked. Molina had no choice but to answer.

"Your friends already know about all this," Molina replied, she tried to usher Arianna up the stairs.

"What?" Arianna tried not to shriek, but it came out quite close.

"They should explain, not me." Molina waited for Arianna to move and refused to add more.

Arianna began to slowly climb the stairs. Everyone made it sound so easy, but it wasn't. Arianna barely understood it herself, let alone explain it. Pausing near the top, Arianna turned back to Molina. "What about Turner and Devin? Why did they leave school early?"

"Turner was low on blood and refused to take it from a human. Devin took him to the nearest safe house."

Arianna tried not to let her smile show as she continued to climb the last two stairs. Turner didn't take the blood after all. She didn't have a right to be jealous. It wasn't like Turner was her boyfriend, but she was happy nonetheless.

Arianna opened the door to their apartment and found Aunt Lilly cleaning as usual. Aunt Lilly smiled and waved with her free hand, ushering Arianna inside. Arianna hesitated at the door. Everything would change again. No matter what Captain Lou said, things would change. Mary Ellen and Tish stood from the couch and dragged Arianna to her room.

"No way, I think she already has too many cute guys. She should let one of us have Chris," Mary Ellen complained to Tish.

"But he was asking her to come to the game, not us," Tish replied, flopping down onto Arianna's floor.

"Are we going to the game tonight?" Mary Ellen asked Arianna, standing in the doorway to her room.

"I have to ask," Arianna remembered. Turning around, Arianna waved to her aunt to turn off the vacuum. "Can I go to a basketball game tonight?"

"That's up to Gabriel. Your plans are with him tonight." Aunt Lilly returned to her vacuuming. Arianna could feel in the air the distaste her aunt had for Gabriel.

"I'll be right back, guys. I have to go ask my uncle," Arianna explained to her friends. "Food should be done. If you eat everything before I return, you guys have to go place a new order."

"But," Tish added, "Lou doesn't like us." Mary Ellen nodded. Arianna smiled and shrugged. Lou was always strict with both Tish and Mary Ellen because it was funny to watch when they were scared. Lou actually was very fond of Arianna's two best friends.

Arianna hurried, with Molina close behind, to the old yellow house two doors down from the diner. Molina paused in the yard as Arianna rang the doorbell. Everything about the house made it seem like a family home. In fact, there was even the sound of children playing outside in the backyard. Molina couldn't pick up a bit of the scent of baku in the house. Arianna opened the door without waiting for someone to answer. Molina stayed in the yard as Arianna entered.

Arianna walked down the hallway to the kitchen, following the scent of Gabriel. Arianna hesitated as she walked into the brightly-lit room. The largest baku she had ever seen was sitting at the table, while a small, bald man was studying his large muscular arm. Her head filled with fearful thoughts of the first night she met a baku. Arianna and Devin were surrounded by men who were all the same as the man in the chair.

"Sure, but you have to leave at nine whether the game is done or not," the baku said. Arianna didn't move from the doorway. He was physically completely different, but Gabriel's voice was exactly the same. The large pale man smiled. His razor sharp teeth glimmered. "I heard you talking with Lilly. My hearing is almost as good as yours when I'm in this form."

"Oh." Arianna stayed in the doorway. It wasn't fear that held her there as she knew it was her uncle, not only by his voice, but his scent. Rather, it was some built-in sense that told her that he was dangerous to get near.

"And that's why baku and dearg-duls don't get along," Gabriel explained, responding to her feelings. "There's no reason to fear me. Don't worry, that feeling will be gone after tonight." Arianna nodded before turning to leave.

Before she made it out the door she paused. "Will I look like you when I turn?" she asked, not turning around to watch his expression. She was trying not to insult him, but she didn't want to turn into a large muscular man either.

The needle broke with Gabriel's movement, and Gabriel laughed as the bald man swore under his breath again.

"You broke another one," the man complained.

"If that's your only fear about tonight, we should be fine. You won't turn into a gigantic albino man," Gabriel reassured her. "Going through the change won't make you any less you than you already are. Nothing can change who you are."

Arianna ran back out the door past Molina, who had been listening to the conversation while she waited. Arianna made it up halfway the stairs before pausing and returning to the kitchen of the diner. With her increased senses, she easily avoided the organized mass of workers to grab food for her friends who were waiting upstairs.

As per normal, Mary Ellen and Tish were already seated on her bed, gossiping as she returned. Arianna sat down on the floor, and they all used her bed as a makeshift table. Arianna looked at her friends again. Neither one was a night human.

"So, spill it," Mary Ellen started to grill Arianna.

"How do you get two gorgeous boys to follow you

around, begging for your attention?" Tish asked. "I need to know your secret."

"I didn't do anything," Arianna replied as Tish and Mary Ellen both shook their heads, mocking her.

"Come on," Tish nudged Arianna.

"Really," Arianna replied. "They just started to follow me around on their own."

"So which one is your boyfriend?" Mary Ellen asked, wanting to know more juicy details.

"Neither," Arianna replied. Again her friends didn't believe her. "Really. Devin works for my grandfather and Turner is my keeper."

"Then they're not your boyfriends?" Tish asked, disappointed they weren't going to get details.

"Your keeper?" Mary Ellen repeated and Tish stopped and stared also. "But don't you guys normally wait years for that?" Arianna stared dumbstruck at her two best friends.

"But? How?" Arianna sputtered.

"We're your best friends," Tish added. "Of course we know what you are."

"Sometimes I wish I could be one also," added Mary Ellen, turning the bowls of fries so they could grab more.

"But?" Arianna repeated.

"My dad is a dearg-dul," Mary Ellen added, noticing her friend's confusion. "Remember all those trips? He was going to the Randolph estate for annual meetings." Mary Ellen picked up a fry and popped it in her mouth like she was having any normal conversation with Arianna.

"And my family has several baku and tengu in it," Tish added. "Though the gene was lost somewhere in my parent's generation." Tish grabbed a fry also.

"Why didn't you ever tell me?" Arianna asked, taking the fries from her friends and holding them hostage. "This past week has been so confusing. No one told me any of this before, and then it was just plopped on me."

"Your aunt asked us not to," Mary Ellen explained like it was a logical answer.

"She told me I couldn't be your friend if I told you," Tish replied with a better answer.

"Then everyone was in on the secret but me?" Arianna asked. Mary Ellen looked to Tish and nodded.

"But we didn't know you were a purebred," Mary Ellen quickly explained. "We just thought you were another dearg-dul who needed to be protected since your parents were gone."

"I'm not just a dearg-dul," Arianna added glumly, grabbing another fry. Her friends hadn't lied to her on purpose, but on orders from Aunt Lilly.

"Of course not. You are the blue-eyed dearg-dul," Tish added to what she had heard through the gossip.

"Yeah, but after tonight I'll also be a baku," Arianna explained. "That's why my aunt probably had to let you be my friend, Tish, even though she hates baku and tengu."

"I always wondered why they would let me be a friend with you once everyone knew you were a dearg-dul," Tish replied. Tish actually didn't take sides like most people and didn't care what Arianna was going to be once she changed.

"That makes no sense. How can you be both?" Mary Ellen asked. "It is so unfair. I just want to be one and you get to be both." Arianna laughed, not being able to reply to her friend and her absurd suggestion.

"It isn't as fun as it seems," Arianna replied. Tish nodded in empathy.

"My cousin complains all the time. He said that it's the blood that drives him nuts," Tish reached over and grabbed another fry. Arianna's mind drifted at the mention of blood. Turner and Devin were coming back now.

"Do you know about everyone in school then?" Arianna asked. How much did her friends know since they were just day humans?

"I don't know who is, specifically," Mary Ellen explained. "But in general, the jocks are mostly lycan and the musically inclined students are baku."

"Dearg-duls are mostly the smart students in student council and tengu are the artist students," Tish added. "You won't leave us for the student council, will you? Now that you can fit in with the other ones?"

"I'm not musically inclined or smart, so I guess I don't fit in with either," Arianna assessed.

"What's it like having a keeper?" Mary Ellen asked, changing the subject after hearing the two boys return.

"Do you get alone time whenever you want?" Tish added. Arianna's cheeks flushed.

"He's not my keeper yet," Arianna explained. "I just agreed last weekend to take him as a keeper someday." Arianna tried to emphasize the word 'someday.'

"What about the blond one?" Tish asked. "Blonds are more my type."

"He's just part of my PPU," Arianna replied, remembering the conversation with Devin over the weekend. Outside the bedroom, he would only be her protector.

"You've kissed them, haven't you?" Mary Ellen was too perceptive. Arianna couldn't reply.

"Which one?" Tish asked, wanting the details now that they were getting somewhere.

Arianna closed her eyes to answer, "Both."

"Both?" Mary Ellen and Tish asked in unison before they all burst into laughter.

Maybe some things won't change, Arianna thought, watching her friends.

"Which one do you like?" Mary Ellen asked when she finally caught her breath.

Arianna shook her head *no*, she wasn't going to talk. Arianna began to blush as her friends jumped on her to tickle the truth out of her. Arianna squirmed and laughed more as they continued to tickle her and asked questions which she refused to answer. After all three girls were exhausted, they just lay on the floor and continued to giggle.

"Girls," Aunt Lilly said as she knocked on the door. "The game starts in fifteen minutes, if you're going."

TWENTY-THREE

Arianna stood between her two best friends as they cheered the basketball team on. Devin had protested her choice of seat within the crowd of people, but she ignored him and decided to have a good time with her friends. Arianna wanted to be normal. Around her, the crowd was mainly lycan like Tish and Mary Ellen had explained. Down in the far corner was the baku, Andrew, from the morning choir room. He wasn't watching the game at all, but just her. Arianna felt uncomfortable, but he wasn't the only one watching her. Turner stood right behind her, cheering for the team and keeping her distracted from all the glances her way.

"It's 'cause I'm so good-looking," he explained, and Mary Ellen agreed.

"Just keep ignoring them," Tish replied. "Or see it as a sign of worship. You're a goddess to them," Tish teased. Arianna tugged on her friend's ponytail.

"I can ignore most of them, but I find Andrew's stares hard to ignore." Arianna looked across the gym and found him smiling more after her comment.

"How about this," Turner slid his arms around her waist, and Arianna blushed at the public display of affection. Andrew's smile faded as he glared at Turner.

"Not your boyfriend?" Mary Ellen teased Arianna.

Arianna wanted to push his arms away, but with all the stares and curiosity around her, Turner's arms were like a shield. Until the timer buzzed to end the game, Arianna stood with Turner's arm around her. Cheers erupted around them as their school won by only three points. Turner raised an arm to cheer with the students around them but made sure to keep one around her. Arianna was actually relieved to not be left alone in the gym full of night humans.

"Let's go congratulate Chris," Tish suggested. "Since he invited you to the game and all."

"She could at least leave one cute one for us," Mary Ellen complained. Arianna punched her friend playfully on the arm.

Tish grabbed one hand, and Mary Ellen the other, as they dragged Arianna across the court, which was now filled with people congratulating the team. Turner followed close behind. Arianna was so glad to use the excuse that she had hurried across the gym to explain her red cheeks to the captain of the basketball team, who was standing in his group of friends.

"Hey girls," Chris said, walking over to them.

"Great job," Mary Ellen added, smiling sweetly at the large guy towering over the three girls.

"Hey, we couldn't disappoint when we had such cute fans," Chris responded.

"Who are you calling cute?" Turner asked, hitting Chris up for a high-five.

"The youngest Winter son," Chris added, smiling at Turner. "Are you hanging around? We could always use another guard."

"I think we head back in a couple days. Sorry man," Turner added. "Not technically enrolled here."

"Too bad. I heard you're pretty good," Chris replied and Turner shrugged. "So, is it true?" Turner smiled in response to the vague question. "Man, you royalty always get the good ones." Arianna turned a brighter shade of red, knowing they were talking about her. "This is sort of embarrassing, but would you mind coming to meet my parents?" Chris asked, turning to Arianna. "They're seated up towards the top in the parent's section." Arianna looked around the room. Devin was in the corner near the door.

"It's part of who you are now," he said quietly, urging her forward.

Turner smiled and grabbed her arm. "Of course," Turner replied, also hearing Devin.

Arianna climbed the stairs slower than her four longer-legged friends. While Mary Ellen and Tish chose to trail behind with Arianna, the two boys climbed ahead, continuing their conversation about the game. At the top of the stairs sat a couple that looked like they were ready for a fancy dinner, not a basketball game. Arianna couldn't fail to see the resemblance between Chris and his father.

"Hey Dad," Chris hugged the man who was smiling proudly at his son.

"Great game," he added. "And the winning shot, even. You played so well tonight."

"How could we not play well when we have the Randolph heir watching?" Chris added. Arianna was unsure if she liked the sound of that, the Randolph heir. "Mom, Dad, this is Arianna." The two parents stared in both shock and awe at Arianna.

"And I'm Turner Winter," Turner added. "Sherwood? From the east coast?"

Mr. Sherwood was pulled away from staring at Arianna to finally respond and shake Turner's hand. "Yes, yes," the gray-haired man replied.

"I think I have a cousin living over that direction that talked about Sherwoods," Turner explained. "A winery, if I remember right." Turner turned on the charm, and fit right into the world she was now part of, where everyone knew everyone but she knew no one. Mary Ellen and Tish talked to Chris as Arianna drifted over, watching the people still milling around the school basketball court. The people were mainly human or lycan. Every now and then was a deargdul, and in the corner Andrew still sat with his constant baku companions. His blue eyes twinkled under his dark curls. An older man arrived through the exit door, and multiple heads turned to the slick-haired baku that entered with his personal guards. Andrew stood immediately, and followed the man as he left. At the door, Andrew paused and didn't turn around as he said one word.

"Tonight."

Arianna shivered at the message meant for her.

"Sorry we can't join you," Turner said, grabbing Arianna's hand and pulling her close. "We have a previous engagement to attend."

"Would you mind...?" Mrs. Sherwood barely whispered her request.

Arianna looked to Turner to try to understand what they were talking about, as she had been distracted by Andrew. Turner smiled before checking with Devin, who nodded his assent.

"She'd like to see your eyes," Turner explained. Arianna blushed more. The center of attention was getting more and more embarrassing. Her friends had stopped talking with Chris, and were now also staring at her.

"It's so embarrassing," Arianna complained, though in reality, she just didn't want to scare her friends. Everything would really change if they saw her as a blue-eyed monster. The more perceptive Mary Ellen understood and grabbed Tish's arm.

"Let's go get our coats," Mary Ellen suggested. Tish suddenly understood and agreed. Once they were back down the bleachers, Arianna turned to the Sherwoods. Her blue eyes gleamed in the well-lit gym. Mrs. Sherwood grabbed her husband's arm in shock. Around her, Arianna heard the talking stop as every night human in the room turned to her.

"We need to leave," Devin said quietly from his position on the floor, as Molina's boots clicked from her pacing behind the door.

Arianna released her dearg-dul form and turned around to find everyone in the room staring at her. Awe and wonder filled the night humans as they bowed their heads towards her when she passed through them. Turner kept a tight grip around her as they made their way through the people milling around that were now frozen, watching her. Devin met her halfway, and created a protective bubble around her with Turner. Turner and Devin ushered Arianna outside to a waiting car. Tish and Mary Ellen said their goodbyes as they left also. Arianna climbed into the car and sat next to her uncle.

"This is it?" Arianna asked as the car began to move. "I get to join yet another secret society?" she joked to hide her nervousness.

"There's no rush," Gabriel replied. "We don't have to do that tonight."

Arianna sighed. It made no difference now. She was already different. The people that walked down the streets were now different from her. Humans were different. Arianna watched each passing face: a girl smiling at a boy, a child holding their parents' hands, an old man crossing the street. They had one thing in common: humanity. The stares in the gym told her that. As much as she wanted to return to her normal life, she couldn't. She was no longer human.

TWENTY-FOUR

Arianna walked into the dimly-lit yard behind her uncle. The backyard of her uncle's house had a large tent and tables put up. She wasn't surprised to find more than a couple of hundred people milling around the backyard. Curious eyes looked up to her briefly, but most people continued chatting away with the person they were talking to. Towards the middle of the crowd, Andrew sat with the greasy-haired man from the gym. He was dressed in a formal tux, like the rest of the guests, but unlike all the curious glances, he continued to stare. Arianna shrank behind her uncle, and tried to hide behind his large frame. Molina walked around the perimeter, obviously irritated to be around so many of her enemies. Devin and Turner stood in the shadows, each watching the situation calmly.

Gabriel ushered Arianna to the front of the tent, past all the guests. Now standing in front of another large crowd, Arianna wanted to hide, but Gabriel wouldn't let her.

"You don't have to do this today," Gabriel explained again, noticing her hesitation.

"It's the crowd," Arianna replied. She could feel the hateful glares from the people that now realized she was a dearg-dul. Gabriel also noticed the stares.

"After tonight it should get better," Gabriel explained, and Arianna nodded. Arianna focused on the one person not staring hatefully, Andrew. His face was stoic, like the rest of the people around him, but he didn't have any hate towards her. Instead, he radiated the complete enjoyment of being near her, as he had in the choir room. Arianna looked across the crowd to him, and he smiled slightly.

"Then let's do it," Arianna replied, hiding her shaking hands. "What do we have to do?"

"We need to do a blood test on you while you are awake and sleeping, in front of witnesses. Then, you will drink baku blood to cause the transformation," Gabriel explained, his back still turned to the hostile crowd. Arianna nodded and wrapped her hands in her skirt to keep them from shaking.

"Does it hurt?" Arianna asked, remembering the pain of transforming into a dearg-dul the first time.

Gabriel shrugged. "We use the blood of the high baku to transform people. Our ancestors say that if you use the strongest blood it won't hurt. With your level though, no matter what we do, it might hurt some for you." Arianna nodded at her uncle's honest reply. "Are you ready?"

"Let's get this over with," Arianna replied.

Gabriel turned and faced the guests. "Greetings everyone, and welcome to my home tonight. I hope you are all enjoying yourselves." Gabriel's gaze challenged anyone to object to his choice of guests. Molina took the brunt of the glares as she passed behind Arianna on her walk around the perimeter. Keeping her cool, Molina didn't glare back. "I've asked you all here today to witness my niece as she joins us." The room broke into whispers. Arianna listened from one group to the next.

"Baku are male."

"Is she really his niece?"

"But she's a dearg-dul."

"Has the old man finally gone mad?" Arianna turned toward the sour voice beside Andrew. The greasy-haired man finally spoke. Andrew stared up at her.

"No. She's baku, Uncle. I saw her asleep today," Andrew

replied. "And a very powerful one. More powerful than anyone before."

"But only one baku had that power. Travis's daughter," the man replied. "I thought she was dead."

Gabriel turned his head to the man who made the comment. He contained the anger that was beginning to flow out of him. The crowd quieted, assuming the anger was for their noise. Only Gabriel was listening to the greasy man.

"Sixteen years ago, my nephew had a child. His wife was murdered the next day, and he went into hiding to protect his child. Travis was the strongest baku to come along in a century, but even more, his child was stronger than anything anyone had ever seen or heard of. Later, he was murdered also, so her grandfather and I decided to hide her," Gabriel explained, and the murmur began again. Arianna turned to Andrew and his uncle, but the man didn't say a word. "A week ago, she turned sixteen. We could no longer hide her, because she changed into her mother's linage, dearg-dul. Today we will complete the change for her father's linage, baku."

"That's impossible," someone in the front row commented.

"Improbable," Gabriel corrected. "Not impossible."

"But she can't be both," someone else complained.

"This is why I have called so many witnesses," Gabriel replied. "For she is both. Let's begin." Patrick walked to the front of the room with a bowl of water.

"We need a drop of blood," Gabriel explained. Arianna nodded and easily pierced the skin on her finger with her own sharp dearg-dul teeth before placing her hand in his. Gabriel dropped a bit of blood into the bowl and swirled it around. A faint blue shimmer occurred as it diluted into the water. "Dearg-dul." Gabriel confirmed. "Next we need to put you to sleep and take another drop. Sit in that chair,"

Gabriel pointed to a chair. A slight mist began to be blown onto it. Arianna walked over and sat down. She scanned over the crowd as she waited. She felt sleepiness coming over her, but every slight sound kept her eyes awake. The crowd watched and waited. Arianna waited in turn.

Turner walked to the front of the room. "She won't fall asleep that way," he explained, as several people in the room hissed at him for talking. Gabriel nodded. "You just need her asleep, right?" Gabriel nodded again. Turner stretched out his hand to Arianna, who ignored the sleepy sensation and stood to take it. Outside the mist, her senses completely returned, and she was no longer sleepy.

"I kind of have a problem sleeping," she explained to her uncle. Turner pulled the chair out from beneath the mist and sat down, still holding her hand. Arianna sat down on his lap and carefully unbuttoned the top buttons of his shirt. His skin was warm as she laid her face against his chest. It was warm and safe in his arms. Arianna unconsciously smiled as she pressed her face deeper into his chest. In a room full of hateful and curious stares, there was nothing but love radiating from Turner. In what seemed like an instant to her, the beating of Turner's heart had lulled Arianna to sleep.

Turner stared at the crowd, challenging anyone to speak further, but everyone just watched in shock as the realization spread from row to row. As she slept, everyone felt the strong sense of baku coming from the sleeping dearg-dul. Gabriel walked over and held the bowl in front of Turner. He gently picked up her other hand and pierced her fingertip. One drop of blood fell into the bowl. A flash of light instantly lit up the whole tent. No one in the room could contain their amazement. The crowd began to feverishly talk to each other. Everyone in the room was happy, with the exception of one person, Andrew's uncle. As Gabriel waited for the crowd to quiet, Turner could feel the hateful stares return to him as he held their precious baku. Gabriel moved in front of Turner to block the glares.

"Arianna is a purebred dearg-dul. She has full dearg-dul powers and is learning how to use them. Circling the tent is her PPU. She won't be assigned baku guards as her grandfather and I handpicked her PPU together. She has taken on one keeper, Brenton Winter. They are not to be touched in any way or form." Disagreement vented through the crowd. "Anyone who lays a hand on any of the humans, dearg-duls or lycan associated with Arianna will have to deal with me." There was no more dissent through the crowd. "Now I ask that the three purebred baku here be the witness for this. You can wake her," Gabriel added to Turner.

Turner lifted Arianna's head and gently stroked her face. Arianna groggily blinked her eyes.

"Time to get up, sleepy," Turner said softly, before leaning in and kissing Arianna's forehead in front of the crowd.

Arianna was instantly awake to the hateful glares of the people around her at Turner. She blushed as he pulled back and smiled victoriously. He lightly set her on her feet. Arianna felt her cheeks still burning.

"Stupid wolf," Devin muttered, also grinning. Arianna finally noticed the glares were meant for Turner and not her. "Join them," Devin urged Arianna who was looking around the room for Gabriel.

Three men were standing in the front of the crowd next to Gabriel. Andrew, his uncle, and an unknown man were standing side by side, all talking to Gabriel. Arianna walked up next to her uncle at Devin's suggestion.

"Sign here and here," Gabriel held out forms. "This way," he added, after all three had signed.

Gabriel led the way back into the house. "Pick a room to wait in," Gabriel directed the three men. "We'll be here, in the kitchen." The men all nodded and left. Arianna stood, watching her uncle as he opened the refrigerator. Pulling out three vials from the bottom shelf, Arianna was surprised to see the fridge was full of food, not blood. Gabriel laughed. "Baku require less blood than dearg-duls," he explained, "since we can only transform at night." Arianna nodded.

"So, what comes next?" she asked. Turner and Devin sat at the kitchen table as Molina continued to pace.

"One of these should do," Gabriel explained, putting the vials on the cupboard in front of Arianna. Arianna wrinkled her nose at the blood. "Baku blood."

"Your blood?" Arianna asked.

"Not my day human blood, as you have tasted before. My baku blood."

Arianna looked at the three vials. Each radiated the same sour smell of power that her grandfather's blood did. Arianna stopped at looked at the second vial. It looked identical to the other two, but it was somehow different. Arianna uncapped it and took a sniff. It *was* different. Gabriel took her hand, and with quick, painless jabs, immediately made blood to blood contact.

'What's wrong?' he thought.

'This just seems strange,' Arianna replied. *'I don't think it's your blood.'*

Gabriel picked up the vial and took a sniff of it also. He couldn't tell the difference.

'I don't know why, but it just doesn't seem like it's yours,' Arianna explained.

'Do you know whose it is?'

Arianna closed her eyes and tried to watch the people outside the house. Gabriel smiled, fascinated with watching how she saw the world as it flickered by. The scent wasn't outside. Arianna moved her search into the house. The white flickering of Devin's heartbeat made her pause. She slowly looked to Turner and sensed it again.

'*It's like them. The blood is from someone that loves me the way those two do,*' Arianna explained. Gabriel smelled the vial again. Now he could slightly sense what Arianna had felt immediately. '*And he's in the house.*'

Arianna used her incredible senses to find Andrew in the front room. He was sitting on the couch, in his baku form, intently listening to the kitchen. A smile crossed his face as Arianna found him.

'*It's Andrew's baku blood,*' Arianna paused. '*You know how we were rating everyone before?*'

'*Yes.*'

'*You and grandpa were at an eleven or twelve. Andrew is at a sixteen.*'

Arianna now watched as Gabriel searched the house and found Andrew's uncle upstairs. The irate man was pacing around an upstairs bedroom. '*The old man has no clue. What a cunning boy,*' Gabriel commented.

'*Please explain,*' Arianna begged, not understanding.

'*It seems Andrew hid his own baku blood in mine for you,*' Gabriel replied. '*The higher the power of the blood you drink, the less painful the change is. That's why all baku changes are done with my blood. I'm currently the strongest baku. At least that's what I thought. Because I'm still in charge, I can assume that even his uncle doesn't know his true strength. The strongest baku is always the leader.*'

'*Why would he hide that then, if he could be the leader?*'

'*I don't know. You'll have to ask him that yourself. I can only speculate that there are secrets in that family that we don't know.*' Arianna nodded, as she finally noticed Devin and Turner tensely watching their silent conversation.

"Drink one vial now, and then, after you change, drink the other two vials. It should be enough to last you through the evaluation by the present purebreds," Gabriel explained, and the tension eased in the room.

"Which one should I drink?" Arianna asked, knowing

that Andrew was intently listening to the conversation.

"Are you sure about what you told me?" Gabriel asked. Arianna nodded. "I don't smell any poisons, so it should be safe."

"I can go ask him," Devin replied, understanding the situation. Turner stared from Devin to Gabriel.

"That's not needed," Arianna replied, taking the vial with Andrew's blood and drinking it. Arianna fell to her knees and the pain rushed over her, forcing her eyes shut.

TWENTY-FIVE

Arianna slowly opened her eyes to find herself in Devin's arms. An overwhelming sense of concern came over her as she watched his face. Arianna turned slightly and looked up at her uncle, who, unlike Devin and Turner, actually appeared to be happy. Arianna sat up slowly and took Turner's outstretched hand. In a fluid movement she was standing eye-to-eye with Turner, her arms wrapped around his neck. The sensation she felt as their hands touched made her not want to let go. As she grazed over the skin at the back of his neck, she paused. The warmth that was radiating from him caught her attention. Arianna paused and smiled. She felt nothing but an overwhelming warm sensation of love from Turner. He smiled back and put his hands at her waist. Arianna shivered. Everything seemed to be amplified a hundred times from what she felt in her human form. Arianna was completely blind to the world around her as she gazed at Turner. His emotions read loud and clear. It felt like direct energy to her, more powerful than any blood she had drank.

"I'd love to let you explore the changes you experience when you are a baku, but I need to get you evaluated before the blood is used up," Gabriel explained. Arianna pulled back, momentarily embarrassed by her blunt actions, which had been almost instinctual.

"I think I might like the baku Arianna," Turner replied, as Gabriel ushered Arianna upstairs. Arianna paused on the stairs to look back at Turner and Devin. While normally Devin was too reserved for Arianna to sense, she could now tell that he felt the same way as Turner. Devin stared back at Arianna. His face was as stoic as usual, and focused on his task, but his heart was not. Gabriel stepped in between Arianna and the two boys.

"Drink these," Gabriel handed Arianna the two vials. Arianna tried to look past her uncle, but he forced the blood in front of her face. Arianna took the vials and obediently drank the sour red liquid. "That should last you until later." Gabriel pushed Arianna down the hallway, toward a closed door. Arianna cautiously opened the door. Even from the doorway, Arianna could see perfectly into the unlit room.

"Since I sponsored you, I cannot enter the room with you, or the test will be forfeit," Gabriel explained. Arianna hesitated at the doorway. A rather large baku was sitting in a chair, reading a paper in the dark. His long, scraggly white hair hung free to his waist. He paused as the door opened, and Gabriel pushed Arianna forward.

"We're right behind you," Devin said quietly.

"We won't let you out of our sight," Turner added.

The baku offered Arianna his hand as she walked slowly into the room. She had only had a glimpse of the baku on the night she changed into a dearg-dul. The refined man sitting in the chair reading was a stark contrast to the growling monsters she had seen. He folded his glasses and set them down on top of the paper.

"Even in this form my eyes are bad," the man explained. "Welcome, prized baku Arianna." The man motioned to the seat beside his. "I am Rafael. I am the current head of the Haggerty family. My job tonight is to assess your strength. We all know from the tests conducted earlier that you are a purebred baku, but we need to figure out what your rank will be within the community."

"How can you do that? I still don't even have my dearg-dul strength under control. I doubt I'm any good at this baku stuff," Arianna replied, catching her reflection in the mirror across the room as she walked over and sat next to the inviting man. She hadn't noticed that she was now standing almost eye to eye with Turner, who was slightly shorter than Devin. Her normally shoulder-length blond hair fell down to her butt, and was now a slightly blond-tinted white color. Her complexion was snow white, which made her lips and blue eyes stand out even more than normal. Arianna stopped and stared at her blue eyes, and then glanced back to the man waiting for her.

He studied her with his purple tinted eyes. "Correct. We baku do not keep our eye color when we change. Those are peculiar blue eyes." He drifted off into silent thought. "Everything about you says you are a purebred baku, except for those eyes."

"They seem to get me in trouble everywhere I go," Arianna replied.

Rafael held open his hand. "Would you permit me to look inside your mind?" Arianna sliced her thumb against her palm and reached over for his hand. "What do you see in this room?" he asked aloud.

Arianna looked around the room. Everything was clear: the furniture, the books, the slight light coming from the party below in the corner of the window. And then she stopped looking. Turner was standing against the doorway, eagerly watching her. Arianna held herself still as she wanted to run back over to him. Gabriel reached forward, and pulled Turner from her view.

Rafael chuckled. "Teenagers," he nodded his thanks to Gabriel. "And what about below, in the party."

Arianna closed her eyes and drifted down to the sounds of the party. People were talking joyously to their neighbors. Each conversation seemed like it was taking place in the same room as Arianna. Sounds slowly became distinct voices. She could make out the shapes and sizes of each person by following their blood flow.

"Good, good," Rafael replied. Reluctantly, he let go of her hand, knowing that his decision was already made up the moment he saw her sleeping.

"That's it?" Arianna replied.

"Each of us test in our own way. I can tell from that where you should be ranked," Rafael replied. Arianna stood to leave. As she neared the door, Rafael added, "Your father would be proud."

Arianna wanted to stay and ask him what he meant, but Gabriel already was ushering her to the next room. Standing at the window, Andrew's uncle didn't even turn to her as she entered. Arianna could easily feel the contempt coming from the man, and he didn't try to hide it. She moved further into the room and stood in the middle, alone.

"Arianna Grace, only child of Travis Grace, purebred baku," he replied, still not looking at her. "From such a prestigious family. Eighty-two baku in written history, five ahead of my own family." Arianna continued to stand still, trying not to provoke the man further as he vented. "And now they have the prize: a female baku." Arianna felt him struggle to contain his temper.

"Close your eyes," the man ordered. Arianna did as he asked. She listened as he slowly drew near and walked around her. More contempt radiated from him. The man paused behind her momentarily.

"I wouldn't do that if I were you," Devin replied. Arianna turned around to find Devin, Turner, and Molina all holding swords at the man's throat.

"Isn't it taboo for one baku to bite another?" Turner asked.

"No one bites her," Molina replied. "Without killing me first." Arianna shivered at the complete evilness and hatred that filled the room. All three of her guards radiated enough hate to match the man behind her.

The man smiled. "Then I guess I cannot vote on this matter." Arianna turned to her uncle, who was gripping the doorway to keep himself from rushing in. Arianna hurried over to him in an attempt to calm his rage. She wrapped her arms around his waist.

"I'm safe," Arianna said quietly, and she felt as the rage completely disappeared. "They wouldn't let it be otherwise." Arianna walked out of the room, leading her uncle away. "Andrew is downstairs, right?" Gabriel nodded, still unable to completely contain his anger. At the bottom of the steps, Arianna stopped.

"He wants me to come in alone," she explained to the four people following her.

"No way," Turner was firm.

"He's right," Devin said, smacking Turner for being so blunt. "It's not safe to leave you alone."

"Uncle, do you feel anything bad from that room," Arianna asked. She could feel something herself, but didn't want to tell Turner or Devin that the only thing she sensed from the baku waiting in the room was love.

Gabriel sighed. "I'll monitor the room. If there's even a hint of malice, we will be there in a moment. I'll not be standing back again." Molina nodded. Turner and Devin had no choice but to let her go in, alone.

TWENTY-SIX

Arianna closed the door behind her before turning around to view Andrew. He was leaning, shirtless, by the window across the room, staring at the sky. His pale, chiseled body glowed in the slight light coming through the panes. While she had originally thought all the baku looked the same, she could now make out the slight difference. Andrew's long white hair had a slight curl that reminded her of his day human form. Arianna felt her heart race a little as she looked over at him with her perfect night vision.

"Did you know that there are over three hundred billion stars, just in our galaxy?" Arianna asked in a whisper. Andrew turned his gaze to her. Arianna stood still, her skin tingling. Instantly, he was standing only inches in front of her. Arianna jumped slightly, startled. In another instant, Arianna was across the room with Andrew, who was holding onto her next to the window.

"Every last one of them is waiting to see you, to know if it could possibly be true," Andrew added quietly, looking at the people still milling around the patio.

Arianna turned her head sideways and continued to stare only at Andrew.

"You've known about me for a long time."

'Forever,' Andrew thought.

"How can...?" Arianna began ask, but stopped as a multitude of questions filled her mind. There was so much she wanted to know from him, yet at the same time, nothing needed to be said.

'I've waited a long time to find you again,' Andrew explained.

"Again?"

'We were kids the first time we met. I didn't know what baku were at the time, but I knew you were special.' Andrew's hands gently pulled Arianna closer. While she stood almost eye to eye with Turner in her baku form, she was now a head shorter than Andrew. Arianna instinctively leaned her face against his chest. Her lips gently grazed the smooth, white skin in front of her, and he shivered in response. Andrew stopped his story when he felt her touch.

Does he feel it too? Arianna wondered.

'Yes,' Andrew replied. Andrew's hands gently traced her back. Leaning slightly forward, he kissed the top of her head.

Complete happiness poured off of Andrew as she tipped her head back to look closer at his face. There was no need to see his expression to read the emotions he was emitting, but Arianna looked anyway. Andrew's eyes were closed, and he took a deep breath. She could sense that his fluctuating power was coming back under control.

'Why are you holding yourself back?' Arianna finally asked, understanding that they were communicating only with their minds and no blood contact.

'It's just a little harder with you so close,' Andrew replied. *'No one knows what my true power is, not even my uncle, and he's raising me. If I let go, for even an instant, Uncle will make a claim to be the top family. With his greed, he doesn't deserve such a high spot. I respect Gabriel, and I know he is a better fit to run the baku clan.'* The slight contempt beneath Andrew's feelings surfaced. Arianna reached up and touched his face. It was as smooth as she imagined. Love returned to Andrew's face as he smiled down at her.

'*Sorry,*' Arianna apologized, finally realizing how close they were standing. She tried to back away, but he wouldn't let go. Andrew pulled her closer to kiss her. Arianna wanted to protest, but the same feelings of love she felt earlier won out. Arianna wrapped her arms around him as he lifted her off the ground, into his arms. Arianna traced the hard muscles of his chest as he pulled her on the couch on top of him. She couldn't stop her hands as they wandered over his body. The touch of his skin made her heart flutter, but at the same time, made her want to continue. Andrew smiled at the response and kissed her again. She didn't protest this time. He easily won his battle.

A cough behind the closed door brought Arianna back to reality. Quickly, she slid off Andrew and sat down on the ground, feeling a slight blush return to her cheeks. She tried to bring her focus beyond the door to her uncle and waiting protectors, but the slight beating of the heart behind her kept pulling her attention. Andrew laughed aloud.

"We need to get downstairs to finish this," Gabriel added from behind the door. Arianna stood and continued to blush as she hurried over to the door. Andrew was right behind her, now fully dressed, and back to his human form. Arianna hesitated to open the door, feeling like she just cheated on the two men on the other side. Two men that had been protecting her since the moment she joined this new bizarre world in which she was now living. Andrew stepped in front of her and opened the door. Arianna waited to feel the jealously hit her, but nothing came. Turner and Devin still were radiating the same loving feelings as before she had entered the room. Arianna turned to Turner and tried to question him, but he just smiled.

"You're never going to be mine alone," he replied a little reluctantly. Arianna grabbed his hand and felt the loving warmth emitted from it.

Gabriel led the group back down to the family room,

where the other two purebred baku were waiting.

"What is your vote?" Gabriel asked Rafael.

"I'd say her power is double that of yours," Rafael replied. "She will need excessive lessons on how to control it, but with even a little skill, she will surpass anyone that we've ever seen or even read about."

"And yours?" Gabriel turned to Andrew's uncle, who was now back to his greasy-haired human form also.

"I cannot render a decision. I wasn't allowed to complete my assessment," he replied, smiling wickedly at the three people standing behind Arianna.

"It's taboo to drink another baku's blood," Turner replied.

"Not if they are offering it," the man shot back.

"I don't recall Arianna offering it," Devin moved in front of Arianna slightly, challenging him. He smiled, ready for a fight. Gabriel placed his hand on Devin's shoulder and ignored Andrew's uncle.

"And your vote?" Gabriel turned to Andrew.

"I agree completely with Rafael," Andrew replied. His uncle looked on in horror at the young man, as if he were committing a sin.

"Then the vote is two to one. Arianna will be given the number one position, and everyone will move down a rank," Gabriel replied. "She will function as the head of the baku, and I'll be her aide."

"But," Arianna replied. "I know nothing of this world."

"Don't worry," Gabriel turned back to her. "Until you are comfortable with it, I'll help to keep things running." Andrew continued to ignore his glaring uncle. "So, let's go outside and tell everyone the good news." The three purebred baku led the way to the garden. Arianna hung behind and found herself frozen in her tracks.

"What's wrong?" Turner asked, coming back to grab her hand and pull her along.

"There's someone out there, sleeping, for me to feed on," Arianna guessed about the delicious smell. "I don't want to."

"Sorry, but you don't get much of a choice on that now," Turner replied. "It's part of who you are for the rest of your life." Arianna remained in her spot, and even with pulling on her arm, Turner was no match for her strength in baku form. "It's really not that bad. You feed on Devin and I all the time. Just tell them you would like to pass on that meal and have brought your own." Arianna had to smile at the offer.

"I can't feed on you guys right now," Arianna said quietly, as Devin returned inside also.

"Then just tell them you refuse to eat," Devin added. "It's not like you haven't done that before." He winked at her, and she finally smiled. "No one can make you do something if you don't want to. Didn't you hear Rafael? You're the strongest baku around. You need to follow your instincts." Arianna smiled and took his outstretched hand. With both of her protectors on either side of her, she walked back outside.

"Finally joining us?" Gabriel asked, noticing that she was warily looking over at the sleeping ten-year-old. "It's time for you to complete your transformation."

Arianna looked down at the child. With each beat of her sleeping heart, she looked more and more delicious. The blood flowing around inside the child pulled her closer. Arianna drew near and paused as she looked at the child's face. Dark ringlets circled her round face. Even one drink would probably kill the child. Arianna reached underneath the child as the audience hushed. Pulling her from the sleeping mist, the child began to stir, and all that was enticing Arianna vanished. The child groggily rubbed her eyes as Arianna walked into the crowd. Near the middle of the crowd, a dark haired couple with their teenage son stared at her. She walked over and handed the child to her father.

"A child is the most valuable thing you will ever see. Keep track of her," Arianna said, turning to walk back.

"Thank you," the mother whimpered.

"But our debt," the dark-haired teenager beside her pleaded. The father grabbed his arm, and he stopped talking.

The crowd began to whisper. No one had ever refused their sacrifice before.

"Without blood, the transformation won't be complete," Gabriel explained as Arianna stepped on the stage. Arianna shrugged.

"That means I need to drink some blood?" Arianna asked, and Gabriel nodded. Arianna's baku form faded. "I can take blood whenever I want. I fed earlier today. I feel fine right now."

"But you won't if you keep avoiding drinking blood," Gabriel replied.

"I'll feed when I get home," Arianna replied, reaching for her uncle's hand. *'It's not safe to feed on either Devin or Turner, as they need to protect me with someone hostile around.'*

Gabriel looked down at her hand, which wasn't making a direct blood connection. *'That is true. When did you figure out how to do this?'* he asked. *'Only high-level baku can talk through blood without a direct connection.'*

'Aren't I a high-level baku?' Arianna teased.

'I meant a highly trained baku,' Gabriel replied. *'And you do need blood. The baku transformation probably used up most of your blood from this morning, and that's why it wasn't painful to transform. If you keep denying what you are, you will get hungry, and then it won't matter who it is. If they have blood, you will attack them.'*

Arianna let go of her uncle's hand and looked at the

crowd. She didn't want to be the monster everyone feared, but most of the people were beginning to look tasty. Arianna turned back to Turner.

"I think we should leave," she added to him. He nodded and offered his hand to her. Turner led her back inside the house with Gabriel right behind.

"If she needs to feed, we need to leave," Devin explained. Gabriel nodded. "I'm sorry for our quick exit, but we need to protect her most of all." Gabriel agreed. Devin led the way through the house to the front door. "Please explain to your guests she's not trying to be rude, but there are two sides of her that need to be taken care of. If you arrange everything with uncle, she will be present at all the baku functions required of the family." Devin moved to open the door but stopped. Andrew was standing in front of the door.

"If you need a little snack, you can have my blood," he offered. Arianna turned red, remembering their meeting inside. He just calmly smiled and turned his wrist up towards her. "In my human form it's not as strong as pure baku blood," Andrew turned to answer Devin's unspoken question. "And don't worry, Puppy, I'm not trying to drug her." A slight growl escaped Turner's mouth. "It would be extremely rude to leave now, before meeting the people you are going to have to spend your life protecting." Andrew smiled up at Gabriel as his last remark was directed more towards him than Arianna. Arianna closed her eyes and felt the rush of his blood through his body. As much as she wanted to deny the fact, she was, indeed, hungry for blood. Her dearg-dul form flickered before she returned to being human.

"Do you trust him?" Devin asked. Arianna nodded. It was his blood that changed her to begin with. He could have poisoned her then. And she could not deny the loving feeling she felt before continuing to radiate from him.

Andrew's hand gently stroked the side of her face.

Arianna closed her eyes and felt the rush of his blood through his veins. Without thinking, Arianna took his wrist and bit down.

TWENTY-SEVEN

Arianna walked back out to the party of people that hated the dearg-dul they felt feeding inside the house. The mood changed as she returned, for they sensed the new, and very powerful, baku. Arianna sat beside her uncle and tried to ignore the curious glances she received throughout the meal. She tried to follow the conversation he was having with Rafael, but her mind kept wandering to Andrew, who sat silently beside his obviously upset uncle. He didn't fear her dearg-dul form, even as she was taking his blood. He merely smiled and thanked her when she was done. As blood was brought to the tables for a toast, a flash of dearg-dul instinctively washed over her. Arianna tried to suppress her dearg-dul form as the people around her hissed their disapproval. Arianna pushed away the glass of blood in front of her and stood up.

"I need to use the restroom," she said, her uncle stared curiously.

Arianna walked back into the house and didn't go down the hallway to the bathroom. Inside she turned and went to the family room where Andrew had been waiting earlier. He was right. It had the best views. She walked back to the window where there was a good view of the people outside.

"Not enjoying your party?" Gabriel asked, as he silently followed her. He wasn't far behind her when she entered the house.

"Not really. This sort of thing just isn't for me," she

222

replied.

"And that has nothing to do with how the people out there react to your dearg-dul form?" Gabriel knew the truth.

"How can they hate a part of me but love the other part?" Arianna wondered, not really looking for a reply. "Dearg-dul," Arianna turned into a dearg-dul and immediately felt the seething hatred from the people at the party before reverting back to human. "Or baku." Arianna turned into her new baku form and felt the overwhelming love. Arianna returned to her human form and looked at her uncle. "Your response doesn't change. Why can you look beyond what I am and they can't?"

"I wasn't raised to hate dearg-duls, as this generation was. You know that I was a friend of your grandfather's long ago. I may be leading the war against him, but I hate neither him, nor his followers." Arianna nodded at the facts she already knew, but it still didn't change the situation. "Besides," Gabriel added. "You are not *just* a dearg-dul or *just* a baku. You are both, and you will always be both. In dearg-dul form you can walk through daylight like a baku can. I'm just guessing, but I bet you can change into baku form even during the day just like a dearg-dul can. You cross the boundaries between the two night humans. There's nothing for me to fear or dislike. You are you."

Arianna reverted back to her dearg-dul form and closed her eyes. She could still feel traces of her baku blood running through her veins. Opening her blue dearg-dul eyes, she stared over at her uncle. "I can feel it. You are right. I'm both at one time." Arianna closed her eyes again and tried to change over to her new baku form. Arianna noticed, as she opened her eyes, that her uncle actually looked surprised as he stared back. Arianna felt the change. Where she had been mostly dearg-dul and a little baku before, she was now evenly split. "This is my true form, isn't it?" Gabriel smiled and nodded.

"You are not one or the other, you're both," Gabriel replied.

"Took her long enough to figure that out," Devin replied, stepping from the shadows.

"I couldn't explain to her how to do that," Gabriel replied. "She truly is the first of her kind."

Arianna continued to stare at Devin. She closed her eyes and opened them again. Arianna didn't doubt the connection she was feeling. Arianna could sense his blood without seeing him, and knew exactly how far away he was. Arianna closed her eyes and searched the party. Turner was standing outside the doorway, and Andrew was still sitting beside his uncle. Things felt different now. She could always sense her uncle before and those she had drank their blood, but now she was even sensing the slightest movements as Andrew flicked his hair out of his eyes. Arianna turned back to Devin and her uncle.

"It seems she can control it now," Gabriel explained to Devin. "She didn't even use any of her blood to do that." Devin smiled.

"About time. That will make my job so much easier," Devin replied.

Arianna's thoughts continued to jump between the people she could now feel before she realized what Gabriel had said. "I'm not using up my blood?" she asked.

"Not now," Gabriel replied.

Arianna stared at him. She hadn't changed anything, but he was right. She didn't feel exhausted at all. Arianna looked to Devin, and he nodded in agreement. She closed her eyes and began her search across the country. Nothing changed. She wasn't tired at all. She found her connection easily, Grandfather. His heart beat slowly. Arianna looked down at her watch. It was early in the night, but he seemed to be resting. Arianna waited a second before she heard it.

'Ari?'

'*Grandfather? Are you not sleeping?*'

'*Ari, promise me you will never leave Devin's side. He is all you have left to protect you. Gabriel and I failed you in the past. I'm so sorry. We cannot keep you safe. Devin will never fail you.*'

'*What are you talking about?*' Arianna felt the soft prick of her finger as Gabriel entered into the conversation.

'*Grandfather, what is going on?*'

'*Randolph?*' Gabriel asked. '*You can communicate with Randolph?*'

'*Joining the conversation, kid?*' Randolph asked weakly. '*Quite a child we have there, huh? There's a blood connection with over a thousand miles between us.*'

'*Old man, quit rambling. What's happened?*' Gabriel demanded. Arianna felt Gabriel's concern.

'*Poison,*' Randolph replied.

'*Details, now, before she starts to use up her blood,*' Gabriel ordered.

'*Lord Winter and I have been poisoned. We are currently in my wing of the house under lockdown. I do not know who poisoned us, but we do know that the Tricity has been left unguarded with Lord Winter here. It's an inside job.*'

'*How long?*' Gabriel asked.

'*Six, maybe eight hours, max. Two different poisons were used. I can tell that I'm the cure for him, and he's the cure for me. I explained that to Bran, but he won't take my blood and be cured. We both refuse to let the other die, so now it's a challenge of who passes out first.*' Arianna felt the heartbeat turn faint before it started back up again. '*Take care of the child. She will be amazing.*'

'*How could she not?*' Gabriel asked back. '*She's Travis's child.*'

'*And Tiffany's.*'

'*Hold on old man. We will be there soon.*' Gabriel broke

his connection, bringing Arianna back to the world around her.

"Get your plane ready," Gabriel ordered Molina, who was now standing next to Devin and Turner watching Arianna and Gabriel. "Lord Randolph and Lord Winter have been poisoned."

TWENTY-EIGHT

Arianna stared out at the crowd of people that were blocking their chances of a quick exit. Gabriel had explained that the party was over, but they refused to move. Each person there had felt the presence of Arianna's new form and was curious. Arianna pulled at Gabriel's arm as he looked like he was truly getting angry.

"They are just all curious," Arianna replied.

"We don't have time for this," Gabriel reminded her. The crowd was complaining, and Arianna listened to the various conversations.

"We are leaving to go help Lord Randolph," Arianna said to the crowd, and they booed. No one wanted to let their precious female baku go wandering over to a clan of dearg-duls. "You just don't get it. I can feel how much you hate my dearg-dul form, but it's part of me. I'm both dearg-dul and baku." As Arianna spoke, she changed into her new night human form. The crowd was silent. "I belong to both sides. So if you continue to hate the other side, you hate part of me."

"You can't let her go to the dearg-duls," a brave man in the middle of the crowd spoke up. "They'll kill her for being part baku. Gabriel, please keep her safe. Don't let her go."

Gabriel felt the genuine worry in the man's voice. He replied calmly, "With the signatures of Rafael and Andrew, she is now the head of the family. I cannot disagree with her decisions." He was as anxious to get to her grandfather as

227

she was, but he could never tell the crowd that.

"She's still a minor," Andrew's uncle commented. "Even as head of the family, as a minor, your decision is final." He didn't want Arianna to stay around, but he could also tell that Gabriel was anxious to go.

"That is true," Gabriel replied with a smirk as he had the upper hand. "And her guardian is her closest blood relative, Lord Randolph, her grandfather." Gabriel finally let the secret out and the crowd became silent. "Arianna is the child of Travis Grace and Tiffany Randolph." Andrew's uncle glared at Arianna. "We won't be returning until we get everything sorted out at the Randolph estate and Tricity. Patrick will be coming with me, so Rafael will be left in charge of the daily duties of the clan."

"You are saving her grandfather, so be it, but why Tricity also?" A tengu spoke up and asked about the city that was the center of their sworn enemies.

"I feel the hatred everyone here has for my grandfather. That hatred also seems to be aimed at Tricity, but I doubt even one of you have ever been there. How can you judge that something is not worth saving if you have never seen it?" Arianna scanned the crowds, and no one would meet her glare. "Tricity is a place where any night human is welcome. They don't discriminate against you, even if you choose not to visit. They welcome anyone to their city, and will as long as Lord Winter controls it. Can you even imagine someplace where you can walk around freely, unafraid that a day human that does not know will see your night form? Everyone there, night human or not, knows about this world. It's the most inviting place for our kind that exists. If you can truly hate such a place, you are stupid, because you have never truly felt the freedom of a place where you can be yourself." Arianna followed her uncle through the crowd that was now parting for them; he paused beside the family that was going to sacrifice their daughter.

"If you want to repay your father's debt, then become Arianna's tengu for the year, and I'll consider it repaid," Gabriel said to the dark haired teenager, the older brother of Arianna's sacrifice. His mother wanted to protest, but he held out his hand.

"Is that a deal?" the teen asked, and Gabriel shook his hand.

As they neared the cars waiting in the driveway, Andrew stepped forward from the shadows to follow them. Gabriel ushered Arianna into the waiting car and turned to the young man.

"Do you need some help?" Andrew asked sincerely. Gabriel paused at the car door and stared at the young man.

"You'd do that to impress a girl?" Gabriel replied.

"I've already impressed her. I'm offering to help because it's something she wishes to do," Andrew replied.

"And yet you also are still a minor, and I doubt your uncle will allow you to help us," Gabriel moved to get into the car.

"Actually, technically, I'm not," Andrew pulled out a paper from his coat. Gabriel looked at it and gave it back.

"Then head over to the airport with Patrick. He will need the most help at Tricity. I'll go to the Randolph estate and put everything in order there. Turner's older brother isn't cut out for leading warriors. Get to their house and help him get the city back under control," Gabriel ordered, and Andrew nodded. Arianna looked through the open car door to see Andrew nod and disappear as easily as he came.

After a quick ride to the airport, Gabriel ushered Arianna from the car and into the waiting plane. Arianna sat nervously beside Turner as the plane took off. Turner reached over and took her hand to comfort her.

"We will get there in time," Turner replied. Arianna wondered where the confidence came from, as his father had also been poisoned.

"It might not matter," Arianna replied, remembering that her grandfather said that one would have to die to save the other.

"Ari," Gabriel interrupted, as the fasten seat belt sign clicked off. "You need to take some blood after doing everything tonight." Arianna wanted to protest, but Turner stopped her. Turner began to unbutton the top of his shirt.

"But I don't use up my blood now," Arianna said.

"You still use it up, just not as fast," Devin explained. "Listen to your uncle."

"Feed, and then rest." Gabriel directed. "This might take a while to sort out." Gabriel tossed two packs of blood to Turner to drink before returning to his seat next to the young tengu from the party. Arianna listened to Gabriel talk to the boy as she bit down on Turner's neck.

"That doesn't bother you?" Gabriel asked as the new teenage Thomas stared across the aisle.

"I've never seen a dearg-dul feed before," Thomas replied, still curiously watching the scene. "It's not like everyone described. He doesn't fear her at all. In fact it seems as if he is actually enjoying it."

"What are you waiting for Turner to do, run in terror?" Gabriel replied with a laugh. Thomas nodded slightly.

"Does it hurt at all?" Thomas wondered.

"Actually, no," Gabriel replied, and Arianna was happy to hear someone actually say that.

"Not even a prick, like a shot?" Thomas was astonished.

"Not when there's a connection between two people. It would hurt, let's say, if she were fighting and bit someone, but as she is now, it does not hurt," Gabriel replied, still laughing at the young man beside him. "When you choose a partner someday, baku do the same, but they just put you to sleep first." Thomas nodded and continued to watch until Arianna was finished. She slid her head down to Turner's chest and dozed off to sleep as he ripped open the packet of blood for himself.

TWENTY-NINE

Arianna stepped down from the car and onto the long driveway that led to the Randolph estate. Molina and Devin were in front of her surveying the area, and Gabriel was behind her, protecting their backs as he made his own assessment. Nixon and Jackson were on one side, with Mica and Turner on the other, forming a complete circle around her.

Molina briefed everyone as they began to slowly walk up the driveway, approaching the mass of injured people spread out on the estate lawn. "Mori said that the rebellion has been stopped for the time being, and many people are hurt. He is trying to track where it started to find out who is the leader, but someone erased all the surveillance footage. His advice is to proceed with caution, as the rebels may still be inside the estate." The people on the lawn who were still conscious and able to move had organized into two lines to welcome Arianna back. From the front of the house a tall, thin man ran down the steps.

"Molina, Devin," the man called. "There's been a rebellion. Lord Randolph is safe, along with Lord Winter, in complete lockdown in his apartment while we try to sort out all of the traitors. We are so fortunate Miss Arianna was not around."

"Situation?" Molina asked the head of the estate security.

"At least fifty injured. I've found almost as many killed, but I haven't been any further inside the house than the front rooms. We currently can't get into Lord Randolph's quarters to assess the situation there, but I expect there are no causalities inside, as he was at dinner with just Lord Winter." Molina nodded, not giving away any of the information that they had. "Have you been able to make contact with your grandfather?" he asked Arianna, reaching forward to move Molina and Devin out of the way to talk to her. The flash of his estate ring caught Arianna eye.

'Blue,' Arianna said softly to Turner, who nodded and pushed her protectively behind him. Devin and Gabriel caught the same gesture and moved in on the tall man. Arianna swiftly hit the man's knees before anyone else could react. The group all fell to the ground. A high-pitched sound whizzed overhead. Bullets hit the ground behind the group.

"Where?" Molina asked.

Arianna pointed northeast. "Tall building, three people; one whose voice I recognized." Molina was instantly conveying the message to Mori.

Devin looked to Turner, who was still holding down the chief of security. Turner picked up his hand and pointed to the ring. Devin nodded. Gabriel looked at the ring and then to Turner and Devin.

"I have the only blue ring," Devin explained. "The rest are fakes."

"That makes that simple enough," Gabriel replied, as he switched to his baku form and quickly yet silently moved through the front yard, retrieving anyone with a blue ring and bringing them back unconscious. Molina couldn't keep her mouth from dropping as the yard was cleared and they were left with a pile full of traitors. In only minutes, without making a sound, Gabriel had gathered everyone.

"That should be everyone outside. Now, that is done, we need to get to the old man." Gabriel returned to his human form. "How do we get inside the apartment?" he asked

Molina, still-stunned.

"Mori can give Arianna access from the roof. Once she's inside, the system can be opened," Devin replied for Molina.

"But how do I get to the roof?" Arianna asked.

"It's easy for me in baku form, but you have never used that form yet. I brought you your own bird to fly you anywhere," Gabriel pushed Thomas forward. "First, use your connection with Andrew to tell him the way to find the traitors, and then Thomas will take you to the roof."

'Andrew?' Arianna asked, trying to focus on his blood, miles away.

'One second,' Andrew replied, and she closed her eyes to help visualize his movements. He moved quicker than Gabriel, and his movements were just as precise. *'Is everyone fine there?'* Andrew asked.

'Yes, the traitors are all wearing blue Randolph rings. White and red are the only colors that are real.' Arianna explained.

'So, do I get to take out your wonderful friend Devin the next time I see him?' Andrew asked, as he took down two more people on his end of the conversation.

'Devin is the only one that should have a blue ring,' Arianna corrected. *'And no. I'd never speak to you again if you were to harm Devin in any way,'* Arianna threatened.

Andrew laughed. *'I was just kidding. Thanks for the info. We'll have this cleaned up in no time, princess.'*

Arianna opened her eyes to find only Thomas standing before her. Everyone else was going through the pile of traitors. Arianna looked around, Gabriel was gone.

"He will meet us there," Thomas replied, as Arianna finally saw the large black wings on his back. "If I were you I'd hold on tight." He wrapped his arms around her waist. Arianna sucked in her breath and complied, though it felt strange to be so close to anyone besides Devin and Turner. Arianna felt her feet lift off the ground as she closed her eyes; she was afraid of heights. A moment later she was being set down on the roof. "You can let go now," Thomas added.

Arianna blushed, pulling her arms from around him. Gabriel was standing at the doorway waiting.

"Mori got this open, but he will close it again once we get inside," Gabriel explained. Arianna nodded and followed behind him. Gabriel paused in the doorway as he took one sniff of the room below. Gabriel turned back to Thomas, "Go back and tell Devin and Turner to get here as soon as possible."

Arianna heard the door snap shut, and the grinding of the metal protection barrier moving into place as she continued to follow Gabriel through her apartment to the staircase leading below. Arianna paused at the sweet, almost cotton candy-like, smell.

"What is that?" she asked Gabriel in only a whisper.

"Baku can sense death," Gabriel replied. "In myth, baku eat dreams. That includes the dreams of people asleep, and those that lay dying." Gabriel reached back and offered his hand to Arianna, who was still standing at the top of the stairs. "We must go help them, and not let on that we know how bad it is." Arianna nodded and took her uncle's hand. Gabriel led the way into the dimly-lit room below. He seemed to glide across the dining room to the two dying men.

"Is that you, old friend?" Lord Randolph hoarsely whispered.

"Who else could break into your house successfully, old man?" Gabriel replied. "And I brought your granddaughter."

"Ari?" Lord Randolph whispered.

"Grandfather," Arianna replied, before breaking into tears at the sight of her grandfather, who had been so strong, lying withered on the floor, unable to move, or even open his eyes. "I'm here. How do we help you?" she begged.

"Arianna, listen to me now," he paused to breathe. He straightened his frame slightly and opened his eyes as he spoke, showing the last flicker of the man he had been for a lifetime. "I'm an old man, and I've lived a long time. I've seen more than I ever wanted to see and lived more than one lifetime. I regret not staying to protect you, but that was never in the cards for me. I have trained Devin to do that, as he will be able to stand by you always. Follow his orders, and those of your uncle here, and you will be safe." The regalness of the man before her faded as he slumped back down.

"I entrust her to you now," he spoke to Gabriel. "Now, go help Bran. The Tricity isn't ready to be without him." Lord Randolph pointed to a plate nearby that was smeared with his blood. Gabriel stood and took the plate across the room to where Lord Winter lay unconscious. He opened the large man's mouth, and smeared the blood inside. Gabriel returned to Lord Randolph's side and heard more metal clanking as the main doors to the apartment were flung open.

Turner rushed across the room to his father and knelt beside him. Devin did the same to Lord Randolph.

"It's time to keep your promise," Lord Randolph whispered to Devin. He coughed before speaking again. "Please, take her away. She doesn't need to see this." Devin nodded and followed this one last order from Lord Randolph.

"He will be awake in a few minutes. He will be fine now," Gabriel said to Turner, who was still holding his father's hand. "Please join Devin and Arianna." Turner stood and nodded, looking back at his father before helping Devin to pull Arianna into a standing position.

"But," Arianna began to complain. Gabriel tapped her forehead, and Arianna slumped into Devin's arms.

THIRTY

Arianna awoke to the commotion around her. The ballroom was filled with people rushing to help the wounded that were crying out. Devin was in one corner with an injured human, while Turner was running back to him with more bandages. Arianna stood and slowly walked through the mess of people. She could only faintly hear her grandfather's heartbeat. He was still alive. Gabriel was near him. Arianna listened as she walked into the hallway without Devin or Turner noticing.

"You should see it," Gabriel said quietly. "She is magnificent. Everything we hoped for."

"I wish I had the chance," Randolph replied quietly.

"Now, with it complete, we don't need to worry any longer. She had complete control. It's truly amazing."

"Only Tiffany and Travis could make a child that unique." Randolph paused. "I think the time is near."

"It's been a good run, old man."

Arianna heard a shuffling sound beside her that brought her back to the situation around her. A cook was sitting on a table, the flowers that used to sit there were smashed on the floor beside it. Her leg was completely mangled, and someone had placed a tourniquet around her thigh to stop the bleeding. Arianna paused and stared at the woman, he scent was familiar. She smiled, despite her state, as people rushed between them. Two transformed dearg-duls rushed past, toward another down the hallway. All the blood was

236

affecting the dearg-duls at the estate, but Arianna was still human. The blood didn't affect her at all.

"They are alright," the cook said to Arianna.

"Who?" Arianna asked.

"Lilly, Dean, and Captain Lou," the cook replied. Arianna stared at the human, wondering what she was talking about. "I talked to Lou just a few minutes ago. He recognized the smell of gas before the building blew up and took everyone out."

"What?"

"You didn't know yet?" the cook asked. "Sorry. I thought someone had told you—the diner blew up. No one had any contact, but Lou finally called me. He said he couldn't get through to anyone else and that I should relay the message to you. I haven't been in any state to find you this way." She pointed at her leg.

"The diner blew up?" Arianna asked, sitting beside the cook in shock.

"Yes, the attack was planned well on all fronts. They were trying to perform a complete take-over. I think they were targeting you at the diner, and here they were going to kill both Lord Randolph and Lord Winter. At least, that's what Lou thinks." Arianna stared at the cook. "I suppose you don't remember me. I'm Lou's wife." Arianna continued to stare at the woman. She smelled exactly the same as Lou. The cook laughed, and then grimaced at the jostle of her injured leg.

"Don't you need to get some help?" Arianna asked, concerned about the wound running from her thigh to her calf.

"Nah. There are people more hurt than me. I can wait." The cook pointed around the room. Many of the injured were bleeding worse than her.

"If you wait, won't you lose your leg?"

"It's not that bad. After they get to tending to the critical people, I'll get my own little bag of dearg-dul blood and in a week or two it will be back to normal." The cook didn't seem to mind her leg as she waited.

"Dearg-dul blood?" Arianna wanted to know she heard correct.

"Yep. Haven't you noticed how you can drink blood from humans and not leave a mark? There's a healing ability in night human blood that can heal, not only their own kind, but day humans also," the cook explained, leaning back against the wall. "I'm not going to die from this wound. Therefore, I sit here and wait for my turn."

"Can I test something?" Arianna asked the cook who nodded her head *yes*, although she didn't know what Arianna was referring to. Arianna pricked her finger and dropped a drop of blood on the wound running down the cook's leg before the cook could get out a protest. Turner came running from the ballroom with Devin and Molina close behind. Nixon and Mica came from down the hallway as Nelson ran up from the other direction.

"What happened?" Turner asked, examining Arianna to find the source of her blood loss.

"Nothing," Arianna replied. "I just wanted to see if my blood worked like dearg-dul blood on humans." The group heaved a collective sigh of relief.

"Of course your blood works like a dearg-dul's," Molina replied. "I thought we'd already tested that theory."

"Then why don't we use my blood to heal everyone?" Arianna asked.

"Because your blood is much too valuable," the cook replied, everyone looked to the now-healed cook. "Everyone made it out of the diner," the cook reported to Devin, who nodded his response.

"But, if one drop can heal a wound like that, why can't I help at least some of these people?" Arianna pleaded.

"One drop, diluted in water, could heal a lot of people,"

Turner guessed.

"It's against the rules," Molina replied, putting an end to their train of thought.

"But," Turner began his protest.

Arianna involuntarily shivered as she felt grief overcome her, not to Molina's response, but from someone close. Arianna closed her eyes and began to wander the estate with her senses. Arianna paused at her grandfather's apartment. Gabriel was all alone in the room. One tear trickled down her face as she reopened her eyes. She looked straight across the group around her into Devin's eyes. Devin nodded, as the conversation around them continued to argue over why she couldn't use her blood.

"Is this your decision?" Devin asked, interrupting the arguing.

"Yes. I want to use my blood to help," Arianna replied.

"But Lord Randolph's order…" Molina tried to remind Devin.

"We follow the orders of the leader of the family, correct?" Devin asked in reply. Molina nodded in confusion. "Then we will follow her orders." The group stopped, and all turned to Devin for an explanation that wasn't needed.

"We won't let her overuse her blood," Devin replied to Molina, who was still in shock. Devin offered his hand to Arianna, pulling her away and back down the hallway, to the ballroom.

Turner ran and grabbed the closest pitchers of water.

"One drop in each," Devin explained.

"Just one?" Arianna asked.

"Your blood is more powerful than all the dearg-duls in this room," Gabriel replied, coming up behind her. "One drop is more than enough." Arianna followed their orders while not looking directly at Gabriel. Devin and Turner hurried around the room, pouring water into the glasses of the injured people.

"I need to leave now," Gabriel said quietly to Arianna. "I told Patrick and the others to head back, and I must meet them there. All sides have been attacked." Arianna wanted to protest, but remained silent as she still couldn't look him in the eyes. "Everything is changing, and I'm needed at home to make sure it is alright. I'll check on Lilly and Dean when I get back."

"Is he really gone?" Arianna asked.

"Yes," Gabriel replied.

"What does one do when a night human dies?" Arianna asked, still unsure of the world she was living in.

"Celebrate their lives and remember every moment you spent together." Gabriel placed his arm around Arianna to comfort her. "And the answer to that question is: nothing. Dearg-duls turn to dust and are gone in the wind." Gabriel took Arianna's hand and placed a ring in it. "He lived a long life, regretting only the loss of you and your mother. He did his best to make amends." Gabriel nodded to Devin, who was still circling the room. "They'll take care of you." Arianna nodded. "You are in charge now, here and back home too. Don't worry about home for now, as I'll be there to take care of everything. I'm never too far away." Gabriel vanished as fast as he had appeared.

Turner returned with two more clean pitchers of water. Arianna nodded and pricked her finger another time.

Arianna was glad to return to her own room after the long day dealing with the injured. Opening the door to her apartment, Arianna paused, catching the faint scent of her grandfather. She looked absently across the room to the stairway. He was already gone, but there was something of him that lingered on.

"Why don't you go get some rest?" Devin suggested.

Arianna nodded. "I'm sure the council will all be arriving soon. This is only just beginning."

Arianna opened the door to her room and stared around the neatly organized space. The whole mansion had been in chaos all afternoon, but her room looked like it hadn't been touched. On her desk, a small laptop computer was playing the same clip over and over. Arianna paused to stare at the new addition to the room before scanning for any intruder. Arianna walked closer to the computer before sitting down. She could faintly sense her uncle, and didn't fear that the computer was part of a stunt to kidnap her. The screen loop began again. Reaching over, she turned up the sound.

In the main ballroom of the Randolph manor, a small blond-haired girl ran across to an older man. The child giggled and laughed as she caught up to the man. The man reached over and placed the young child on his own feet. As they whirled around the room to the sound of a familiar tune, Arianna finally caught a close look at their faces; it was her grandfather and herself. She watched her younger self gracefully dance around with her grandfather, giggling at every chance. As the song ended, her grandfather paused near enough for the camera to pick up their conversation.

"Papa, again," the young Arianna demanded.

Lord Randolph laughed. "I am an old man, child. One dance is enough for me."

"Again," she demanded, the stubborn child that she was.

Lord Randolph plopped unceremoniously to the ground and lay on his back, giving up.

"Really, I'm old and tired," Randolph complained. Young Arianna climbed up onto her grandfather's lap and stared intently at the old man.

"Hmm," she paused and pushed a bit on his wrinkles in his face. "Nope, not old," she determined, and Randolph laughed, much more happily than Arianna remembered hearing.

"I am old, child, even if you do not think so."

"You can't be old. Old people die. If you die, then there would be no one to take care of me," young Arianna began to sniffle.

"Child, child," Randolph comforted the small child as he hugged her. "You will never be alone. You have so many people that care about you. And remember, Devin promised he would watch over you some day when I am gone." Arianna looked up to the camera before smiling. Quickly, she jumped off her grandfather and ran over to the camera. The camera shook as the person holding it tried to dodge the child running after them.

"And that's why I'm going to marry him," Arianna declared before the camera dropped to the ground. Feet momentarily blocked the view as a young Devin ran from Arianna. Lord Randolph slowly stood, and walked over to the camera while the two children ran around the ballroom.

"You are special. You have the power to change the world, and I am too old to stay around to see it happen. Good luck my child. Your destiny awaits," Lord Randolph said to the camera. "And know that I love you, very much." The computer screen was momentarily black before the loop restarted at the beginning. The same scene began again. Arianna watched the loop continuously until there was a knock at the door. Devin let himself into the room.

"They have all arrived," Devin commented. Arianna stared at the screen and nodded. "If you want to wait, we can deal with this tomorrow," he added. "I can tell them you're too tired."

"It won't change anything, will it?" Arianna asked, finally looking up. "I'll still have to deal with them?" Devin nodded. "Then we deal with it now." Arianna looked down one last time at the child dancing with her grandfather. She smiled and closed the laptop.

"I love you too," she whispered in the direction of the

closed computer before accepting Devin's outstretched hand.

"We do this together, right?" she asked, wavering slightly.

"Together," Turner replied from behind Devin, offering his hand also.

Arianna left the room, not looking back. Destiny was waiting.

ACKNOWLEDGMENTS

As with any work of fiction, there are many people to thank along the way.

To you, the reader. Thank you for taking the time to read this story. If you liked it, please leave a review on Amazon, Goodreads, Barnes and Noble, your blog, twitter, facebook, etc. The greatest help you can do to keep a writer going is to support them by spreading the word about their books and leaving them encouraging words.

Also I would like to thank my editor and cover designer. A good editor is essential to getting the story correct. Thank you so much Kathie for catching all those errors. I will be working hard to better my writing through seeing everything that I have to work on. A thank you also to Ravven for such a pretty cover. I greatly appreciate all those that can do what I cannot, like editors and cover designers. Thank you also Kathy McMichael for your financial and promotional support.

I'd also like to thank my hubby for continuing to push me further down the writing road. I really never planned to let anyone ever see my writing. I have written tons of stories over the years for my own enjoyment. Writing is a great creative means that you can do alone. This particular story was written two months before Twilight came out, and I laughed when the vampire craze took over. Vampires were always a creature I thought you ran from, not kissed! I never considered going further with this story until my hubby asked me to try and put myself out there. So thank you, B. for pushing me off the deep end (or the cliff as I see it sometimes).

ABOUT THE AUTHOR

B. Kristin McMichael graduated with her PhD in biology at Ohio State where she worked as a scientist before taking her passion of writing full-time. Besides writing, she enjoys chasing her kids, playing outside, and baking cookies.

She lives in Ohio with her husband and three children.

BOOKS BY THIS AUTHOR

http://www.bkristinmcmichael.com

- **TO STAND BESIDE HER**

- **The Blue Eyes Trilogy**
  - o The Legend of the Blue Eyes
  - o Becoming a Legend
  - o Winning the Legend

- **The Day Human Trilogy**
  - o The Day Human Prince
  - o The Day Human King
  - o The Day Human Way

- THE CHALCEDONY CHRONICLES
  - o Carnelian
  - o Chrysoprase
  - o Aventurine
  - o Chrysocolla

24262975R00142

Made in the USA
San Bernardino, CA
18 September 2015